ADAM TESTA

© 2020 by Adam Testa
All rights reserved.

ISBN: 978-0-578-76598-3

All rights reserved. No part of this publication may be reproduced, distributed, or transmitted in any form or by any means, including photocopying, recording, or other electronic or mechanical methods, without the prior written permission of the publisher, except in the case of brief quotations embodied in critical reviews and certain other noncommercial uses permitted by copyright law. For permission requests, contact AdamTestaAuthor@gmail.com.

This is a work of fiction. Names, characters, businesses, places, events, locales, and incidents are either the products of the author's imagination or used in a fictitious manner. Any resemblance to actual persons, living or dead, or actual events is purely coincidental.

Content warnings: violence, adult language, politics, religion

First Edition

Cover design by Codex Art and Apparel
Independently published by Adam Testa | Phoenix, AZ

*To Zachary,
this book is proof your childhood dreams
can come true. Believe in yourself and trust others
who believe in you.*

PROLOGUE
Bryce Reynolds
June 17, 2018

PLUMES OF GRAY SMOKE BILLOWED from the rubble, glowing red and blue in the flashing lights of the emergency response vehicles.

Neighbors gathered at a distance. Fire and utility crews worked the scene.

Summer winds fanned the blaze, adding risk of spread to nearby residences. A crackle and creak pierced the air, silencing the spectators' hushed chatter.

"Back! Get back!"

Firefighters scurried away from the structure. A ceiling beam cracked and fell to the ground, stirring embers and drawing gasps from the crowd. Bryce Reynolds, leaning against a fire engine, didn't flinch. Soot and sweat streaked his face. He raised a plastic water bottle to his lips.

When you walk through fire, you shall not be burned, and the flame shall not consume you, Bryce thought to himself. In times of duress, he found comfort in the Word, solace in his faith. His calling had brought him this far. He trusted it to carry him forward.

A firefighter sauntered toward him from the frontline. He reached for a refreshment of his own. Bryce remained focused on the smoldering scene ahead.

"Hell of a blaze," the firefighter said. "Haven't seen one this bad for a while. And after 20 years, I've pretty much seen it all. But a young pup like you? You can't have been at this more than a few years, huh?"

Bryce tilted his head in recognition. "Believe me, I've seen more than most my age." *Most 27-year-olds haven't had a front-row seat to watch their friends and family die.*

"Well, at least we can agree the poor bastard never had a chance," the man added.

Bryce identified him by the patch on his jacket. "Do any of us, Smithers?"

The man returned a stone-faced gaze.

"'For the living know that they will die, but the dead know nothing, and they have no more reward.'"

"That from the Bible or something?"

"Ecclesiastes 9:5."

"You might wanna watch where you're spouting that. I'm not sure his wife's up for a sermon at the moment." Smithers pointed over his shoulder, where a group consoled the grieving widow. "Did you know Tommy?"

"Can't say so," Bryce replied.

"Thomas Sheridan. A good man, did a lot for this community. Ran some kind of internet company working with the government. Not really my thing. I just know he was always giving money to the schools and helping those in need."

"Sounds like he died a hero." Bryce took another drink and turned his gaze back to the fire.

"Yeah, just lucky Colleen wasn't hurt, too. That's his wife, the one standing over there." The man looked at Bryce, who didn't react. "Said she left for the grocery store about 20 minutes before we got the call. Few minutes later, she might have been inside, too."

Bryce waited a moment to respond. He turned and extended a handshake. "Well, Smithers, I'm going to check with the incident commander and see if we're still needed."

Smithers accepted the handshake and checked Bryce's ID tag. "Sure thing, Anderson. Pleasure meeting you. Tell the boys in Coal City we appreciate the support. I didn't even realize you'd been called out here."

Called, maybe, but not the same way as you. Bryce walked away without speaking.

He glanced over his shoulder. Smithers had returned to his previous position. Bryce moved away from the scene, uninterested in continuing his charade.

Once the fire engine separated him from the crowd, he removed the insulated jacket. The breeze hit the damp polo shirt underneath, sending chills through his veins. He tore the gloves from his hands and tucked them under his arm.

Confident he'd moved far enough from the scene, Bryce leaned on a vehicle and wiggled his feet from their rubber confines, removed his drenched socks and slid out of the protective turnout pants.

How can anyone tolerate these uniforms?

He walked along the empty road barefoot with the gear cradled in his arms. The sweat on his skin glistened in the rays of the overhead streetlights, underscoring his muscular physique. He turned the corner and headed toward a parked vehicle.

The lights of the new-model Audi S6 flashed when he unlocked the doors. Bryce opened the rear driver's side door, exposing a black leather interior free of clutter aside from a packed duffel bag on the seat.

He shoved the jacket, boots and pants on the floorboard and opened the bag, removing a clean pair of socks and a dry T-shirt. Standing in the street, he removed and replaced his polo before taking a seat. His legs dangled from the vehicle door as he slid on the fresh socks and a pair of sneakers he pulled from the duffel.

The rest will have to wait.

Feeling somewhat refreshed, Bryce closed the bag and moved to the driver's seat. The blast of the air conditioning and sounds of alternative rock welcomed him when the vehicle's engine engaged. He sat for a moment, collecting his thoughts.

He tossed his keyring onto the passenger seat, where it landed on a nondescript file folder. Bryce picked it up, opening the flap to see a photo of a portly man with rotund cheeks, messy gray hair and a horrid Magnum-style mustache. The man in the photo smiled as Bryce lifted the image aside.

He focused on the paper beneath, a computer-generated form.

Name: Thomas Edward Sheridan
Address: 927 Lone Tree Lane, Braidwood, IL 60408
Birthdate: 03-24-1962
Enrollment Status: Active

He reviewed the document and tucked it back in the folder alongside the photo. None of it meant anything anymore. Thomas Sheridan had devoted his life to serving others, but in death, it only mattered whether he'd served God.

Bryce shifted the vehicle to drive and pulled away from the curb. He watched the pillars of smoke fade in the rearview mirror, reflecting on the night's events.

For the wages of sin is death, but the free gift of God is eternal life in Christ Jesus, our Lord.

CHAPTER 1
Derek Price
June 22, 2018

"DID YOU HEAR about what the idiot's been tweeting?"

Derek Price sighed playfully, tucking the ZTE flip phone between his shoulder and head. The vehicle's engine hummed in his ears as he continued down the highway. "It's nice to hear your voice, too, Sonia."

"Damn it, Derek. You know I've missed you," the young woman said. "But, seriously, this guy can't stop talking about witch hunts and walls. I just can't believe we're supposed to accept this clown as the leader of the free world."

Dealing with Sonia Torres, especially regarding politics, required a delicate approach. Derek carried some blame himself. From the beginning, he'd encouraged her to follow her heart and pursue her passion. She'd chosen politics.

And, for the 19-year-old only child of an immigrant single mother, having a president take a hardline approach to immigration fueled her progressive spirit.

"First, you know I don't pay attention to Twitter. Second, just remember, a lot of us felt the same way about the last guy, too." Derek paused. "Anyway, how have things been? No fires at the agency while I was out?"

"None I couldn't handle."

The tinge of sass in Sonia's voice made Derek smile. For the past seven years, Derek watched Sonia grow from a troubled middle-schooler in a community mentoring program into an active, intelligent woman. He'd played many roles in her life: mentor, father figure and, lately, boss.

Since graduating high school, Sonia had learned how to balance life. She enrolled at Joliet Junior College and cared for her ailing mother. And, for the past year, she had helped Derek at -30-, the public relations firm he launched after leaving journalism.

I wish I had that much drive when I was her age.

Sonia's voice crackled through the phone's speaker, bringing Derek back to reality. "So, how was the trip?"

Derek glanced at the bustling corn fields out the window of his Honda CR-V as it barreled down the interstate. Two weeks at a remote cabin in South Dakota had left him longing for home and ready to start the next chapter. "Cathartic."

"I know it's still hard, but I love you, and I'm here for you, whatever you need." Sincerity replaced the sass in Sonia's tone.

Derek's excursion hadn't been one of pleasure; he'd needed to escape. Three days ago marked the first anniversary of his wife Madeline's death. A healthy woman in her prime, her life had been cut short by an errant driver without so much as a 9-1-1 call.

The loss had left Derek empty. He'd fallen into a fit of depression and despair. Sonia propped him up as best she could, taking over operations at -30- and staying by Derek's side. *And she did all that while grieving herself.* Madeline had treated Sonia like her own daughter. The two had bonded over shared interests, particularly technology, which eluded Derek.

Derek's gaze turned to his hand on the steering wheel, to the faded cobalt wedding band he continued wearing. The ring, once a symbol of his marriage, had become a visual promise to himself to focus on the future while remembering the past.

"By the way," Sonia's voice came through the speaker. "I have a special surprise for you."

"Should I be worried? Because I'm a little worried. Do I have to feed it?"

"You'll have to wait to find out. Dinner tomorrow, usual spot? Don't forget it's your turn to treat."

"Sounds great." Derek ignored the fact it was always his turn to treat. "I've got a few things to catch up on around the house in the morning, but dinner works."

"It's summer. 'NCIS' is all reruns."

Derek smiled. "I'll see you at 4."

"Four? You're such an old man," Sonia quipped.

You don't have to remind me. Derek's 50th birthday loomed in the not-so-distant future. "Stodgy, old white man. Poster child for the Republican Party, huh?" Derek couldn't help himself. He knew when and how to push Sonia's buttons.

"Seriously, Derek! This guy thinks the entire world's out to get him. And he can't stop tweeting about it!"

"I have no love lost for the guy, but you have to admit, he's done a lot of good things for this country, too."

"Derek, I swear, you could watch Nixon say 'I am not a crook' and believe the guy. I don't know how, after everything you've been through, you still want to see the best in people."

I did watch Nixon say it, even if I was only 3. "Call it a curse." He paused. "Four o'clock tomorrow. I'll see you then. Oh, and Sonia, one more thing. Respect the office, if nothing else."

Derek visualized Sonia's fists clench.

"I'll start just as soon as he does!" She paused, mimicking his behavior. "Oh, and Derek, one more thing. Text me next time. You know I hate talking on the phone."

Derek snapped the phone shut. He smiled as he made his way down the interstate, less than 30 miles from the front gates of Shadow Ridge.

Tyler Norris

TYLER NORRIS BOPPED his head to the classic rock playing through his Beats headphones. The 20-something drummed his fingers on the edge of the desk, staring at his three-monitor display.

Working for SHADOW hadn't been on his radar when he graduated from Northwestern University with an information technology degree. He'd never heard of the organization; few people had. But, when the opportunity had presented itself, he couldn't have fathomed turning it down.

A mix of live video feeds and data refreshed on his screens. Six months into his role, he'd learned what to watch and when. Other young upstarts looking for their big break filled the surrounding cubicles, but the analysts rarely conversed while on duty.

Deep Purple's "Smoke on the Water" played in Tyler's headphones, but the field director's words repeated in his mind. "Mr. Norris, I have an important project for you." *An important project. For me.*

He'd waited all day, hopeful to report progress. Now, finding himself lost in Ritchie Blackmore's guitar rhythms, Tyler convinced himself the day would be a bust. Then, a small pop-up box in the screen's corner caught his attention and sent his heart racing.

"SHADOW RIDGE GATE ENTRY." The letters appeared in white font against a blue background. Tyler moved his mouse and clicked the button. Video feeds faded as a new set of information appeared, including a portrait photo of an older man with salt-and-pepper hair. His smile drew attention to a mostly gray beard; his green eyes appeared welcoming.

The man's name appeared in large letters next to the photo: "DEREK PRICE."

"Oh, shit," Tyler muttered.

He jumped from his seat with childlike abandon, ripping his headphones' auxiliary cable from the computer's headphone jack. Ian Gillan's voice blared through the speakers, sending echoes of the song's chorus through the office.

Tyler rushed to silence his computer, ignoring snickering from adjacent cubicles.

Music muted, he raced down the row of cubicles toward the field director's office. Breathing deeply as he arrived, Tyler knocked on the open door. "Sir, you wanted to know when Derek Price arrived at Shadow Ridge." He waited. No response. "He's home, sir."

CHAPTER 2
DEREK PRICE
JUNE 23, 2018

"WELCOME HOME, neighbor!"

Derek shifted his attention from the envelope in his hand to the woman across the street. Knowing the letter's contents without opening it, he welcomed the distraction. The woman set a trowel down and climbed to her feet.

"Don't stop on my account. I'll come your way." Derek admired the rainbow of colors created by the coral bells, hibiscus and daylilies Karen Conrad tended in her flower bed. He crossed the street and greeted his friend with a hug.

"How you holding up?" Karen's face appeared three shades of red. Sweat dripped under the brow of her beige sun hat. She tilted her hands outward as she embraced Derek, trying to keep the dirt to herself.

"Better than you, it seems." Derek smiled. "I'm doing okay. The time away helped."

"Glad to hear that. You haven't missed much around here."

"Well, I appreciate you keeping an eye on things."

"That's what neighbors are for, right?" Karen looked at the pile of mail in Derek's hand. "Still no luck?"

Derek gazed down at the top envelope, noting the logo in the corner. The H in Shadowen looked like a house, a distinct symbol of the real estate developer's brand. "Unfortunately, no. I'm starting to think you might be stuck with me."

"That wouldn't be such a bad thing, now would it?"

Derek looked at his home across the street. A giant willow tree shaded the front porch. Dark blue window treatments accented the recently replaced white siding. A "for sale" sign swung from its post in the morning breeze. The house held countless memories, but Derek's sense of home had faded in the past year.

"I suppose not." He gestured toward Karen's flowers. "Especially with such exquisite views."

Karen chuckled. "You're too much sometimes, you know that?"

Derek grinned. "Well, I'll let you get back to it. Get inside before it gets too hot out here."

"Bit late for that," Karen said. "It's really nice to have you home, Derek. I've been thinking about you. I know it's not easy, but I'm here if I can do anything to help. Us neighbors have to look out for each other."

"I appreciate it, Karen." Derek turned and headed back across the street. He looked at the house, then down at the letter. *Here we go again.*

* * *

DEREK STOOD in his great room, surrounded by stacks of half-full boxes. He'd spent yesterday resting and catching up on -30- emails but planned to spend the morning packing. The house would eventually sell, and he'd be ready when it did.

She's going to flip out when I tell her at dinner. As much as the rejected buyers bothered Derek, Sonia became more emotional with each denial. He reminded himself of her age and lack of perspective, focusing on using his situation as a learning opportunity. *At least something good might come of it.*

Derek meandered down the hallway, leading from the great room to the office and owner's suite. Framed photographs, certificates and plaques hung on the wall. He'd resisted dismantling his self-professed "hall of fame." The collection held no actual value, but to Derek, these items represented a life's journey.

His foray into journalism had begun in junior high, but Derek traced his passion for the field to June 1976. At age 6, Derek had seen reports of Arizona Republic reporter Don Bolles's death on the news, but he didn't understand the implications until several years later.

Combining a childish desire to earn a living as a private eye with his love of writing, Derek had become fascinated with Bolles's story. The investigative reporter had earned fame for uncovering corruption, bribery and the influence of the mafia in Arizona politics. Bolles's story had ended with a car bombing, purportedly orchestrated by the mob.

Bolles's willingness to die for his cause had inspired Derek to pursue a journalism degree from Southern Illinois University Carbondale. His "hall of fame" and associated memories were all that remained of his newspaper tenure.

I should reach out to Steve, see how he's doing. Derek looked at the photo of himself and Steve Erikson, a former colleague at The Daily Herald, standing on stage at the 2007 Philip Meyer Awards. Their collaborative series exposed corruption across townships and earned recognition as an award finalist. Much to their disappointment, however, the effort had resulted in little change to the state's bloated municipal structure.

Maybe Sonia needs this one for her room. Derek's gaze moved to a photo of him and then-U.S. Senator Barack Obama outside Assembly Hall at the University of Illinois. He'd met Obama several times on the campaign trail, and while he had never embraced the man's ideology, he'd recognized his stature as a rising political star.

As Derek moved to the next image, his left thumb instinctively spun his cobalt wedding band around his ring finger. This photo contrasted the others. There were no politicians or newspaper colleagues. Rather, Derek and Madeline stood alone atop Starved Rock, aglow with glee. Long before Merriam-Webster accepted the world "selfie," Derek reached out with a cheap Kodak point-and-shoot and snapped the couple's first photo.

Maddie used to hate this being here. She'd joked about the photo's placement among memories of Derek's professional career. But he had always reassured her that the story they wrote together was his finest work.

And he recognized fine work. His career had entailed more than meeting future presidents and exposing low-level corruption. His investigative efforts had led to new legislation, the recall of elected officials and significant changes in government transparency. He'd never concerned himself with accolades, though. Derek's satisfaction came from shining a light on those operating in darkness.

He removed the photos from the wall and carried them back to the great room, carefully placing them in a box near the fireplace. As he closed the lid, a series of knick-knacks and smaller photos lining a cutout shelf caught his eye.

Engagement photos, wedding prints, a vacation snapshot with Sonia and her mother. These images told the other side of Derek's story. There, between a picture of Madeline feeding a giraffe at Lincoln Park Zoo and a shot of himself wearing a Cubs jersey at Wrigley Field, sat a small but distinct ceramic figure.

I can't believe she kept this around. I can't believe I've kept it.

The craftsmanship and level of detail still amazed Derek. He picked up the figurine, held it in the palm of his hand and ran his fingers across it. The creature had the carved head of a lion, body of a goat and tail of a serpent. A flood of emotions washed over him as his fingers tightened their grip.

CHAPTER 3
DEREK PRICE
SEPT. 1, 2007

IF THERE'S ANYTHING worse than mandatory Saturday shifts, it's trade shows.

Derek struggled to recall an experience more uncomfortable than walking into McCormick Place for the 2007 Technology of Tomorrow trade expo. His colleagues often mocked his traditional methods and resistance to the modern age. He acknowledged they'd have had a field day with this sight.

"Should I get your AARP application ready?" Steve Erikson frequently joked, to which a colleague usually replied, "You know, he's not even 40 yet." The jokes didn't bother Derek. He practiced the art of sarcasm and replied in kind.

The monstrous map of booths hosting companies from across the country, however, proved to be no laughing matter. The noise of thousands of vendors and attendees chatting reverberated through the room, amplified by the venue's elevated ceilings.

This will be fun.

Derek stood near the entry of the exhibit hall, scanning the booths for anything interesting. He spotted industry giants such as Microsoft, Verizon and Facebook, which had recently opened its platform to a global audience. Steve Jobs, founder of Apple, which eight months ago revealed a new phone people believed would change the world, would present the keynote speech at 3.

That would give Derek's story a big-corporation perspective. He wanted to use his man-on-the-street interviews to spotlight smaller or lesser-known companies.

If I have to do this, I'm at least going to do it right.

After all, he didn't buy into Apple's hype. The new iPhone seemed little more than an elaborate iPod with a price tag that would have sent his father into cardiac arrest.

Derek continued searching for interview subjects. He walked up and down aisle after aisle of vendor booths, seeking something beyond generic logos, slogans promising a new future and nerdy computer programmers awkwardly navigating sales pitches.

Then he saw her.

Standing behind a company booth, the woman tossed her auburn hair over her shoulder as she laughed. Her cheeks raised when she smiled. Younger women rarely appealed to Derek, but something about this one — he guessed 10 years his junior — captivated his attention.

Trying his best to not stare, Derek diverted his attention to the promotional banner beside her.

Well, that's different. Thick white lines against a forest green background formed the border of the company's logo, a creature Derek recognized from mythological lore. The beast bore the head of a lion, the body of a goat and the tail of a serpent. "CHIMERA TECHNOLOGIES. Modern Problems, Mythological Solutions."

As Derek contemplated using this company for one of his interviews, he accidentally caught the woman's attention. *I'm sure I look like an easy mark standing here staring.* He pivoted and walked away from the booth. *I'll find another interview.*

"Excuse me?"

Derek hesitated but kept walking.

"Excuse me, do you have a minute?"

The voice grew louder. Derek stopped, craned his neck and saw the woman approaching. He feigned a confused expression as if to say, "Me?" A closer look made Derek's heart flutter. The woman's light brown eyes shined, and the dimples on her cheeks blushed when she smiled. She extended a handshake.

"Hi, I'm Madeline. Madeline Griffin."

A slight laugh escaped Derek's lips. "Your last name is Griffin, and you work for a company called Chimera? I bet that helped you land the job." *That's what you go with? You didn't even introduce yourself.*

If Madeline had heard that joke before, she didn't let on. "No, I thank my father for that one. Perhaps you've heard of him? Name's Zeus." The right edge of her lip creeped upward in a playful smile. "I didn't catch your name."

"Derek Price, Daily Herald. Sorry, not much to work with there."

"I'm sure we could find something, but it'll cost you." Her smile widened.

Derek smirked. "So, Chimera, huh? Tell me about that. What do you guys do?"

"On or off the record?" Madeline quipped.

She's good. "Well, you know, being featured in the same article as that Jobs guy might earn you some bonus points with the boss."

Madeline glanced toward the Chimera booth, where a portly middle-aged man with an outdated mustache talked to an expo attendee. "Well, that's Thomas over there. I can go get him if you'd rather go straight to the top."

"Oh, absolutely not. I wouldn't want to bother him. He looks rather busy."

"Well, he's quite good at looking busy." Madeline smiled. "Let me give you the official spiel."

Derek listened while she rattled off the company's standard sales pitch and attempted to explain her role as a business analyst. He scribbled notes about Chimera's multi-faceted approach to serving government clients, but his attention focused more on his interview subject than the subjects she discussed.

He surmised the company provided services including website development, emergency alerts and records management to municipalities of all sizes. Madeline even let slip that Chimera had been preparing for international expansion. Derek gathered enough to write his article, but he wanted to learn more of her story.

I'm probably keeping her away from her boss too long. He glanced at the booth. Thomas sat behind the table watching people walk past. *Or maybe not.*

"I'm sorry. I'm taking all your time," Madeline said. "You have other people you need to talk to, huh?"

"It's not a big deal. I've enjoyed our chat."

"Me, too, Derek. It's been a pleasure. I look forward to reading your story tomorrow."

"Pleasure's been all mine, Miss Griffin," he said. "Just one more question before I go."

"Sure, what's up?"

"With all your government connections," Derek paused, casting a furtive glance each direction, "can you confirm aliens exist?"

Madeline grinned. "Tell you what, give me your phone number, and I'll do one better."

She had Derek's full attention. "Yeah, what's that?"

She leaned in close and whispered in his ear. "I'll tell you who was on the grassy knoll."

CHAPTER 4
Sonia Torres
June 23, 2018

THE "PRINCIPLES OF MACROECONOMICS" textbook sat on the bed unopened. Sonia Torres laid next to it, her legs crossed, her back propped against the headboard. The glow of her MacBook lit an otherwise dark room.

She needed to study for Tuesday's exam but couldn't focus. Instead, she scrolled through her Twitter feed, reading headlines from CNN and responding to the occasional meme.

Why is economics even required for a marketing degree? While Sonia had developed a passion for politics, her experience working with -30- had made her interested in business, as well. She hoped to combine the two one day by becoming a campaign manager.

A knock at the door attracted her attention.

Luciana Torres stood in the doorway, propping her hand on the frame for support. "Good morning, mija."

Sonia switched on a bedside lamp. "Morning, mamá." Her mother's body appeared frail. She seemed to grow weaker by the day since her diagnosis, but Sonia admired her resolve and spirit. "Anything I can take care of today?"

"No, no, no. You have your own work to do." Luciana pointed at the textbook. "I do wish you would make time for yourself, though. Be a teenager. Maybe meet a nice boy."

Sonia's face blushed. She brushed off the remark. "Mamá, we've talked about that!"

Luciana grinned. "I know, I know." She paused. "Will you be home for dinner?"

"No, I'm catching up with Derek tonight."

"Oh, that will be nice. Please tell him hello for me. And give him a hug. I know how hard it must be."

If anyone does, it's you, mamá. Sonia's father, Hector, had died more than a decade ago, just after the family immigrated to the States. Luciana had balanced raising a child on her own with learning a new culture. Along the way, Sonia had developed her own perseverance.

"I will, mamá." Sonia grabbed the economics book and flipped it open. "But I should probably study first."

Luciana smiled. "I'm proud of the woman you've become, mija." She walked away from the room. Sonia closed the book and tossed it aside, turning her attention back to her laptop.

* * *

DEREK PRICE

DEREK SLID his wedding band up and down his ring finger as he waited. Propped against a faux-glass half-wall dividing the restaurant's booths from table seating, he rested his arms on the laminate tabletop. A stack of papers sat next to him with the now-opened envelope from Shadowen Real Estate lying on top.

She's really not going to be happy.

Derek checked his watch. 4:02 p.m. He flipped the lid of his phone open and selected Recent Contacts. Sonia's name topped the list. Choosing her number, he punched away repeatedly on the nine-digit keypad. The letters on the screen changed. Sixteen clicks later, he'd formed the words "Late again."

Before he hit send, Derek saw Sonia through the window, climbing out of her 2004 Chevy Cavalier, holding a shiny blue gift bag. He sent the message anyway. She checked her phone as she walked past stone statues of Betty Boop, Elvis and Marilyn Monroe on her way inside.

The door swung open. She looked at Derek and mouthed, "Funny." Seeing Sonia's long, brown hair, a change from her usual shoulder-length cut, reminded Derek of Madeline. Her tan complexion and deep brown eyes, however, contrasted his wife's light color tones.

Derek stood and greeted his protégé with a hug.

"You're blaming me for being late, and you haven't even ordered yet?" Sonia smiled and hugged Derek again.

"Didn't know what you'd want."

Sonia's smile turned into a look of contempt. The two visited this restaurant often — and their orders rarely changed. Double cheeseburger with all the fixings and a Diet Pepsi for Derek, an Italian beef with chili cheese fries and a cookie dough Arctic Swirl for Sonia.

"You know you're not a cheap date." Derek paid the cashier and grabbed the slip with their order number.

"You're forgetting I know how much you make."

"Fair point." The pair passed a mix of clientele on their way back to the booth. High school-aged kids laughed over milkshakes. Senior citizens grabbed an early dinner. *Maybe 4 is too early.* Whether the food or the nostalgia, the Polka Dot drew a diverse crowd.

Sonia slid into the booth across from Derek. She looked at the documents on the table. "Are those closing papers?"

"Well, yeah." He paused. "But not for the reason you hope." His expression turned downtrodden. "Fell through again."

"Again?"

Derek saw at least two other diners look their direction. He waved his hand in a downward motion, reminding Sonia to lower her voice.

"What the hell are you going to do now?"

Before Derek could answer, a voice behind the counter called his order number. *Saved by the bell.* He slid out of the booth to retrieve their meals. Returning a minute later, he took his seat and dished out dinner.

"So, everything went okay with -30-?"

Sonia wore her disdain for the subject change on her face. "Yeah, it was all good. Berkot's had some good engagement with their Instagram campaign, and the Kinders loved the article Country Living did on their B&B. They said to tell you thank you." She stared Derek in the eyes. "Now, what are we going to do about your house?"

"You're relentless, you know that, right?" While he'd never admit it, Sonia's persistence made him proud. The shy, young girl he'd met years ago had faded into the background of a small-town setting she'd never truly fit in. Seeing her now not only stand her ground but push matters showed how much she'd grown.

"Well, you can't just sit here and do nothing at this point. This is the third buyer they've denied. It's just getting ridiculous, Derek. If you don't do something soon, you'll die in that house waiting for it to sell."

She probably isn't wrong.

"Maybe you should stop playing the nice guy card and go back to your investigative days," Sonia continued. "That is, if you can remember how."

Sonia dished it as well as she took it; that part of her personality also reminded Derek of Madeline. *I may have been her mentor, but I think she picked up more from Maddie than I could ever teach her.*

"Fine, I'll let you have this one. From what I've been told, it's the HOA causing the issue, but the title company says they can't give me specifics."

"The HOA?" Sonia's voice elevated, again drawing attention. "Can they even do that?"

Homeowners associations weren't common in the area, but in recent years, builders had introduced the concept as a way of protecting property values and developing upscale subdivisions. Despite living in such a community, Derek had never invested time into researching the ins and outs of their operations.

"That's what I need to find out," he said. "Let me make a few calls tomorrow. I'll check in with my friend Steve. He used to cover real estate for the Herald. He should know."

"Listen to you. 'Make a few calls.' There's the old journalist spirit." Sonia smirked. "You know all that information's on the internet, right? 'Let me make a few calls,' and I'll send you what I find. I'm helping mom tomorrow and have class Monday and Tuesday — stupid economics test. How about I come by Wednesday and we compare notes?"

"Sounds good to me. But do you know what sounds even better?" Derek noted Sonia's inquisitive stare. "This burger I've been neglecting."

Sonia looked at her Italian beef. "You're right, and I hate myself for being this hungry at 4:15." She glared at Derek. "But first, before I forget — your surprise!" She lifted the gift bag from the seat next to her and handed it to Derek. "Open it."

Derek reached inside and pulled out a white box with a picture of a phone on top. Apple iPhone 8. He opened the box and removed the device without saying a word.

"Don't even bother telling me about the time you met Steve Jobs. I've already heard that story a hundred times." She paused, expecting a reaction. "I figured it's time for you to join the 21st century."

Derek looked puzzled. "Don't worry. No one else has the number," Sonia continued. "Once you're comfortable with it, we'll get rid of that piece of junk." She nodded her head toward Derek's flip phone.

Derek looked at the phone and back at Sonia. "You didn't have to do this. I know these things aren't cheap."

Sonia's smile grew wider. "Don't worry about that, either. I expensed it to work." She paused. "It's okay. I know the boss."

CHAPTER 5
Bryce Reynolds
June 26, 2018

BRYCE RECOGNIZED the pianic melody flowing from the Echo Dot on Akumi Kim's owner's suite bathroom vanity but couldn't place the composer. *Beethoven, maybe?*

A lavender candle burned in a glass jar nearby; the smell tickled his nostrils. A tumbler filled with melting ice and drops of dark soda rested on the edge of the tub. The latest issue of Cosmo laid open on the floor, revealing a two-page spread titled "Keeping Sex Fresh in Your 40s."

The scene felt serene, undisturbed aside from the woman's lifeless body sunk just beneath the surface of the bathwater.

Darkness was over the face of the deep. And the Spirit of God was hovering over the face of the waters. Bryce reached down and grabbed Akumi's body under her armpits, lifting her head above water. He focused on her closed eyes. A sense of calm washed over him. *Her busy mind can finally rest.*

He kneeled beside the bathtub and took Akumi's hand in his own. He thought of the times they'd spent together, enjoying each other's company and trading barbs on their spiritual beliefs. As much as Bryce embraced his Christian faith, Akumi practiced devout Buddhism.

He will wipe away every tear from their eyes, and death shall be no more, neither shall there be mourning, nor crying, nor pain anymore. Bryce released her hand, which splashed when it hit the water. "May this road lead you to nirvana."

He climbed to his feet, turned and blew out the candle. He left the music play as he withdrew from the room, pausing in the doorway, absorbing the eerie sense of tranquility for one final moment.

Collecting his thoughts, Bryce dried his hands, walked down the home's narrow hallway, purposefully avoiding the portraits on the wall. He descended the staircase and exited through the front door of the home, cracked open from his earlier entry. Motion-censored security lights engaged. Bryce glanced each direction but continued moving.

He opened the door of his Audi and took his position behind the wheel. His iPhone sat on the seat next to him. He grabbed it and unlocked the home screen. A picture of Akumi Kim appeared, along with her birthdate and address. Bryce stared at her smile, a smile he'd never see again.

He pulled away from the curb, navigating his way through rows of houses. The neighborhood seemed quiet. *No noise, no distraction. No wonder she lived here.* He followed the road's curve and approached the sole brick structure along an otherwise empty entry street.

The light of the gatehouse shined ahead. He lowered his driver's side window. A tall, slender gentleman stepped outside, waiting for Bryce at the gate. As the vehicle approached the mechanical arm separating its driver and the open road, the guard leaned down to look in the window.

"Get your business squared away?"

"Sure did." Bryce could tell the man thirsted for conversation. *The night shift must be terrible.* But he had places to be. "I appreciate your help."

"No problem. It's unusual to see many people — especially visitors — this time of night. Gave me something to do for a change."

"Glad I could help. Have a good night."

"You, too," the guard said.

The gate's mechanical arm lifted. The Audi rolled forward. Bryce raised the window as his vehicle approached a stop sign at the end of the private road. He glanced out the passenger window at the community's granite monument sign and flagpole, illuminated by ground-level spotlights. SHADOW RUN: A SHADOWEN REAL ESTATE COMMUNITY.

Bryce waited to turn. He picked up the smartphone, opened the Maps app and entered his destination. Nashville to Charlotte, about 400 miles. *It's gonna be a long night.* These drives made Bryce long for home, but tonight, he at least had something to think about. The past few weeks had brought several themes to mind: life, death, destiny.

For I know the plans I have for you, declares the Lord, plans for welfare and not for evil, to give you a future and a hope. He wondered how life would be different if he'd chosen another path, if he'd followed God's plan rather than pursuing his own. Would the blood on his hands weigh as heavy on his heart?

Bryce turned the corner, continuing toward the highway. He adjusted the phone from Maps to text messaging, opened the most recent thread and started his reply.

"Update." He kept his left hand on the wheel and typed with his right. "Akumi Kim is dead. Looks like an accident."

CHAPTER 6
Sonia Torres
June 27, 2018

"CAN THEY really fine you for leaving your trash bins out?"

Sonia sat at Derek's dining room table, flipping through a document labeled "Design Guidelines." Derek sat across from her, perusing a document of his own.

"They can, but I've never heard of them actually doing it. The one time I left mine out, they just sent me a letter reminding me of the rules."

And this is supposed to be the American dream? "I just don't understand how they can make such stupid rules." Sonia turned the page. "Oh, look, now they're telling you what flowers you can have in your front yard."

A voice came through the speaker of Derek's new iPhone, positioned between the two on the table. "Every state is different in how it regulates the industry." Derek's friend Steve Erikson couldn't join them in person but answered their questions by phone. "We're pretty much in the middle, but if the concept takes off more, especially downstate, I expect to see more legislation."

If this is what home ownership looks like, I'll be staying in the apartment for the rest of my life.

Derek chimed in. "So, Steve, we've got copies of all these documents. 'Articles of Incorporation.' 'By-laws.' Looks like these are labeled 'CC&Rs.' You know the situation. Where should we be looking for something that might actually help us out?"

"A lot of those are just legal documents that Shadowen had to file with the county to set up the association. You'll want to focus on the 'CC&Rs,' or 'Covenants, Conditions and Restrictions.' That outlines all the rules and restrictions for the community. If there's anything about the buyer application process, you'll find it in there."

"That's the one I'm looking at now, Steve." Derek flipped back to the title page. "Sonia's looking at the 'Design Guidelines.' I'm pretty sure she picked it because it has pictures."

Sonia huffed. "You handed me this one!"

Steve laughed on the other end of the phone. "Glad to see some things never change, Derek. A lot of times, the developer will make a guide like that to show the rules in more of layman terms. I wouldn't spend too much time worrying about it."

Fine by me. Sonia set the papers down and turned her attention to her MacBook. She checked out of the conversation, switching her browser tabs from the National Multiple Sclerosis Society homepage to Twitter. *This HOA business makes macroeconomics sound exciting.*

"Steve, I hate to take any more of your time," Derek said. "But I appreciate your help. Let's get together for a beer one of these days."

"No worries, Derek. I hope you're able to get your issues resolved. Let me know if anything else comes up. Take care, guys." The call disconnected.

Sonia pulled her eyes from the computer, turning to Derek. "You actually pay money to live under all these rules?"

"It's not that simple." Derek clasped his hands on the table. "We pay $375 every quarter for dues — assessments, they call them."

Sonia's eyes widened; she leaned forward. "$1,500 a year for someone to say you can't have a lawn gnome in front of your house? And you just go along with that?"

Derek chuckled. "Like most things in life, it's not that simple. First, consider the peace of mind that comes with living in a gated neighborhood. The sense of security. And there's the clubhouse — the pool, the gym, the tennis courts — and the events they put on."

"Because you're Mr. Active." Sonia smirked.

"You're right. I don't go that often. But Maddie did. She made a lot of friends in the neighborhood that way. People enjoy that sort of thing. That's what they're really paying for. But, yeah, it doesn't make sense when it's just me."

Shit. I didn't mean to open that wound. Sonia picked up the "Design Guidelines" from the table. "So, what do we need to do now?"

"Steve said we should focus on these." Derek tapped the "CC&Rs" with his finger. "I'll give them a read, if you want to take a break."

"Cool."

Sonia returned to her Twitter feed, reading an article from Variety about actress Evan Rachel Wood's hunger strike and laughing at comments about a White House spokesperson being denied service at a Virginia restaurant.

"Aha!" A few minutes later, Derek slid forward on his seat, leaning his face closer to the papers in his hands.

"You find something?"

"Maybe." He didn't look up. "Give me a second."

Sonia stared, waiting for an update.

Derek raised his gaze. "This might be a long shot."

Sonia raised her hands and shook her head. "Well, are you going to tell me or what?"

Derek looked down at the papers, underlining the words with his finger as he read aloud. "An Owner aggrieved by a decision of the Board may appeal the decision to the Declarant or its designee in accordance with procedures to be established by the Board."

Who writes this shit? "In English, please."

"Basically, it means I can challenge their denial." Derek grinned. "It may not get the decision overturned, but maybe I can at least get some questions answered."

* * *

Derek Price

DEREK POWERED the iPhone down and set it on the shelf above his office desk. *At least she saw me use it once.* Sonia had left about an hour ago. Derek spent the time organizing the notes from their working session and clearing off the table. Heightened emotions lingered, stirred by a return to the familiar world of research.

He sat at the desk and opened the top drawer of a file cabinet underneath. Thumbing through a set of folders, he stopped on one labeled "HOUSE". He removed it, set it on the glass desktop and opened it. He shuffled through papers, looking for any document with his HOA's contact information.

Here we go. He removed a small, half-sheet booklet. "Welcome to Shadow Ridge: New Owner Information." Derek flipped through the pages of the book until he found the "Contact the Association" section near the back. Holding the booklet open with one hand, he used the other to pull his flip phone from his pocket.

Moving his eyes from the booklet to the phone keypad and back, he dialed the number for the clubhouse front desk. The phone rang twice before a woman's voice answered.

"Thank you for calling the Shadow Ridge community clubhouse. This is Adrienne. How may I help you today?"

"Yes, hi, Adrienne." Derek paced around the office, avoiding boxes on the floor. "My name is Derek Price. I live over on Elm Street, not too far from there. I've been having some issues trying to sell my house, and I wondered if there's someone there I could talk to about it."

"Absolutely, Mr. Price. Community manager J.D. Moore would be the one you'd need to speak with. I'm afraid he's out of the office this afternoon, but it looks like he has availability tomorrow morning, if that would work for you."

"That's fine."

"How about 9 a.m.?"

"Perfect. Thank you for the help, Adrienne. I really appreciate it."

"My pleasure. Have a great day, Mr. Price."

"You, too."

* * *

Adrienne Palmetto

ADRIENNE PALMETTO BRUSHED the bangs from her face as she cradled the phone receiver against her neck. She reached across the desk and disconnected the call. When the dial tone returned, she pressed a red speed-dial button on the dock.

Three rings later, a man's deep baritone voice answered. "This is Moore." His tone hinged on the line between urgency and comfort.

"Sir, it's Adrienne out at Shadow Ridge. I'm sorry to bother you, but Mr. Price just called."

"And?"

"And I think we might have a problem, sir."

CHAPTER 7
Derek Price
June 28, 2018

LONG-TIME SHADOW RIDGE RESIDENTS affectionately referred to the community clubhouse as The Barracks. The massive, single-story concrete building stood as a monolith of recreation at the community's northern end, near Derek's residence.

A cool morning breeze brushed Derek's face as he crossed Van Buren Boulevard on Elm Street, heading to his meeting with community manager J.D. Moore. Sounds of tennis players calling their scores and children on the playground echoed in the distance. *Lots of activity this morning. Everyone must want to beat the heat.*

Derek approached the parking lot. Ahead and to the left, the tennis courts. To the right, the playground and open lawn space used for community events. He imagined a hustle of activity at the basketball courts on the other side of the building. *This is what I was trying to explain to Sonia. This is why people live in HOAs.*

He crossed the parking lot, weaving between cars, each with a small barcode sticker in the lower-right corner of the windshield. These emblems, much like the one on his CR-V, connected with the gatehouse system to grant access to the community.

Arriving at the glass-paned double doors of the main entry of The Barracks, Derek instinctively swiped the plastic key fob against the small black box on the adjoining wall. The red light turned green, but the door locks were already disengaged. *Business hours, duh.*

The interior of the clubhouse contrasted its unassuming exterior facade. Derek noted the renovations since his last visit. *I guess I haven't been here much since Maddie died.* The walls wore shades of blue, pink and orange, replacing the muted beige and dark green scheme Derek recalled.

A young child ran past Derek, nearly causing a collision. A woman he assumed to be the mother apologized. Derek smiled and waved. *Kids.* The thought he'd have none of his own infiltrated his mind.

He continued his way to the front desk, where a jaunty older woman greeted each person who passed by name. She sported a maroon polo with the Shadow Ridge logo embroidered above the heart. She smiled and rose from her swiveling office chair.

"Good morning, sir. Can I help you with something?"

Derek glanced at the woman's name tag. Adrienne Palmetto. "Yes, Adrienne, I believe we spoke yesterday. I'm here to meet with Mr. Moore."

"Oh, you must be Mr. Price." Her smile turned solemn. "I'm terribly sorry about your wife."

The words caught Derek by surprise. Adrienne clearly noticed.

"We were all so sad when it happened. I was the one who sent the flowers on behalf of the community. No worries if you don't remember. I know your mind must have been elsewhere at the moment. I can't believe it's been almost a year, hasn't it?"

Derek's mind had been elsewhere in the wake of Madeline's death. He recalled the swarm of sympathy cards and flowers, but he'd focused on battling his depression, not admiring the flora. "Thank you."

"You're most welcome. We just adored your wife. Didn't get to see her as much as we would have liked, but she was always so sweet and caring." Adrienne smiled. "With just the right amount of sass."

Seems like Maddie knew everybody around here. "I appreciate hearing that. She was one of a kind."

Adrienne paused. "Well, Mr. Price, if you want to have a seat over there, Mr. Moore will be with you soon." She gestured toward a set of black leather furniture set in the middle of the lobby area. "I hope your meeting goes well and you enjoy the rest of your day."

"Thank you. I appreciate your help."

* * *

Jefferson Moore

"AND THAT COMPLETES our tour." Jefferson Moore led a young family — father, mother and middle-school-aged child — through the fitness center doors and back into the lobby. "Questions?"

Jefferson preferred to show new residents around the community himself. His tour started by exploring the outdoor amenities — the sports courts, event lawn and playground — and finished with a walk through the fitness center and adjoining locker rooms and pool area.

"I'm good. Lynn?" The man looked to his wife, who shook her head. "We're just excited to move in and meet the neighbors."

"There will be plenty of opportunities for you to do so. I'll have lifestyle director Heather Ryan reach out to discuss our youth sports programs for your son."

The young boy's face lit up. "Awesome!"

"Well, if there's nothing else I can do for you at the moment, let me take you to Adrienne. She'll help set up your Access ID fobs."

As Jefferson led the family across the room, his eyes darted to the black leather couch in the center of the lobby. He recognized the man sitting there; he looked just like the photo in his file. A shoulder bag sat on the seat next to him. He stared at a notebook in his hands. *Punctual, prepared.*

"Well, Alex, Lynn, Christopher, it was pleasure meeting you." Jefferson extended a handshake to each member of the family. "Welcome to Shadow Ridge. I know you'll love it here."

"Thank you again, Mr. Moore. We appreciate your time," Alex said.

"Please, Alex, call me J.D." *Even if I hate that name.* He preferred his given name, but the director convinced him using his initials made him more approachable. "You're part of the family now."

Jefferson turned and walked toward the man on the couch. *Now, for the business at hand.*

* * *

Derek Price

DEREK WATCHED the man shake hands with the family at the front desk. Hearing the father call the man Mr. Moore, he surmised the tall, broad-shouldered mammoth of a man to be his community manager. *Not at all what I expected.* He packed his notebook in his satchel.

The man turned, giving Derek a better view. Short, not quite shaved, gray hair lined J.D.'s head; the color of his thin mustache matched. The community manager's face bore the wrinkles of age. His dark eyes appeared heavy with experience and wisdom. The dress shirt pressed tightly against his chest, making his chest muscles pop. *It's like Morgan Freeman's face on Michael Clarke Duncan's body.*

"Mr. Price, I presume?" The man reached a hand forward.

Derek rose from the couch to return the gesture. J.D. had at least three inches on him. Derek guessed he stood 6-foot-3. "Correct. And that must make you Mr. Moore."

"Indeed." The two locked eyes in a show of respect. J.D. tightened his grip as he spoke. "Well, Mr. Price, shall we get to business? I hear we have a problem we need to discuss."

CHAPTER 8
Derek Price
June 28, 2018

NEITHER MAN SPOKE during the walk from the lobby to J.D.'s office. The lack of personal effects in the community manager's workspace struck Derek as odd.

Sitting across a large L-shaped desk from J.D., he felt more comfortable. *He's not as imposing sitting down.*

Derek surveyed his surroundings. A sole picture frame sat on the desk, facing away from him so he couldn't see its contents. Binders with labels such as "2018 Financial Statements" and "Shadow Ridge Lot Files" lined the bookshelf behind the desk. Framed certificates recognizing J.D. as a Professional Community Association Manager and Association Management Specialist hung on the wall.

Well, that doesn't tell me much about his personality.

"So, Mr. Price, what brings you in today?" J.D. clasped his hands and leaned his wrists on his desk. He maintained eye contact and didn't seem to blink.

I'm sure you already know.

"Well, my house has been on the market for the past month. There's been a lot of interest. I've actually accepted three different offers. But, each time, I've gotten a letter from Shadowen that the buyer's application has been denied. I called Title One, but all they could tell me is that it was an HOA decision."

Derek turned his head and glanced out the window, breaking J.D.'s stare. The crowds at the tennis court had already dissipated.

"How much do you know about the real estate business, Mr. Price?"

That's an odd question. Derek turned his gaze back to J.D. The man's head hadn't moved, and Derek wasn't sure whether he'd yet blinked. "Well, I covered the industry a bit back in my newspaper days, but I've been out of that game for a decade now. So, while I'm not an expert, I'd say I'm more informed than your average Joe."

"Then you're aware of the legalities surrounding association membership?"

Talk about cutting to the chase. "A limited knowledge, sir. As I said, I've been out of the game for a while. There weren't many communities like this back then, mostly just condos in the city."

J.D. leaned forward, closing the gap between himself and Derek. "Then I trust you'll accept my expertise on the matter."

He must be former military. Now it's starting to make more sense. J.D.'s directness reminded Derek of his father. Thankfully, he'd learned how to deal with those types early in life. "I respect your knowledge, sir. You've obviously put in the time." Derek gestured at the industry certifications. "I'm just hoping you can explain to me why all three of my potential buyers weren't approved."

The community manager leaned back, placed his palms on the arms of his chair and pressed his weight down for leverage. "Mr. Price, Shadowen Real Estate has made a significant investment in this community, and we continue doing so by providing substantial financial subsidies. Our leadership team does everything they can to protect that investment."

I know a good PR line when I hear one. "And, likewise, sir, I've made a significant investment in my home."

J.D. raised his eyebrows. "I understand that, Mr. Price. But I'm sure you remember undergoing the same application process when you bought the home, correct?"

Derek nodded. His hands hung between his knees. His right thumb and index finger slid the wedding band from his left ring finger. He spun the band between his fingers several times before sliding it back to its rightful place.

J.D. continued, "So you also recall that, given the nature of the process, the results of our background and credit checks are confidential. I'm afraid the board's decision is final, and I'm unable to release additional information regarding any applications."

Why am I not surprised? Derek clasped his hands in his lap and leaned closer. "What about the appeals process?"

J.D.'s shoulders rolled backward. "I'm sorry, come again?"

"The CC&Rs. They say we can appeal grievances with board decisions. I'd like to request an appeal."

J.D. hesitated. "Mr. Price, I'm not sure what you expect to accomplish. The board's decision was firm."

"Well, I'd prefer to hear that directly from them." Derek scooted to the edge of the seat. His face hovered close to J.D. *I'm at least going to meet the people willing to hold a man hostage in his own home.*

"Very well, Mr. Price. I will contact the board to make arrangements. Adrienne will call later this week with a date for the appeal."

Derek put his hands on the edge of J.D.'s desk, using the leverage to stand. "Thank you, sir." He extended a handshake, which J.D. returned. Derek left the office and walked past the front desk and out the double doors of the clubhouse.

* * *

Jefferson Moore

JEFFERSON MUTTERED under his breath as he crossed the office and closed the door. *This isn't over yet.* His meeting with Derek Price caused more concern than it allayed.

He maneuvered behind his desk, took a seat, closed his eyes and inhaled deeply. *This isn't the update she wants to hear.* Jefferson generally thrived under pressure. He'd led his college football team to a conference title and his squadron of men into the throes of battle. But in his mind, this was different. The director had trusted him to handle the situation, and he'd failed.

Jefferson picked up the office phone and pressed the top speed-dial button on the dock. The woman answered after only one ring. "Jefferson."

"Madam Director." He paused. "Our Derek Price problem isn't going away as easily as we would have preferred. I'm leaving Shadow Ridge shortly. I'll brief you this afternoon."

"Jefferson," she repeated herself. "I'm afraid our problem may be bigger than just Derek Price."

CHAPTER 9
DEREK PRICE
FEB. 20, 2010

"CAN WE buy it, please?"

Derek rolled his eyes as Madeline elongated each syllable to drive home her point. He turned his gaze from his fiancée to the realtor and back. *She's loved this place since we passed through the gate.* "If I let you buy this one, can we go back to the condo where it's warm?"

The trio stood in the empty great room of the former model. They'd spent the morning traversing snow-covered roads on a quest to find the perfect home. "Maybe we should widen our search. I hear Phoenix is nice," Derek had quipped earlier in the day.

Since they'd entered Shadow Ridge, Madeline hadn't been able to contain her excitement. Derek listened as she raved about the landscaping, the clubhouse and the welcome reception they had received from residents.

"Well, Derek, there is a fireplace." Her feet tapped on the hardwood floor as she crossed the room. She performed her best Vanna White impersonation, waving her hand in front of the gas-powered fireplace.

The realtor laughed. Derek sighed. "And how much would we be paying the HOA every month for that fireplace?"

Madeline's eyes shot daggers. "Would you rather find another Boyd?"

Boyd Newton owned the property next to their rental and had proven himself an interesting neighbor. He raised chickens, cleaned his rifles on his porch every Sunday, and had left his boat parked in front of the house for the past year — without a trailer.

When she's right, she's right. "You have a point."

They'd looked at three others house that morning and several others through the past few weeks. Derek hadn't seen Madeline this excited about any other.

"And there's all the events and activities. You grew up in a small town. You know what it's like to know your neighbors. I didn't have that chance living in the city. This place just seems so tight-knit. Think about the friends we'll make here."

Sure, we'll fit in canasta and water aerobics between your trips to New York and Berlin. Less than a year after they met at the Technology of Tomorrow expo, Derek had lost his job at the Daily Herald and Chimera had executed its international expansion, sending Madeline on whirlwind trips across the globe.

Derek had launched -30- but business had started slow. He'd put off proposing for several months, anxious to avoid over-committing with so many variables in their relationship. About a year ago, he'd moved from his apartment. Madeline had joined him in his new condo as they took the next step in their life together. Their needs had since changed, as talks of a wedding and children grew more serious.

"Just look at all this space." Madeline walked a wide circle through the great room. The house offered over 2,500 square feet with four bedrooms and two-and-a-half baths. "There's even an office for you."

The space will be nice when we have kids. But he couldn't let her win so easily. "And who's going to clean it?"

Madeline smiled. "Don't sell yourself short, mister. You're pretty handy with a dust rag."

The realtor's phone rang. She pulled an iPhone from her pocket.

Am I the only person who doesn't have one of those now?

"Excuse me, guys. I need to take this." The realtor stepped down the hallway toward the owner's suite.

Madeline walked over to Derek, grabbed his hands and looked into his eyes. "I think this is the one. This just feels like home to me."

Derek stared into her sparkling brown eyes. "Well, let's weigh the pros and cons. Big house, friendly neighbors, beautiful clubhouse. And, on the other side, you've been completely enamored with it since we got here." He pulled her into a hug. "You're not making this easy, you know that?"

Before Madeline replied, the realtor returned. "Sorry, that was the seller's agent for another client. Did you guys talk? What are you thinking?"

"We did, and I'm afraid we have good news and bad news." Derek's expression took a serious turn. "The good news is we want the house. The bad news is you won't have to deal with us for much longer."

Madeline tilted her head back and looked into Derek's eyes. "Seriously?"

"Seriously."

She wrapped her arms around him. "I love you."

"Hey, I couldn't have done it without you."

Madeline's face glowed. "You're right. What would you do without me?"

Derek braced for impact. "Well, for starters, I wouldn't buy a house this big."

CHAPTER 10
BRYCE REYNOLDS
JUNE 28, 2018

IF ANYONE DESTROYS God's temple, God will destroy him. For God's temple is holy, and you are that temple. The Bible left little room for interpretation in its condemnation of suicide. Renowned poet Dante placed the act on the same level as murder in his famed "Inferno."

Bryce stood in Nicole Guzman's kitchen, hovering over the woman's bloody corpse. Dark red blood stained the sandcastle backsplash and pooled in the grout of the white ceramic tiles, cascading a river of blood through the woman's kitchen. He examined the wound — right temple, slight upward angle. *If I didn't know better, I'd assume suicide.*

He moved to the kitchen island, revisiting the half-empty glass of wine and empty merlot bottle. *Nine o'clock seems early, but we all have our vices.* Leaving the glass in place, he picked up the bottle with his gloved hands and tossed it in the recycling bin.

From there, he hustled to the table at the center of the adjacent eat-in kitchen. A page ripped from a Chimera Technologies spiral-bound notebook waited. Bryce picked up the note, reading it a second time.

"To my friends and family, I'm sorry." Letters weaved up and down, scribbled in a state of emotional stress. *Or, to the right eyes, distress.* "I've done everything I can to fight the demons of my past, but I can no longer bear the burden. Cameron, I'm sorry for the lies. I'm sorry for the secrets. I should have been honest with you sooner. To Isabelle, I'm proud of the young woman you've become. I can no longer say the same about myself. Please remember me for who I was, not what I've become."

Bryce had met Cameron two or three times but knew of Isabelle only by reputation. *She has to be 13, maybe 14, by now.*

He read the letter again. *Lies, secrets. There will be questions.* Pushing emotion aside, he went about his work. He grabbed the notebook, lying nearby on the table, and began copying the first lines of the note. Stopping after a few words, he ripped the page from the book, crumpled it and tossed it toward the trash. He repeated the process two more times. *Helps show she had second thoughts.*

Bryce spotted the woman's Samsung Galaxy sitting on the counter. He carried the device back to the body, reaching down with its camera pointed at Nicole's face. *C'mon, work.* The phone's home screen unlocked. Bryce opened Chrome. Macy's website displayed a deep red cocktail dress Nicole would never wear.

He typed "suicide hotline" into the browser's search bar. Words in a large font and a clickable phone number appeared across the top of the page. "Help is available. National Suicide Prevention Lifeline. 1-800-273-8255."

Bryce activated a call but hung up as soon as someone answered. He returned the phone to the table. Satisfied, he moved back toward the woman's body, squatting down to look at her face one last time. Her eyes were open. Bryce wiped his hand across them, pulling the lids shut.

Whoever sheds the blood of man, by man shall his blood be shed, for God made man in his own image. Bryce raised his hand to his face, kissed his fingers and touched them to Nicole's forehead.

He rose to his feet, turned away from the body and walked out the front door. He pulled the rubber gloves from his hands. The sun's morning rays beamed down on him; the East Coast air hung in his lungs. *It just feels so much more natural than Chicago.* Standing outside his Audi, parked two blocks down the street, he pulled his phone from his pocket and dialed.

"9-1-1. What's your emergency?"

"Hi, yes, I live over in Shadow Grove, the new neighborhood outside Asheville."

"Yes, sir, I know the location."

"I was out walking my dog, and, well, I'm pretty sure I just heard a gunshot."

"Sir, can I have your name and exact location, please?"

Bryce didn't answer. He disconnected the call, returned the phone to his pocket and climbed inside the vehicle. He sat for a moment, reflecting on the past two weeks, the three dead bodies.

And this is nowhere near over yet.

CHAPTER 11
DEREK PRICE
JUNE 28, 2018

THE WALK HOME DID LITTLE to improve Derek's mood. His meeting with community manager J.D. Moore left him frustrated with what he considered a lack of cooperation. *At least they're scheduling the appeal.*

Back at his house, he poured himself a drink. He held the glass of water in one hand and his flip phone in the other. Finding Sonia's name on the Recent Calls list, he dialed her number. Voicemail picked up after three rings.

"Hey, it's me. I just got home from the meeting and wanted to fill you in. Call me back when you can." As Derek clasped the phone shut, a shrill noise from the bedroom caught his ear. He hurried down the hall. The screen of the iPhone on his office shelf glowed.

He picked up the device. A text message from Sonia waited. "I told you to text me."

Oh, you're funny.

Derek tried to reply. His fingers fumbled over the buttonless keyboard. A moment later, the screen changed to an incoming call. He slid the green circle to the right to answer, as Sonia had shown him.

"Now, was that so difficult?"

She didn't acknowledge his question. "Tell me about the meeting."

"Not really anything we weren't prepared for. He gave me a line about protecting Shadowen's investment. Don't get me wrong; he seemed like a good guy, reminded me of my dad a bit, but he clearly didn't want to say too much."

"Did you bring up the appeal?"

"Yeah." He paused. "They said they'll call and schedule it."

"We'll see if that actually happens."

Derek rolled his eyes. "We have no reason to believe it won't. Now, how effective will it be? That's the million-dollar question."

"How are they allowed to have this much power? I'd expect this crap from the White House, not the HOA."

He let the comment slide. "With the holiday next week, I'm sure it will be a while before I hear from them."

Sonia hesitated. "What can we do in the meantime? Is there any way we can take these assholes down?"

"Now, there's no need to be overly dramatic. We're not taking anyone down. I just want answers so I can move on."

Sonia huffed. "So, what are we going to do?"

Derek grinned. "Haven't I told you the first rule of investigation a hundred times?"

"You tell me a lot of things. You expect me to remember them all?"

Derek's mood had improved significantly since their conversation began. "Follow the money, Sonia. It always leads somewhere."

* * *

Sonia Torres

SONIA SLUNG her backpack over her shoulder as she walked down the long hallway. She passed classroom doors propped open to improve airflow. Professors lectured on a variety of subjects. Her

English class had been discussing Shakespeare's "King Lear" when she had stepped out to return Derek's call and decided not to go back. *Nothing I didn't learn senior year.*

She started to text her mother but stopped to check the time: 9:47 a.m. *She knows I'm in class until 10:30.* The white lie came to her quickly. "Teacher no showed. Heading to Derek's. Be home for dinner. Love you."

Sonia opened the stairwell door and climbed down two flights to reach ground level. The humid air hit her face when she walked outside. She stopped, turning to look at the white stone building behind her.

Cutting class wasn't her style, but Derek needed help. Besides, dissecting Shadow Ridge's financial records would provide an education of its own. *And this might actually be relevant to my career. "King Lear?" I feel like we're already living it.*

* * *

Tyler Norris

TYLER NORRIS SQUIRMED in his chair. He wore his headphones with one piece on his ear and the other raised slightly, allowing him to eavesdrop on the nearby conversation. He wondered what happened, what role he'd played in it and what repercussions he'd face.

Tyler had worried since field director Jefferson Moore returned to the office that morning without so much as a hello. The field director had come in, grabbed a few items and taken the elevator upstairs to the head boss's office.

Now, Tyler tried not to stare as Jefferson hovered over one of the larger cubicles reserved for middle management. Jefferson and Tyler's boss, senior analyst Angie Farrow, talked in hushed tones. Tyler strained his ears to listen. *At least they're not in his office. Maybe I'm overthinking this.*

Last week, Jefferson had asked Tyler to monitor Shadow Ridge resident Derek Price's activity. Now, he dropped the name multiple times in his conversation with Angie. But Derek Price wasn't the only name being tossed around. Tyler couldn't be positive, but he thought he heard Sheridan, Cross, Kim and Wainwright.

He tried to concentrate on data entry, but the quiet chatter stole his focus. A few minutes later, the whispers stopped. He looked up. Jefferson's hulking frame approached his desk. Tyler's heart raced. *I'm about to be fired; I know it. But what the hell did I do?*

Tyler's eyes remained locked on his computer screen until Jefferson spoke.

"Mr. Norris." The man's voice boomed. "What can you tell me about Derek Price's recent activity?"

"Let me check for you, sir." His fingers shook as they glided across the keyboard. He typed the wrong character multiple times, backspacing to correct his errors. *Just settle down.* Tyler watched Derek Price's photo and profile appear on the center monitor. "Looks like he hasn't left Shadow Ridge for a couple days. He swiped into the clubhouse this morning, which is odd because the doors would have been unlocked already."

Tyler felt Jefferson's stare. "Oh, this is interesting. It looks like he had a visitor come through the gate less than an hour ago."

Jefferson lowered his gaze. "Name?"

"Yes, sir." Tyler clicked a few buttons on the screen. "Her name looks to be Sonia Torres, sir. Frequent visitor, it seems."

The corner of Jefferson's lip raised. "Thank you, Mr. Norris." He turned and walked back up the row of cubicles.

Thank God. For the first time in several minutes, Tyler consciously remembered to breathe.

CHAPTER 12
Sonia Torres
June 28, 2018

"WHEN'S THE LAST TIME you even ate at this table?"

Sonia broke a 10-minute silence. Derek sat at the other end of his dining room table scouring the hundreds of pages she'd printed. After leaving class, she'd headed to Derek's house and began pulling financial records for HOAs, both within and outside the Shadowen portfolio, from the internet.

"I don't know. Maybe before South Dakota?" Derek didn't look up.

I've never seen him like this before. She enjoyed observing him in his element. *He hasn't even made a sarcastic remark in over 20 minutes.* He stared at document after document, tracing lined spreadsheets with a pen and organizing pages in a system she didn't understand. *And I'm not about to stop him to ask.*

The afternoon's biggest surprise for Sonia had been the sheer size of each HOA budget. She'd focused on communities of comparable size to Shadow Ridge, yet annual spending ranged from $200,000 to upwards of $4 million.

Derek attributed the differences to factors such as the privacy gates and the clubhouse. She'd learned not every community offered the same benefits as Shadow Ridge. *Still seems like a shit ton of money.*

"Here's a few more companies for you to check out." Derek finally looked up. "DataLink. Montini Brothers. Labyrinth Systems."

"DataLink, Montini Brothers and Labyrinth Systems?" Sonia repeated the names as she typed them into a Word document on her MacBook.

"Correct." Derek lowered his gaze back to the document in his hand.

His first pass through Shadow Ridge's annual budget had raised no red flags, though line-items varied compared to the other communities they'd examined. Derek had used three colors of highlighter to distinguish the discrepancies. Green meant a difference of up to 25 percent, yellow indicated 26 to 50 percent, and pink marked anything higher. *As long as he understands what he's doing.*

She knew, however, that when he encountered a pink highlight, he switched to another document and called out names of companies he wanted her to investigate.

"DataLink checks out. Based in Denver. Looks like they specialize in facility access systems. You have that thing on your keyring that lets you in the clubhouse, right?"

"Yeah." Derek dug his keys from his pocket, turning the diamond-shaped fob over in his hand. The words DataLink were imprinted on the back of the device. "That checks out."

Damn it. Every promising lead that turned out innocuous added to Sonia's growing frustration. But she persisted, remembering the story Derek had told her about discovering a city clerk embezzling money by looking into city's halls utility payments.

"I've got Montini Brothers for you now. Local company from Kankakee. Heating and air conditioning." She paused. "Maybe we should ask what they have the thermostat set at."

Derek chuckled. "Keep looking."

I was only halfway joking. Just as Sonia considered questioning the effectiveness of their strategy, she stopped. "Hey, this is kind of interesting."

Derek set down the paper in his hand, stood and walked behind Sonia's chair to see her screen, which displayed an error code saying the site couldn't be reached. "What am I looking at here?" He turned his gaze to Sonia.

"Labyrinth Systems. Their website doesn't seem to exist anymore. I still see references in my search results, but it looks like the domain expired." She looked at Derek and smiled. "Do you need me to put that in Derek terms for you?"

He snickered. "Funny. I get the gist, and I know you understand the rest."

"I'm just wondering what kind of company doesn't have a website in 2018." *Shit, I shouldn't have said that.* She'd begged Derek to let her set up a -30- company website. He'd only agreed late last year.

"Maybe they're just updating it or something?"

Doesn't seem he took that the wrong way. "Maybe. Give me a few minutes. I've got an idea."

Sonia's fingers flew across the keyboard. She transitioned between tabs with sites for State of Illinois agencies, the Better Business Bureau, LinkedIn and Glassdoor. From the corner of her eye, she noted the look of reverence on Derek's face. *He'll never admit my way worked, though.*

"Anything interesting?"

"Well, kind of." Sonia stopped typing and looked at Derek. "Labyrinth Systems was a registered LLC, but they let their business license drop last year. There's nothing from the BBB and no employee reviews on Glassdoor. They have a LinkedIn page, but it hasn't been updated in almost two years, and the few posts that are there look like sales materials."

"None of that really helps us, though, does it?"

Sonia smiled. "Oh, there's more. Labyrinth Systems is actually a subsidiary. Paperwork is all filed under the name Thomas Sheridan. Let me see if I can find the parent company."

Derek held up his hand to stop her. His jaw hung open, but he didn't speak.

"What's wrong?"

"You don't need to look it up."

"What? Why? Do you know the name, this Thomas Sheridan?"

Derek hesitated. "I do. He was Maddie's boss. Labyrinth. Chimera. It's too much to be a coincidence, right?"

Madeline's boss? I thought she worked with the government, not HOAs. "Sure seems that way."

Derek's face scrunched, stressing the wrinkles on his forehead. His eyes squinted; his lip tremored. "It just doesn't make any sense."

Sonia turned back to the computer and began another search. *What?* "Chimera's website is gone, too."

"That's the weird part. Chimera shut down right before Maddie died. Caught everyone by surprise. Everyone knew Thomas was planning to retire soon, but Maddie was confident Andrew would take the reins."

Sonia nodded, not knowing what to say.

Derek adjusted his head, looking her in the eyes. "So, why the hell is my HOA paying a company that doesn't exist?"

CHAPTER 13
DEREK PRICE
DEC. 18, 2014

"HOW'S THAT for a bowl full of jelly?" Derek elbowed Madeline beneath the table.

"Oh, stop it." She laughed.

The couple watched Thomas Sheridan stumble his way onto the portable stage in the basement of Al's Steakhouse. The red Santa suit almost blended with the brick background. Derek guessed Thomas wished he could fade into the wall. *That get-up is awful. He must have lost a bet with somebody.* "You can't tell me he doesn't look miserable right now."

Isiah Cross, the young red-headed man seated next to Madeline, spoke. "I haven't known the guy that long, but I think that's his default setting."

Thomas grabbed a microphone and tapped it twice. "Is this thing on? Good." He looked across the room. "I just wanted to say thank you. First, to Monique and Nicole for planning this wonderful event. Second, to all of you spouses here with us tonight. I know our work often takes us away from home, so it's nice to have a chance to get together and celebrate."

"I'm pretty sure he means us." Derek leaned across the table, addressing Isiah's wife Katherine, who smiled and nodded.

Thomas continued from the stage. "This has been a remarkable year for all of us at Chimera. We welcomed a few new team members. Isiah Cross, Akumi Kim, would you please stand for a moment?"

Isiah rose from his seat, as did a 40-something Asian woman on the other side of the room. Derek watched Isiah smile and wave like an experienced pageant contestant.

"Quite the charmer you've got on your hands," Derek said to Katherine.

Thomas paused while Isiah and Akumi took their seats. "This has also been an exceptional year for us operationally. But I think to fully appreciate all we've done, we have to look back at where we started."

"Hold on to your seats. He's going to tell the origin story." Madeline's crooked smile said enough.

Thomas raised his palm into the air. "Why Chimera? I can't tell you how many times I've been asked that question. Why all the mythology references? Well, I'm sure Vince over here will tell you it's because I think of myself as a god, and Andrew will say I'm as bullheaded as a minotaur."

He waited while the crowd laughed. "But the reality is simple. Mythology is about ordinary people doing extraordinary things. Humans interacting with gods and slaying beasts. And that's what we do every day — we help normal people overcome Herculean tasks and feel like they belong on Mount Olympus. And you make that possible."

Not a bad little speech. Derek applauded with the rest of the audience.

"Now, if I can continue, I've put together a short presentation to highlight those accomplishments." The crowd's applause turned to jeers and booing. "I'm kidding. I'm kidding. We'll save that for Monday's staff meeting." Thomas smiled. "We all have better things to attend to tonight. Enjoy yourselves, everyone, and have a Merry Christmas!" The audience applauded once again.

"Better speech than I expected," Isiah said to Madeline.

She grinned. "He's had practice. He gave the same speech two years ago."

As Thomas left the stage, a waiter carrying a tray of salads stopped at the table, placing a dish in front of each guest. Derek and Madeline enjoyed small talk with Isiah and Katherine over the opening course. When the women excused themselves to the restroom, the men took advantage of their first real chance to interact.

"So, Madeline says you're an entrepreneur. Marketing, is it?" Isiah seemed young, maybe early 30s. His scraggly red hair appeared orange in the incandescent light.

"More public relations, really. Traditional media, coaching, consulting. Trying my hardest to avoid this new wave of digital marketing everyone's on about. If things keep going that way, I'll have to hire some young kid to work for me, I suppose." He paused. "So, you're new to Chimera? What do you do here?"

"I have the distinct pleasure of serving as sales director." Isiah chuckled. "Not what I ever expected I'd be doing when I was growing up. You know, I actually studied journalism for a semester at Mizzou." Isiah grabbed his glass and sipped his chardonnay.

Mizzou's a good program. "Only a semester?"

"Yeah, I learned I'm better at talking than writing. So I found a career more suited to my skills. Now, Madeline gets me in the door, and I talk them right into the deal." He laughed.

I'm surprised he didn't end up doing TV news. "You from Missouri, then? I grew up in southern Illinois. Graduated from Carterville High and SIU. Had quite a few friends over at SEMO."

"I'm actually from Nebraska. Wanted to get away and see the world — you know how that goes, I'm sure. I didn't really plan to stay in the Midwest, but when I met Kat, I knew I'd follow her anywhere."

Katherine and Madeline returned to their seats. "Are you telling that BS story again?" Katherine leaned in and kissed her husband. "I've offered to move several times, but we love Kansas City, and we're in a great school district for the girls."

At the mention of children, Derek put his hand on Madeline's knee under the table.

"And besides," Katherine continued, "with as much as he's traveling now, I'm not sure it would matter where we lived."

Derek clapped his hands together. "Now, isn't that the truth?"

Madeline playfully smacked his arm. Isiah laughed. "Yet they have no problem using our airline miles, right?" She shook her head and smiled as she spoke.

The couples continued talking through the main course — rosemary chicken breasts with fresh vegetables and a baked potato. *Of course they bring us to a steakhouse and serve chicken.* The four laughed and carried on conversation.

"We'll all look back at tonight as the beginning of a beautiful friendship," Isiah toasted at one point.

As the evening drew to a close, Thomas Sheridan returned to the stage sans Santa suit. He thanked everyone again for attending and called the members of his team forward for a group photo. Derek laughed as Madeline, Isiah, Thomas and nine others attempted to arrange themselves. Most of the men stood in the back, though Isiah's diminutive stature forced him into the front row.

Derek leaned across the table, closing the gap between himself and Katherine. "Is it me, or does this look like the group that's going to save the world?"

Katherine chuckled and smiled. "With my husband involved? You'd better believe they'll try."

Derek paused thoughtfully. "Yeah, and if my wife has anything to say about it, they'll either do it or die trying."

CHAPTER 14
DEREK PRICE
JUNE 29, 2018

"WELL, JOE, I think everything's ready to go. I'll send the press release Monday and let you know what I hear. If you need anything else in the meantime, just give me a ring back."

Derek paced across his front porch, enjoying a change of scenery after spending the morning cooped up in his office. He hadn't stopped thinking about the odd connection between Thomas Sheridan and his HOA, but he'd forced himself to concentrate on -30- projects.

"Perfect. Well, have a great weekend. Enjoy the time with your grandkids." Derek closed the phone. His gaze drifted across the street to Karen Conrad's house. A stack of Amazon boxes sat on the porch undisturbed. *Those were delivered yesterday. I should make sure everything's alright.*

Derek descended the two steps from the patio to the sidewalk and made his way across the street. As he approached the home, he noticed the flowers in Karen's yard drooping. He climbed onto the porch — nearly identical to his — and knocked on the door.

Now that I think about it, I really haven't seen Karen since the day after I got home.

Derek waited a minute and knocked again. A few seconds later, Karen opened the door. A mesh screen separated the two. She wore pajamas. Her hair appeared disheveled, as if she'd just climbed out of bed. He couldn't quite tell through the screen, but Derek thought her eyes looked bloodshot.

"Oh, Derek, it's you."

"Hey, Karen. I just wanted to make sure you're okay. I saw you had packages left on the porch."

"They brought those yesterday. I fell asleep and forgot about them. Thanks for reminding me. I haven't been feeling myself lately."

You don't look yourself. "Is there anything I can do to help? Do you need medicine? Warm bowl of chicken soup? Campbell's finest."

Karen smiled. "No, I just need time to let it pass. But thank you. I appreciate you thinking about me."

"Hey, us neighbors have to look out for each other, right?" Derek returned her smile and said goodbye, stepping off Karen's porch and heading home. He paused, looking again at the flowerbed. *I should come back and give those some water.*

* * *

BACK INSIDE, with deadlines behind him and the weekend ahead, Derek couldn't stop thinking about the illogical relationship between Chimera Technologies, Labyrinth Systems and Shadowen Real Estate.

He'd tried distracting himself with television, music and the logic puzzle book he'd fiddled with since Christmas. He wanted answers and wondered if he'd find them in his office closet. *Maddie must have had some idea about all of this.* Six weeks ago, Derek would have known exactly where to find the box of Madeline's belongings, but, at some point, the mountains of cardboard started blending together.

It has to be here somewhere. He rummaged through the closet, building new stacks of boxes. At one time, he'd wondered why he'd held on to the trinkets, notebooks and junk. But, in this moment, he hoped his reluctance to dispose of Madeline's materials would pay dividends.

Here we go. The box sat on the carpet at the bottom of the closet. Derek carried it from the office to the dining room and ripped tape from the cardboard lid. *What do I actually expect to find?* He'd been so engrossed with finding the box he hadn't considered the actual value of its contents.

A stack of thank you and best wishes cards from when Madeline left Chimera. Notebooks and pads, covered with pristine penmanship and less-than-stellar doodling. Derek smiled as he glanced at the entries:

*Lady Maria's catering ****1/2.*
Gift idea for Thomas — improv classes.
Remind Isiah gingers shouldn't wear orange.

Derek placed his left thumb between his middle and ring fingers, rubbing it against his cobalt wedding band. *What I would give for just one more day.* He wiped a single tear from his eye.

Setting the notebook aside, he returned to the box, where he found an 8x10 print of a familiar photo. Twelve people awkwardly posed in front of a brick wall in the basement of Al's Steakhouse. *Oh man, what a night.* From Thomas's ill-fitting Santa suit to meeting Isiah and Katherine, that night held special memories. He looked across the smiling faces.

Maddie, Thomas and Isiah, obviously. There's Andrew and Vince. Nicole and Monique. Akumi. What was his name? Brian? Brad? Something like that. I can't remember. He struggled to identify a few of those pictured, especially those who had left Chimera through the years.

"Not everyone's cut out for our line of work," Madeline used to joke.

To which Derek would respond, "You mean not everyone can keep a secret, right?"

If anyone could help explain the connection, they're probably in this photo. Derek's mind immediately went to Thomas and Isiah. For better or worse, the two men were entangled in his mind after the situation at the funeral. *Or maybe Andrew.* Derek's real problem wasn't who to call; it was how to reach them. *I have Isiah's number saved.*

Derek and Isiah hadn't talked in over a year. Isiah had even missed Madeline's funeral, but Derek understood, mournfully appreciating the similarities of their situations. Only months before Madeline's death, Isiah's wife Katherine and their two daughters perished in a tragic accident when a semi-trailer blindsided their vehicle. *I buried a wife; he buried a family.*

Derek pushed the thought from his mind, returning to the box. Removing papers by the handful, he dug deeper, looking for a specific spiral-bound book containing Madeline's contacts. He spotted its dark blue cover at the bottom of the box.

Madeline's organization wasn't always the most logical, but Derek flipped to "W" and found the information he wanted under the heading "Work." He scanned a list of names — some he recognized, others he didn't. Looking at his watch, Derek thought twice about bothering anyone with such a trivial matter on a Friday evening. *I'll make some calls in the morning.*

He closed the book, satisfied with having a new thread to pull.

CHAPTER 15
Sonia Torres
June 30, 2018

"HEY MAMÁ, did you see there's an MS Walk happening in September? Maybe I should set up a team and we'll fundraise. I'm sure Derek would sponsor us."

Sonia sat at the small round table in the apartment kitchen while her mother washed dishes at the sink. "That's sweet, mija, but you have enough on your plate. You should see if someone else has a team you can join."

"This is important. Besides, I'm not that busy." *Except for the English paper due next week, the ad campaign I'm working on for Derek and the fact I still haven't decided what to do for the Fourth of July.* "I'm going to register."

She clicked the "Join the Walk" button on the Greater Illinois Chapter page on the National Multiple Sclerosis Society website and followed the on-screen prompts. "Done! I set our goal at $10,000. Now I just have to invite everyone to join our team."

Sonia switched the browser to Twitter, where she copied and pasted her team's donation link.

"Sonia, dear, I'm worried you're taking on too much." Luciana set the dish towel down and moved to stand behind Sonia, laying her hands on her daughter's shoulders. "It's summer. This is supposed to be your time to enjoy yourself, to spend time with friends."

Spending time with friends doesn't pay the bills.

"Don't worry about me, mamá." Sonia reached up and patted her mother's hand. "Everything is under control. I'd tell you if anything was wrong."

"I know you would, mija." Luciana bent down and kissed Sonia atop her head. She turned and walked back to the sink.

Sonia closed Twitter. Another open browser page appeared on her screen. She did a double-take at the Joliet Junior College website, ensuring her mother hadn't seen it. She gave it another quick look before pulling the MacBook shut. The words were etched in her mind. "ECN 102 Macroeconomics: D."

There's still one more test before the final. I've got time to raise it.

* * *

Derek Price

DEREK SECOND-GUESSED himself from the moment he woke up. Finding Madeline's address book had felt like a minor victory, but to do anything further, he needed to interject himself into someone else's life.

These people worked for a company that shut down over a year ago. They were Maddie's friends, not mine. Except Isiah.

Derek thought about the young hotshot from Kansas City he'd met four years ago. That Isiah had radiated confidence and screamed personality, always finding himself at the center of attention.

But Isiah had changed. Life had taken its toll. The version Derek had last seen had experienced pain and suffering beyond his years. At his most vulnerable, he had pushed away the people who'd tried to help. *He flipped a switch at the funeral. That's the part I'll never forget.*

Even if Isiah had answers, Derek debated if calling would cause more harm than good. Sitting on the leather couch in his great room, he held his flip phone in one hand and Madeline's address book in the other.

Just start with one call. Start with someone you know. Not Isiah.

Derek dialed the number listed for Larry Peterson. They'd met at a Chimera picnic several years ago and bonded over their commonalities. Both men of a certain age, Larry had spent his childhood in western Kentucky, close to Derek's hometown.

Three rings later, an automated greeting connected. "We're sorry, but the number you have dialed is no longer in service." *Maybe these were business numbers. Maybe none of them will work.* Derek realized, however, the numbers had distinct area codes and weren't centralized to Chimera's Chicagoland base.

One more try won't hurt. Derek dialed the number listed for Andrew Wainwright, Chimera's anointed one and Thomas Sheridan's presumed successor. Within five years of earning his bachelor's degree, Andrew had added an MBA and been named chief operating officer of Chimera. Madeline had raved about Andrew and predicted a bright future. Derek had understood why.

The phone rang twice. The line clicked as if someone answered, but Derek heard only silence. "Hello?" No response. "Andrew?" He pulled the phone from his ear. The screen flashed a Call Ended message. Confused, he hit redial.

This time, the call rang through to voicemail. *Maybe he's in a meeting or something?*

"We're sorry, but the voicemail for the user you're trying to reach is full. Please hang up and try your call later."

That was weird. Maybe he'll call back. Derek sunk into the couch with his arms stretched to either side. He closed his eyes. *I'm not going down that road. I'm not calling him.* His mind quieted for a moment. *But I know he'll know. He has to know.*

Derek straightened his pose, looked down at the phone in his hand and entered Isiah's number. His thumb hovered over the call button. *He probably won't answer. I'm sure he's changed his number.*

The first ring. *Maybe it will be disconnected, like Larry.* The second ring. *Or go to voicemail, like Andrew.* The third ring. *See, he's not going to answer.* The fourth ring.

"Hello?"

Words formed in Derek's mind, but none escaped his lips.

The man's tone changed. "Hello?"

"Isiah," Derek mustered.

"Speaking, but I'm not interesting in whatever you're selling."

Derek's voice broke. "No, it's not that at all. I'm not selling anything." He paused. "Isiah, it's Derek Price."

Well, this is the moment of truth.

"Derek Price! Long time, no talk, buddy. How the hell have you been?"

How the hell? More like what the hell?

CHAPTER 16
BRYCE REYNOLDS
JUNE 30, 2018

ENTER BY the narrow gate. For the gate is wide, and the way is easy that leads to destruction, and those who enter by it are many.

Bryce stared at the two bodies sprawled before him, surrounded by signs of struggle. A broken lamp, an armchair lying on its back, blood on an area rug.

Staring at the splatter staining the top of a glass end-table, Bryce contemplated the choices that had led each man's life to this point. He traced his own path to one specific moment, when he had consciously assaulted his father. The familiar scene triggered a memory.

* * *

JAN. 13, 2007

BRYCE RULED the school. A well-respected sophomore and standout athlete, his dreams consisted of multimillion-dollar sports contracts, fancy cars and beautiful women. His home life, however, told a different story.

His father, Garrett Reynolds, suffered from a potent combination of alcoholism and a bad temper. He often commiserated his problems with his friends Jack Daniels and Johnnie Walker, and when they couldn't console him, he'd turn his attention to his wife and son.

The Alcoholics Anonymous meetings had seemed to help. After a particularly violent incident, the police had intervened, though Bryce's mother had refused to pressed charges. A month had passed since Garrett's last drink.

Then Bryce fell ill during basketball practice. Rather than bother his parents, he caught a ride home with an older friend whose varsity practice had finished. Walking down the sidewalk, he heard screaming inside the southern Maine home.

Damn it.

He barged through the door to see his mother's frail body slam into the living room wall. She shrieked through the tears. His father drunkenly staggered toward her with his fist cocked back, ready to swing. "Stop it, Dad!" Bryce dropped his backpack and rushed to position himself between his parents.

His mother cried out in abject terror. "Bryce, no!" Garrett's fist connected with Bryce's face.

Bryce dropped to the floor. *I'm going to make sure that's the last time you ever lay a finger on either of us.* He climbed to his feet, staring into his father's empty eyes and waving his hand to taunt his opponent.

Garrett threw another punch. Bryce ducked. As the arm flew above his head, Bryce pushed himself forward, tackling the older man. Both collapsed to the floor, tangled in a web of flailing limbs, struggling for advantage.

Bryce's arms strained as he pinned Garrett to the floor. He felt his control fading. Garrett pushed upward, lifting his head and shoulders from the ground, sending Bryce toppling. Bryce released his grip, acknowledging he'd lost the dominant position.

"You're going to pay for this, you little asshole." Saliva foamed at Garrett's mouth. The smell of whiskey made Bryce wince.

Bryce maneuvered his way to a seated position. Garrett lunged. Bryce shifted his weight to the right, sending his father flying past on his left. *Who's the asshole now?* He watched Garrett's body fall.

The world stopped.

Garrett's head smashed into the corner of a glass coffee table. His temple bore the brunt of the blow.

"Garrett!" Bryce's mother rushed to her husband's side. She turned to Bryce, a look of terror on her face. "What did you do?"

Bryce noticed the blood on the glass. He rolled to his knees and grabbed his father by the shoulders. *Fuck. What did I do?* "Dad? Dad, are you okay?" No response. *This wasn't supposed to happen.*

"What the hell were you thinking, Bryce? What did you do? What did you do?" His mother's words trailed off into tears.

For the first time in his life, Bryce Reynolds had killed a man.

* * *

JUNE 30, 2018

FOR IF WE LIVE, we live to the Lord, and if we die, we die to the Lord. So then, whether we live or whether we die, we are the Lord's.

Bryce broke his stare from the blood-stained glass. He looked at the corpse at his feet. An older man, in his 50s. Blond hair, green eyes, three gunshot wounds to the chest. *We must have crossed paths before, but I can't remember when.*

The second body, on the other hand, he knew well. He'd traveled to Springfield specifically to find this man, Andrew Wainwright. Bryce squatted next to Andrew's body and pulled the phone from the dead man's pocket. "Missed call," the screen read.

Would things have ended differently if he'd been able to answer the call?

Bryce rose to his feet and exited the house. The streets were empty. In the distance, he heard children playing. He climbed behind the wheel of his Audi, parked in Andrew's driveway, and sat in silence for a moment. *Precious in the sight of the Lord is the death of his saints.*

He pulled out of the drive and down the street, admiring the white fences lining the road. *The Land of Lincoln, if I've ever seen it.* The dichotomy between the serene community and the nearby state capitol always struck a chord with him.

Until next time, Shadow Cove.

CHAPTER 17
Derek Price
June 30, 2018

"DEREK? You there?"

Derek sat on the edge of the couch in stunned silence, caught off-guard by the enthusiasm in Isiah's voice. *I guess everyone processes grief differently.*

"Yeah, sorry, I'm here." The words stammered from his mouth. "I've been alright, I guess. You?"

"Oh, you know, just living the dream."

The dream? It feels more like a nightmare to me. Derek had feared reopening old wounds for Isiah, but he seemed to be the one suffering.

"By the way, man, I'm sorry I missed Madeline's funeral." Isiah broke the awkward silence. "I was in a dark place after losing Kat and the girls. I didn't feel like I knew who I was anymore."

After the way you went off on Thomas at the funeral, none of us knew who you were. "I don't know if I'll ever truly understand your pain, Isiah, but, believe me, I can relate. I know things were rough, but it seems like you're doing better now."

Isiah paused. "They never caught the asshole who did it, did they?"

"No, they closed the case a few months back. Not enough evidence to keep it open."

"Damn, man, that really sucks. Can you imagine living life knowing you were responsible for something like that and not coming forward? It takes a special kind of person to be that heartless."

"Ain't that the truth?" Derek let the conversation lull. "So, anyway, you sound good. What have you been up to?"

"To be honest? Living my best life, man. After the funeral, I started therapy. Great therapist here in KC. She helped me figure out how to move on."

Maybe I should have gone that route myself. Derek held his left hand out in front of him, staring downward at the worn ring.

Isiah continued. "She encouraged me to find a project to focus on, something to take my mind off my grief. Not something stupid like cleaning the garage; it had to be something with purpose. She called it my North Star."

"How's that been going?"

"Oh, man, Derek. I can't tell you how cathartic it's been. I've been hacking away at it for a year now, and I can finally see the light at the end of the tunnel. It feels good, man. I feel like I've given a little something back to the world."

Once I get settled down in a new place, maybe I need to find a project. "That's great, Isiah. I'm glad things have turned around for you."

"I appreciate that." He waited. "How about you? What's been keeping you busy?"

There's the opening I needed. "Well, I've been trying to sell the house."

"Leaving good old Shadow Ridge, huh? Heading back closer to the city?"

"I think I'm going to stay around here. Just looking to downsize, find a better place for, well, just me."

Isiah's voice crackled. "Believe me, I understand. I swear I still hear Kat in the kitchen or Kelsey and Deandra laughing from their bedroom. Sometimes it seems like we can't leave the past behind us."

Man, he knows exactly how I feel. "Exactly. So, I've been working to get away, but I'm having issues with my HOA. That's actually why I was calling. I found something in the community budget that seems to connect Chimera to Shadowen Real Estate."

Isiah chuckled. "Labyrinth, right?"

The response took Derek by surprise. "Actually, yeah."

Isiah laughed again. "You want the Reader's Digest version? That's what happens when someone's ego gets in the way of business. The longer version goes something like this. A year or so after I joined the team, Chimera was really taking off. Thomas bought a house in an HOA community, and one day, he comes into the office spitballing ideas about how we could adapt our systems for real estate developers."

Real estate? Chimera worked with government clients. "I guess I'm struggling to connect the dots here."

"Think about it. HOAs are really like small cities. You have a manager instead of a mayor. You have specific rules that act like laws. I mean, you even pay to live there. Sounds a bit like taxes, right?"

I'd never thought of it that way, but it actually makes sense. "Yeah. I'm just surprised Maddie never mentioned it."

"I'm not. The whole idea sort of split our team."

"Really?"

"Well, it wasn't just the idea; it was Thomas's approach. He expected us to do it on top of our current jobs. He wanted us to build him another empire."

Why would Maddie never have mentioned any of this? "So, where does Shadowen fit in to all of this?"

"They were Thomas's guinea pig, the first developer he signed on for the project. In fact, they might have been the only one he ever got on board before everything went to hell. I really don't know. I went back once after the funeral to get my things. Andrew met me in the lobby with a box. After that, I was just done with all of it."

Whatever happened, it must have gotten really bad after Maddie left. Derek didn't want to push too hard. "Understandable." He hesitated. "Well, hey, I don't want to take too much of your time. But it's been good talking to you. I'm really glad everything is working out for you."

"You, too. Listen, buddy, I'm here if you need anything else. Good luck with the house ordeal. It sounds like a shitshow if you ask me, but I'm sure you'll figure it out. I'll talk to you soon, Derek. Maybe I'll make it back to your part of the world one of these days."

"Sounds like a plan. Take care, Isiah. Stay out of trouble."

Derek didn't know if his last words were directed at Isiah or himself.

* * *

Sonia Torres
July 2, 2018

"HEY, ME AND TORRIE are heading up to Kankakee on Wednesday night for the fireworks. Brad is supposed to be there with his friends. You in?"

The young girl's high-pitched voice reverberated through the speaker of Sonia's iPhone, lying next to her on her bed. *I wish she would have texted me, but it sounds like she's driving.* Sonia held the MacBook in her lap, half-listening to the call.

"I wish I could, Em. But I've already made plans with Derek to go to Shadow Ridge that night." She refreshed her Twitter feed.

Maybe I could reschedule with Derek? I'd just feel bad with everything going on.

"C'mon, Sonia. I'm heading back to Ann Arbor in a few weeks. I've hardly spent any time with my bestie this summer. I need my fix before I leave."

Guilt trip, party of one. "I know, and I'm sorry about that. Everything's just been so crazy."

"Besides, isn't Derek old enough to be your dad? Don't you think it's a little creepy to spend time with him like that, especially since he's your boss, too?"

"It's not like that at all. And you know that, Emily." Sonia only used her bestie's full name in serious situations. *Derek's like a dad to me. I owe him everything I have.*

Emily huffed. "Fine, whatever." She paused. Sonia said nothing. "Well, if you can make time for me in the next few weeks, you know how to get hold of me. Have fun with your friend. Enjoy the senior discount."

Sonia ended the call. *I love that girl, but, man, she can be a total bitch sometimes.*

CHAPTER 18
DEREK PRICE
JULY 4, 2018

POP! The balloon burst, struck by a dull-tipped dart.

"Again?"

Derek smirked when he saw Sonia's mouth agape with frustration. He'd just popped his third consecutive balloon. "It's simple. You just have to accept that the game is rigged and stop trying so hard."

"What? Rigged how?"

Oh, she'll love this one. "By the Russians, of course."

Sonia pouted and feigned leaving.

"You're not getting away that easily. You're the one who dragged me out here to begin with."

The carnival worker behind the booth handed Derek a stuffed eagle. *Now isn't that patriotic?* He handed the toy to Sonia. "Here's a consolation prize. Everyone's supposed to get a trophy, right?"

Sonia squinted and shook her head. "Is it time for the fireworks yet?"

Derek gazed at the orange glow of the setting sun. "Probably another hour." The two walked down the midway on the event lawn outside The Barracks. People gathered around them, enjoying festival food, playing games and listening to the DJ play songs from Taylor Swift and Maroon 5.

"Oh, by the way, did I tell you they called about the appeal?"

Sonia stopped. "No, what did they say."

"They want me to go up to their headquarters on Monday."

Sonia's forehead scrunched. "They want you to go to them? That's ridiculous. They should come to you!"

"I don't disagree. But I guess since Shadowen still runs the community, their executives are all on the board."

Her voice grew louder. "Wait, so the people who run this community don't even live here? This whole thing just keeps getting more ridiculous, Derek."

Believe me, I get where you're coming from. "I talked to Steve about it. He said it's not uncommon at all. Eventually, the board will turn over to homeowners and Shadowen will pull out. But, as long as they're building new houses, they have a controlling interest."

Derek resumed his pace and continued talking. "Anyway, let's not worry about that anymore. For milady, tonight's festivities await." Derek bowed his arm. Sonia slid hers into the opening. Together, they made their way to the grassy area where Sonia had scouted the perfect location for their blanket.

The two spent the next half-hour chatting and laughing, waiting for the fireworks to begin. The crowd filled in around them. Families, couples, even a few groups Derek surmised were just friends. *Seems like most of the community is out here tonight.*

"How's your mom doing? You should have brought her with you."

"She's doing okay. You know, every day is a new challenge." Sonia looked to the ground for a second before raising her head again. "I asked her to come with, but she said she was tired and just wanted to rest."

Derek nodded. *Poor girl.* He knew Sonia well enough to read the emotions on her face. *She probably needed a night away as much as I did.* "Hey, how about a snow cone?"

Sonia smiled. "Cherry, please."

"You got it." Derek stood and made his way toward a row of food trucks selling everything from burgers and fries to ice cream. He grabbed himself a hot dog and Diet Pepsi from What's Up, Dog, and stepped into line at Tropical Ice and Thunder.

With three people ahead of him, Derek let his eyes wander. He scanned the crowd, still surprised by the sheer number of people. He recognized a few faces. *Maddie probably would have known half the people here.* Then he spotted an unmistakable figure.

Community manager J.D. Moore's massive frame towered above those sitting on blankets and chairs. *I wonder how much he has to do with these events. He doesn't seem the fun-and-games type.* J.D. appeared to be a man on a mission. Derek followed his trail as he weaved through the crowd before stopping in front of a couple sitting in blue camping chairs.

The woman stood up and moved close to J.D., presumably to avoid the noise of the crowd. Derek thought he'd seen the woman before, but she stood with her back to him, limiting his view. Taller than average, she had long, curly blond hair and a toned build. *Maybe I've seen her at the gym.*

J.D. stood with his arms folded in front of him, his head tilted downward. *Not the most approachable pose in an audience of residents.*

"Sir, can I help you?" The teenage boy leaned out the window of the food truck. Derek realized he'd reached the front of the line.

"Sorry about that. Cherry snow cone, please."

"Just the one?"

"Just the one."

Waiting for his order, Derek peeked back to where J.D. and the woman had been talking. She'd taken her seat. J.D. had disappeared.

"That'll be three dollars, sir."

Derek pulled a five-dollar bill from his pocket and handed it to the kid, who tried to hand him change. "Keep it."

"Thank you, sir. Have a great night."

"You, too." Derek returned to the blanket where Sonia greeted him — or rather the snow cone — with a wide smile.

Ten minutes later, the first explosions rocked the night sky with colorful bursts of red, white and blue. An announcement over the PA asked all attendees to rise for the National Anthem. Derek and Sonia stood. Derek held his hand over his chest and hummed along with the tune.

The fireworks display continued with spinning, swirling and shattering blasts of color set to a mix of pop and patriotic music, drawing "oohs" and "aahs" from the crowd. The show wound down with a three-song combo of "Party in the USA," "Born in the USA" and "Living in America."

Derek and Sonia remained seated as the crowd dispersed around them. "No sense trying to fight our way through this mess," he said.

Two intoxicated men walking past their blanket started shouting at each other. One man shoved the other, accusing him of getting in his way. The second man responded by attempting to tackle the aggressor. Both fell to the ground wildly throwing punches.

Sonia laughed so hard she snorted. "That's 'Merica right there, if I've ever seen it."

Derek smiled. "Can't all be winners."

Sonia used her hands to push herself off the ground. "You ready yet or what?"

Derek rolled to his knees and stuck out his hand. "Just as soon as you help me up."

"You really are an old man."

Derek collected the blanket and led Sonia away from the event lawn. Others stopped to watch the fight, and two police officers jogged past them as they cut across the basketball courts on the north side of The Barracks to avoid the chaos of the parking lot. Carnival workers deflated bounce houses and disassembled game booths. *Being a carny must be a hell of a life.*

Movement in the shadows at the edge of the basketball courts caught Derek's eye. Just past the light post, masked by the shadows of night, J.D. Moore stood talking to the blond woman Derek had seen him with earlier. J.D.'s hands flailed. *That's not the look of a calm man.*

J.D. stopped. His head lifted Derek's direction, as if he'd just noticed the onlooker. He raised his hand and nonchalantly waved. Derek returned the gesture.

"Who's that?"

"That's J.D. Moore, the community manager I met with."

"That's your community manager? The dude's a beast!"

Derek turned his attention away from J.D. "Let's just keep moving."

They reached the sidewalk and headed south toward Derek's house. He slowed his pace and turned his head toward Sonia. "Thanks again for dragging me out here tonight. I needed this."

"Someone has to take care of you, right? Besides, there's nowhere else I'd rather be."

That's a nice sentiment, but I'm not sure I believe it.

* * *

Jefferson Moore

"THIS IS URGENT. You need to handle it tonight."

Jefferson cast a furtive glance at his surroundings. He'd led Sarah Evans to the edge of the basketball court, away from the crowd and outside the glow of the overhead streetlight.

Her head bobbed; her face held a stern expression. "Understood, sir. Would you like me to handle this alone?"

"That won't be necessary. Reynolds is on his way. He knows how to handle these situations. Let him take the lead."

She nodded. "Yes, sir."

"And Evans," Jefferson paused. "I trust you'll handle this matter with the utmost discretion."

Jefferson's gaze averted from Sarah's face and curly blond hair to two figures in the distance. He recognized Derek Price but could only assume the young woman's identity. Forcing a smile, Jefferson raised his hand to wave.

He turned his attention back to Sarah. "Let me know when it's done."

CHAPTER 19
DEREK PRICE
JULY 5, 2018

DEREK'S LEGS SEARED with pain. His breath caught in his lungs. The early morning air hit his sweat-drenched undershirt, sending chills through his veins. But he had no choice; he couldn't stop running.

I should have spent more time at the gym. Derek didn't consider himself out of shape. He thought he maintained a decent physique for a man his age. But running down Elm Street, he questioned if any amount of cardio could have saved him.

He dared not stop. Even turning his head to look behind him could have cost him his lead. He didn't need visual confirmation to know his pursuer had gained ground. He sensed him getting closer.

The surrounding houses appeared familiar, yet different. Derek felt both at home and completely lost. *Where is everybody? There has to be someone who can help me.*

A shrill noise hit his ears. He bit his lower lip, fighting back ringing pain in his head. *Shit, that's my phone.* Without slowing his pace, Derek reached into his pocket and grabbed the iPhone. He cast a quick glance at the screen. ISIAH CROSS. *How does he even have this number? It doesn't matter. Maybe he can help!*

He fumbled the phone in his fingers. The device wobbled and bounced, smashing onto the asphalt. He heard the screen shatter but couldn't chance stopping to look. *Damn it.*

Derek's pace slowed. His energy was running out. His pursuer closed the gap. *This is it. It's over.* He stopped, bent forward with his hands on his knees, catching his breath. He closed his eyes and accepted his fate.

"So this is how it ends, Mr. Price?" The man's deep baritone voice echoed around Derek. "I told you to leave matters alone."

Derek opened his eyes and saw The Barracks in the distance. *Not like it would have helped, anyway. He runs the place. He'd have just followed me inside.* Stretching to an upright position, Derek turned around and looked upon his pursuer.

J.D. hadn't so much as broken a sweat. His dress shirt and black slacks remained dry and wrinkle-free. He wore loafers, which had somehow avoided even the slightest scuff marks.

How did he keep up with me in that outfit?

Derek's eyes followed J.D.'s hand as it raised the beige Sig Sauer 17. Derek traced the line of sight to his own chest, which tightened in response.

"This is for Madeline." J.D. pulled the trigger.

Madeline.

* * *

MADELINE.

Derek jolted upright in bed. His body convulsed. His heart pounded. He labored to breathe. Lying still in the darkness, his mind worked to separate nightmare from reality.

Reaching for an opened bottle of water on the nightstand, his shaking hands spilled water as he moved it toward his lips. *What the hell was that?*

The green light of the bedside clock read 2:48. Derek swung his legs over the side of the bed. He knew he needed more rest but also recognized he'd have trouble going back to sleep. *I just need to clear my head.*

The past few weeks hadn't gone as Derek had expected. He should have been moved out, settled in a new place and focused on -30- projects. Instead, he wrestled nightmarish visions of his own death — at the hands of his community manager, nonetheless.

Derek put his feet on the floor and climbed from the bed. He walked down the dark hallway and into the great room. *I'll kill myself if I'm not careful.* He raised a hand to shield his face and hit a switch. His eyes adjusted to the light, allowing him to avoid stacks of boxes on his way to the kitchen.

He poured himself a glass of water, hoping to cleanse the nightmare from his memory. He chugged the first glass and poured another. Feeling refreshed, he headed back toward bed. But as the great room plunged back into darkness, Derek noticed a light across the street through the window panes of the front door.

Karen's up late. He stood behind the glass, watching. *Wait, there's someone out there. Why is Karen out so late? Should I check if she needs help?* A second figure entered Derek's view. This one appeared to be a man, emerging out the gate on the side of the house, as if he'd exited through the backdoor. He carried something in his arms.

Derek's gaze followed the two figures down the sidewalk to a black sedan. The woman opened the vehicle's rear door, triggering the interior light and allowing Derek to see what the man was carrying. *Wait, is that Karen? What in the actual fuck is happening?*

The woman shut the car door and turned. Derek's heart skipped a beat as he saw her curly blond hair. *That's the woman from earlier, the one J.D. was talking to.*

Derek tried to move, but his legs wouldn't cooperate. *I need to call the police. My phone. Where's my phone?* Standing in the entryway, paralyzed with shock, Derek wondered if he'd woken from one nightmare into another.

* * *

Bryce Reynolds

"I THINK I saw a light come on in the house across the street."

Bryce sat behind the steering wheel of the black Audi, looking across the center console at Sarah Evans. "I didn't notice anything."

"I hope you're right. We need to get out of here either way." Sarah swiveled her head on her shoulder, looking at Karen Conrad's unmoving body stretched across the backseat. "Jefferson's going to want an update. Should I tell him what I saw?"

Lying lips are an abomination to the Lord, but those who act faithfully are his delight. "You have to. I know you're still new at this, but keeping secrets from the boss never ends well."

"Do you think he'll be upset? He told me to be discreet."

Bryce turned his attention to the road ahead, shifting the vehicle to drive. "This isn't my first rodeo. Have a little faith. I'll handle it."

CHAPTER 20
DEREK PRICE
NOV. 21, 2015

"CONFIRMED VISUAL, 12 o'clock. Caucasian female. Late 30s. Long dark hair. Eyes undetermined."

"Will you knock it off?"

Derek hovered behind the front door of the house, watching through the inset glass panes as three men unloaded a moving truck across the street. Madeline stood at the kitchen stove, waving an oven mitt over a fresh peach pie.

"Odd time to move, this close to Thanksgiving, don't you think?" Derek's eyes didn't leave the glass.

"You don't know her situation. Any sign of a husband or kids?"

"Negative. Subject is alone, commander." Derek could sense Madeline's glare without turning to see it.

The house across the street hadn't been vacant for long. About a month prior, Dennis Milward had moved his family to Baltimore. He and his wife, Frannie, had been the first friends Derek and Madeline made in Shadow Ridge, so losing them as neighbors stung.

Hopefully, this new one works out alright.

"You should go ask if she needs help with anything, especially if she's alone." Madeline carried her perfectly crusted pie into the great room.

Derek's eyes broke their stare. "Maybe she needs help with that pie."

Madeline walked past Derek without responding, balancing the pie in one hand while she opened the door with the other, and stepped onto the porch. "Come along, dear." She watched the ground in front of her while descending the front steps and crossing the road.

That's smart. Protect the pie at all costs.

The woman saw them approaching, pointed toward the house while talking to a mover, and removed the gloves from her hands. She smiled as she greeted Derek and Madeline. "Hi, I'm Karen, Karen Conrad. You must be the neighbors."

Madeline handed Derek the pie and extended a handshake. "Sure are. I'm Madeline Price. This is my husband, Derek. We just wanted to say welcome to the neighborhood."

Karen shook Madeline's hand. "It's nice to meet you, Madeline." She looked toward Derek and nodded. "And you, too, Derek."

The conversation carried on with small talk. Karen, who had recently left her role as a manufacturing engineer at Honeywell's St. Louis location, bonded with Madeline over their shared experiences as government contractors. Derek chimed in with stories of his frequent visits to St. Louis while growing up in southern Illinois.

I remember plenty of late nights driving home from shows at Kiel.

"Derek, can I take that from you? Your arms have to be tired by now." Karen reached out and grabbed the pie from Derek. "Do you want to come in and have a slice? There's no way I can eat this all by myself."

Madeline objected, but Derek stopped her. "It would be rude to leave our new friend all alone on her first day in town, right?" He smiled.

"I do have to warn you," Karen turned her head toward the moving truck. "I'm not sure they've gotten the table out yet, and I'm certain all I have handy are paper plates."

"That's never stopped him before." Madeline elbowed Derek's side. "If caveman's hungry enough, he'll use his hands if he has to."

The three moved inside. The table had, in fact, not been unloaded yet. Standing in the kitchen eating peach pie off paper plates with plastic forks, Madeline made the invitation.

"Hey, if you don't have family in the area, you're more than welcome to have Thanksgiving with us. It's just the two of us, our friend Luciana and her teenage daughter, Sonia."

Karen smiled. "That would be great. The last few Thanksgivings have been pretty lonely since Dad died. Being an only child with both parents gone can make the holidays really awkward."

"Well, we'd love to have you." Madeline put her hand on Karen's arm. "But, before we get to Thanksgiving, I think I'm going to need to go for a run tonight, if you know what I mean." She lifted the plate of pie in her other hand.

"Would you mind some company? I could use a run myself. Might be a nice way to see the neighborhood. Derek, care to join us?"

Derek laughed. "I'll leave that fun to you ladies. I've got a few 'NCIS' reruns on the DVR calling my name."

Madeline shrugged. "He'll be asleep before Gibbs even smacks DiNozzo." She poked Derek in the stomach. "But, you know, a little exercise wouldn't hurt you."

Derek looked at Madeline, then turned his gaze to Karen. "I'm going to let you both in on a little secret, okay?" He glanced around, as if to make sure no one could overhear. "We're all going to die someday. In the meantime, just enjoy the damned pie."

CHAPTER 21
DEREK PRICE
JULY 5, 2018

"THANK YOU, deputy. I understand and appreciate your time."

The red and blue lights of the police cruiser parked across the street lit the night sky. *I hope I didn't wake any of the neighbors.* Derek waited as the Grundy County deputy stepped off his porch and across the street. He watched as the lights of the squad car stopped spinning and the vehicle pulled away from the curb.

Derek paused before returning inside, taking one more look at Karen's house. Darkness filled the windows. *Even if they don't believe me, I know what I saw.* He turned and walked through the front door of his home.

He pulled his flip phone from his pocket and debated whether to text Sonia. *I'm sure her ringer's off. She'll see it when she wakes up.* He started to type. "Crazy night. Call me in the morning. Need to talk." He hit send, closed the phone and made his way back to the owner's suite.

Where's the damned NyQuil? Derek rummaged through a plastic bin of medicines under the sink. *Here we go.* He tossed the measuring-cup lid aside, opened the bottle and took a swig. *That should help.*

He climbed into bed. His conversation with the sheriff's deputy replayed in his mind. *No signs of forced entry or struggle. No one inside. No evidence of wrongdoing. An empty promise to follow up later in the day.* The thoughts faded. Derek's eyes closed, and he fell asleep.

* * *

DEREK STIRRED and rubbed his eyes, trying to clear his blurry vision. *What time is it?* He looked at the clock: 8:13. *Wow, I actually slept in.*

He sat up and leaned his head back against the wall. *Did last night really happen, or did I dream all that?* A few minutes later, he forced himself out of bed and made his way to the kitchen. *Maybe a little breakfast will help clear my mind.*

He scrambled three eggs, put bread in the toaster and poured a glass of orange juice. Waiting for his meal to cook, he walked back to his office. *If she texted me back, I'm sure she did it to the stupid iPhone.* He was right.

Grabbing the phone from its place on the shelf above the desk, he read Sonia's message. "Everything okay? Call when you're up. I'll try to answer." A circular yellow smiley face ended the message.

I'll call her after breakfast. I need to get my head on straight. He set the phone back on the shelf and returned to the kitchen.

Derek plated his food and sat down at the dining room table to enjoy it. After he finished, he headed toward the office for the phone. The noise of a running engine and people talking outside caught his attention. Peeking through the great room blinds, he saw a pickup truck parked in front of Karen Conrad's house. Two men in blue jeans and denim shirts stood outside talking.

What the hell is happening now? Derek scurried to his bedroom, pulling on the outfit he'd worn the night before. Powering his way through the house, he threw open the front door, stormed outside and scurried down the steps.

The men had moved onto Karen's porch, but from this vantage point, Derek could read the lettering on the driver's side door of the silver Dodge Ram. SHADOWEN REAL ESTATE HOME SERVICES. *Seriously, what are they doing here?*

"Excuse me?" Derek maneuvered around the truck's bed.

The men on the porch stopped. "Can I help you, sir?" The older man spoke. He stood maybe 5'6" with a stocky build, black hair hidden by a baseball cap and a goatee.

"Yeah, I live across the street. This is my friend Karen's house. I don't think she's home at the moment. I just wondered if there's something I could help you with." *Or, you could just tell me what you're doing here.*

The younger of the men glanced at the older, who nodded in return. "Got called out for a power-down. Resident had to leave town. Called the office to have us come out and shut down the utilities. Raise the AC a little, unplug the TVs. You know, trying to save energy and all that."

"That's funny; I talked to Karen the other day, and she never mentioned going anywhere." *Especially not in the way I saw her leave.*

"I'm sorry, sir. I don't have any other information. We just go where the office tells us to, you know?"

"Well, I appreciate the info." *Even if you didn't tell me anything.* "I hope everything's alright with Karen."

He walked off the porch and across the street, stopping when he reached the sidewalk. He cocked his head on his shoulder for one more look, but the two men had disappeared inside the house. *None of this makes any sense.*

* * *

DEREK RECOGNIZED a familiar face as he walked through the double-door entry of The Barracks.

Adrienne Palmetto rose from her seat behind the front desk and greeted him with a smile. "Mr. Price, it's good to see you again."

"Good morning, Adrienne. Don't they ever give you a day off?"

She blushed and dismissed the remark with a wave. "Let the young ones have the holiday break, I say. An old lady like me isn't going anywhere." She paused and took her seat. "What can I help you with today?"

Derek scanned the racks of brochures and flyers on her desk. "I'm hoping you can tell me about Shadowen Home Services."

"Why, certainly. Home Services is one of the benefits available to residents here in Shadow Ridge. If you're ever going to be out on vacation and need someone to watch your house while you're gone, they can do so. They'll check for leaks, adjust your thermostat and just keep an eye on things so you don't have to worry while you're away."

That would have been handy a few weeks ago. How have I never heard of this program before? "And how much notice do you need to set all this up?"

Adrienne's gaze moved to her computer screen. "Let me print you a Home Services flyer. That way you'll have all the information. But, generally, we ask for a week's notice so the team can assign it out."

Derek put his hands on the desk. "So, if I decided I needed help tonight, what are the odds someone could be at the house tomorrow?"

Adrienne stopped typing and looked at Derek. "Well, I suppose if it was an emergency, we'd do everything we could to be there. But I wouldn't make a habit out of waiting so long. Something coming up that has you worried, Mr. Price?"

Not anything I can bring up to you right now. "Not really. I just saw the Home Services truck at my neighbor Karen's house this morning and wondered what it was all about."

Adrienne tilted her head to one side. "Oh, you must mean Ms. Conrad. That makes sense why you're asking. She called us yesterday with a family emergency. She's not sure when she'll be back. I just hope everything's alright with her sister."

Sister? "Me, too, Adrienne." Derek held his gaze. Adrienne's expression never changed. "Well, thank you for your help."

"My pleasure, Mr. Price. Have a great day."

Derek walked across the lobby and out the double doors of The Barracks. *Something isn't right here, and whatever it is, Shadowen Real Estate seems to be at the center of it.*

CHAPTER 22
DEREK PRICE
JULY 5, 2018

"AND YOU'RE SURE that's what you saw? You weren't having night terrors or some weird hallucination from that food truck hot dog?"

I thought at least you'd believe me. Derek leaned back on the couch and closed his eyes. Sonia sat in the armchair, bent forward, hands clasped. "Yes, I know what I saw. After the dream I had, I was wide awake. I wouldn't make something like this up. Hell, I'm not sure I could if I wanted to."

"And you said something weird happened when you went to the office. What was that all about?"

After he'd returned home from his ominous discussion with Adrienne Palmetto, Derek had called Sonia to explain his text. At first mention of the alleged abduction, she had panicked and told him she'd be right over.

"I thought I was losing my damned mind until then. But she said something about Karen's sister." He paused and straightened his pose. "Karen never mentioned a sister. I'm pretty sure she told us she was an only child. Don't you remember when we had Thanksgiving that year?"

"Derek, I was 16. Do you think I paid attention to anything you guys said that night?"

Fair point, I suppose. "It just doesn't add up."

Sonia scooted forward on the chair. "So what are we going to do about it? Isn't your appeal on Monday? You're not actually going to barge in there and accuse your HOA of kidnapping your neighbor, are you?"

I'd be lying if I said I didn't think about it. Derek scoffed. "Of course not. Don't be ridiculous." He smirked.

Sonia smiled. "You want to be prepared when you go in there, though, right? We should do some more digging into Shadowen, widen our net."

Well, would you look at that? "You sure you don't want to go into journalism?"

Sonia tilted her head and lowered her lip. "I'd prefer to make a decent salary. Now, if you want to write Dick Durbin's office a letter on minimum wage and fair pay, you know I'm more than happy to help."

Derek stood from the couch. "I'm going to go grab my notes from the office. Want to set up at the table and see what we can find?"

"Whatever you say, boss."

A few minutes later, the two were at Derek's dining room table, which had become their war room in recent weeks. Derek had brought two glasses of water and a bowl of M&Ms from the kitchen. Sonia had set up her MacBook and opened the Shadowen Real Estate website.

"Here's your first question: Why are they using a WordPress template that looks like it's from the '90s?"

Derek shot her a look. "You realize you were barely alive in the '90s, right?" *She has a point, though. If Shadowen was working with Thomas, couldn't he have helped them with that?*

"Anyway, let's see what we can find here." She'd positioned the computer so both she and Derek could see the screen. "Seems like a pretty average company site." She moved the mouse to the drop-down navigation menu and selected "ABOUT US."

"What's it say? The text is too small to read from back here." Derek waited for the age joke, which never came.

"'Founded by Geraldine Shadowen in 2009, Shadowen Real Estate develops master-planned communities throughout the Midwest and the South, offering first-class lifestyle and security services to homeowners.' They make it sound so exciting."

Derek nodded. "It is kind of interesting, though — starting a new real estate business in the midst of that recession was risky." *Not to mention being founded by a woman.* Real estate development was primarily a man's game, as Derek had learned in his reporting days. "What else does it say?"

Sonia scanned the page. "Just a bunch of marketing junk. Nothing too interesting." She moved the mouse back to the menu and selected "LEADERSHIP."

A new page loaded. A photo of an older woman appeared. Derek placed her in the mid-60s. Her white hair, wrinkled cheeks and welcoming smile made him think of his late mother.

Sonia read the text beside the photo aloud. "'Founder and CEO Geraldine Shadowen holds a master's degree in psychology from Columbia University. Prior to launching Shadowen Real Estate, Geraldine served as a clinical psychologist for the U.S. Army. There she met her husband, Randall. The two have been married over 40 years.'"

Derek's left thumb moved instinctively to his wedding band. "Military psychologist to real estate mogul seems like a bit of a jump, right?"

"Yeah, there's more. 'Randall Shadowen's passion for home-building and construction inspired the launch of Shadowen Real Estate. After retiring from the military in 2008, Randall planned to launch a real estate design and consulting agency, but a debilitating injury derailed his plans. Committed to helping her husband fulfill his dreams,

Geraldine recruited the industry's best and founded Shadowen Real Estate.'"

She stopped reading and looked at Derek. "That's actually kind of sweet."

He nodded. "Yeah." *But it makes it harder to believe this sweet old woman with a crippled husband is somehow involved in Karen's disappearance.*

Sonia changed the page again, this time selecting "COMMUNITIES" from the website menu. "Here's a list of all the communities they run." She held her finger to the screen as she read down the list. "Shadow Cove, Shadow Falls, Shadow Grove. Noticing a theme here?"

From a branding perspective, it makes sense. "Yeah, it's a pretty smart business move. No matter what part of the country you're in, you can easily identify their properties."

"That might also make this easier." Sonia's fingers flew across the keyboard.

Derek's eyes couldn't keep up. He diverted his gaze and took a drink of water. "What exactly are you trying to do?"

"I'm searching for each community to see if anything out of the ordinary pops up."

Derek leaned forward in his chair. "You mean like news articles?"

Sonia snickered. "Something like that. But it goes beyond the media. I'm searching blogs, message boards. There's something called Nextdoor that seems to pop up a lot."

I'm still amazed she can search this fast. Of course, nothing beats an in-person interview. "Anything interesting?"

"Maybe." She stopped scrolling. "Here's a Reddit post about two deaths in this community, Shadow Cove, near Springfield. A bunch of the posts have been removed, but it looks like it's being investigated as a murder-suicide. Let me see if there are any details."

She scanned the comments in the News thread. "It doesn't look like names are being released yet. That's weird, right? It's been over a week. Why wouldn't that have been made public yet?"

"It's not normal, but it's also not out of the realm of reality. Sensitivity to the family, concern that details being released could hamper the investigation. It's certainly awful that it happened, but I'm not sure it does anything to help us."

"Okay." Sonia started typing again. "Oh, here's one that's local."

"In Shadow Ridge?"

She shook her head. "No, that new place over in Braidwood. Shadow Farms."

Derek scooted his chair closer. "What happened over there?"

"Fatal house fire just a few weeks ago. This article says they're still investigating, but they think it was a gas leak." She clicked the link to read the full article from the Kankakee Daily Journal. "One fatality."

Her last words trailed off in Derek's mind. His eyes focused on the photo on the screen. Next to a horrifically poignant image of a firefighter emerging from the burning building was a portrait of the victim — an older man with gray hair and a bad mustache. *Holy shit. Is that Thomas?*

"Derek, what is it?" Sonia must have seen the shock on his face.

His eyes didn't move from the screen. "That's Thomas Sheridan."

Sonia looked confused for a moment. Then her eyes widened and her mouth opened. "Madeline's boss? The one connected to Shadowen?"

Yes, that one. "When did this happen?"

"Looks like June 17."

I was in South Dakota. No wonder I hadn't heard about it. "I just don't know what to say."

"Say 'this is getting fucking weird,' Derek. Your friend gets taken from her house in the middle of the night. Your HOA makes up some bullshit story about her sister being sick. And now this happens? This can't be a coincidence."

She's right. It doesn't add up. "We can't jump to conclusions. That's exactly why people don't trust the mainstream media anymore. Cable news channels rush to be the first on air without bothering to stop and confirm anything."

"Well, what else can we do?"

Derek sat in silence for a moment. He stood up and paced the dining room floor. "I think we're done for now, Sonia. I need time to process all of this."

"But your appeal is on Monday. Don't you want to figure out what's going on before then?"

Of course I do, Sonia. But what else am I supposed to do right now? "I've got a few days to figure that out. You should probably go home and see if your mom needs you for anything."

"But I want to help."

Damn it. Just let it go. "You have helped. I just need some time. I'll check in with you tomorrow."

Sonia stood and packed her laptop. "You sure you're going to be okay?"

"I'll be fine, I promise."

I hate lying to her.

CHAPTER 23
DEREK PRICE
JULY 6, 2018

DEREK HAD SPENT the previous night alone with a bottle of scotch and his thoughts. *I appreciate Sonia's help, but I can't get her wrapped up in this.* He had woken up with the nerve to make the call he needed.

"Hello?"

"Isiah, it's Derek Price."

"Hey, buddy, what's up? We go a year without talking and now it's twice in one week."

Maybe I should have reached out sooner. "I just wondered if you'd heard about Thomas."

Isiah hesitated. "Yeah, man, a few people messaged me when it happened. I wasn't sure if you knew when we talked. I thought maybe that's why you were bringing him up."

"It just really caught me by surprise."

"Well, it couldn't have happened to a better man." Isiah paused and sighed. "I'm sorry, Derek. I shouldn't have said that. Thomas and I had our problems, but, man, what a way to go."

Things must have been even worse between them than it seemed. "That's for sure." *How far do I push this?* "I'm just still shocked Maddie never mentioned any problems with him or his plans for Labyrinth." *I guess that far.*

"You knew her better than anyone, Derek. Do you think she could hold ill will against anybody?"

"You're right, I suppose. She had a way of getting along with everybody, huh?"

"She was always the first one I'd call when I needed something. I can't tell you how much I miss her, Derek. After losing Kat and the girls, knowing Madeline was gone, too — man, talk about emotions."

Derek paced the great room floor. "Not to change the subject, but there's something else I wanted to ask you about." He paused. "Well, I suppose in a way it's all connected."

"I'm an open book, my friend. Ask away."

How much do I tell him? He'll think I'm insane if I tell him everything. "So, how much do you know about Shadowen Real Estate? I know you mentioned they were Thomas's guinea pig. Were you involved in any of that?"

Isiah chuckled. "Only as much as I had to be. That all went down probably two, two-and-a-half years ago. Shadowen had been up and running for a while, but they were nowhere near as big as they are now. I think it was just Shadow Ridge and maybe one or two other places. Andrew knew how pissed I was about the whole thing, so he took the lead on it and let me focus on actual Chimera business."

Damn, maybe he won't have as much insight as I hoped. "Do you know anything about their CEO, Geraldine Shadowen? I'm meeting the Shadow Ridge board at their office on Monday, and I'm trying to avoid walking into a minefield, if you know what I mean."

"The old lady, right?" Isiah paused. Derek didn't respond. "I met her maybe once or twice, not enough to provide any deep insight. Honestly? I remember her being super sweet and friendly. But you don't make it to her level in the business world by being nice, so take it with a grain of salt."

I imagine he's got a point, especially as a woman in real estate. "I appreciate the candor."

The two continued their conversation. This side of Isiah continued to amaze Derek. Whether therapy, time or a combination of the two, he really had seemed to turn his life around.

Listening to his friend, Derek contemplated his own journey.

I thought I was ready to move on, but now, I'm not so sure I'm there yet.

* * *

Geraldine Shadowen

GERALDINE SHADOWEN SAT alone in her top-floor office. She'd granted the majority of her team an extended holiday weekend, keeping only essential personnel on the clock. *They've worked so hard these past few weeks, and I imagine it will get worse before better.*

She leaned back in the oversized office chair and admired the suburban landscape out the window. Her focus returned to the stacks of paper on the oak desk. Signed documents, lot files and a spreadsheet listing dates and times Derek Price's Access ID fob and gate-entry decal had been used at Shadow Ridge were sprawled out before her.

Her hands held another paper, an aged newspaper clipping. A photo of a young woman with light skin and long dark hair stared back at her. The word "OBITUARIES" stretched across the top.

She read to herself, "Madeline Elizabeth (Griffin) Price, 39, of rural Grundy County died Wednesday, June 21, 2017, in a vehicle collision. Madeline was born on Aug. 15, 1977, at Mercy Hospital and Medical Center in Chicago. She is preceded in death by her mother, Jessie Lynn (Tennant) Griffin, and survived by her father, James Griffin of Orland Park, and her husband, Derek Price."

She set the obituary down and reached for the picture frame on her desk, staring downward at a photo of herself and her husband, Randall, in his wheelchair. *I couldn't imagine what my life would be if I'd lost you that day.*

A tear formed in her eye, a memory in her mind.

* * *

Feb. 13, 2007

"IS THERE ANYTHING I can help you with, dear?"

"No, I think I'm okay. Chicken's in the oven and the corn's boiling on the stove." Geraldine double-checked the counters to ensure she hadn't forgotten anything. Satisfied, she joined her husband in the living room.

"I know this isn't how you wanted to spend our anniversary." Randall leaned forward in the recliner. "We'll go out for a nice dinner this weekend."

"After this long, I'm just glad we're both still here to celebrate." Geraldine smiled. "And you're the one that just had to play tennis this morning."

Randall placed his hand on his back as he repositioned himself. "And I would have won, too, if I hadn't tripped!"

The front door of the house swung open. Geraldine gasped and stepped backward. Randall winced as he jumped to his feet. A young man stepped inside the house, wearing black jeans and a gray sweatshirt with the hood pulled over his head.

"Tony? Is that you?"

The young man raised his hand. Geraldine screamed when she saw the black Smith & Wesson in his hands. The man's hood fell backward.

"Tony, what's going on? What are you doing here? This is my home, damn it!"

Tony's hand shook as he pointed the weapon at Randall's chest.

Randall took a slow step forward. "Tony, listen to me. You don't want to do this. You have your entire life ahead of you."

"You took my life away from me." The young man's voice cracked as he spoke. "The Army was my way out. My way out of that shit-hole town. That fucking mess I call a family. This was my chance to start over. And you took it from me!"

"Randall," Geraldine called out. "What's happening? What is this all about?"

Randall took another step. "Tony, I don't know what you think happened, but I spoke on your behalf at the hearing. I defended you."

Tony flailed the gun through the air. "I don't believe you. I don't fucking believe you. And, stop. Stay where you are. If you take another step, I will shoot you."

Geraldine rushed out of the room to retrieve the cordless phone from the bedroom. She found it on the headboard and dialed 9-1-1.

The gunshot rattled the house. Geraldine dropped the phone.

"9-1-1. What's your emergency?" She didn't hear the operator's voice echoing from the floor. She ran back to the living room and found Randall sprawled on the floor, blood pooling around him. Tony had disappeared.

"Randall!" She kneeled at his side, grabbing his hand. Tears poured from her eyes. "Randall. You're going to be okay. You'll be okay, I promise."

His hand squeezed hers. He looked into her eyes. "He's a good kid, Geraldine." Randall closed his eyes and lost consciousness.

* * *

July 6, 2018

GERALDINE RETURNED the picture frame to the desk and picked up the Samsung Galaxy lying next to it. She opened her contact list, selected a name and pressed dial. Only one ring.

"Geraldine?"

"Yes, Jefferson, I'm sorry to bother you."

"It's no bother. What can I help you with?"

She paused. "I'm preparing for Monday's meeting. Can you tell me again exactly what happened with Derek Price?"

CHAPTER 24
Derek Price
July 8, 2018

THEY REALLY OWN this entire building? Entering the Shadowen Real Estate high-rise, Derek admired his surroundings. The entry level featured an open-floor design free of offices and meeting rooms.

The artwork on the wall ranged from modern abstract to classic Renaissance fare. Handcrafted pottery and sculptures accentuated glass-topped coffee tables surrounded by different styles of furniture.

To his right, two baristas stood behind the counter of Shadow Roast, the building's coffee shop. *Clever.* Derek approached two uniformed guards behind a curved desk at the center of the spacious room. "Hi, I'm here for a 9 o'clock meeting with Shadowen Real Estate."

"Name?" The overweight man fumbled for a clipboard behind the desk.

"Derek Price. I live in Shadow Ridge. I'm supposed to have a hearing with the board this morning."

"Found it." The man looked up from the clipboard. "Have a seat, sir, and we'll let the Shadowen team know you've arrived." He gestured toward a set of art déco chairs.

"Thank you." Derek took a seat and pulled a notebook from his messenger bag, reviewing his notes and list of questions one last time. He squirmed, unsure which made him more uncomfortable: the awaiting confrontation or the plastic seat of the chair. *Stay calm. They're people, too.* He swung his legs the other direction. *But they might be the kind of people who kidnap a helpless woman in the middle of the night.*

He lifted his eyes to see the second security guard — this one younger, taller and with a leaner build — approaching. "Mrs. Shadowen asked us to send you upstairs. You can take this bank of elevators," he gestured to Derek's right, "to the ninth floor. There will be a receptionist there to meet you."

"Thank you." He put the notebook away, stood and headed for the elevator. Waiting for the elevator to arrive, he noticed a blackboard directory with removable letters between the bays. *Looks like they're not the only ones using this space.* The upper three floors housed Shadowen Real Estate, but two through seven listed other businesses such as a lawyer and a CPA.

Ding! The elevator arrived. The metal doors opened and two occupants stepped out. Derek entered alone and pressed the button for the ninth floor. The door slid shut. Derek nervously shuffled his messenger bag to the other shoulder.

As the car reached the fourth floor, he slid his wedding band from his hand and squeezed it in his palm, sliding it back into place as he arrived at his destination.

This is it. The doors opened to reveal a much smaller lobby, decorated with two armchairs, a coffee table, two end-tables and a reception desk. A young blond girl with her hair pulled back smiled from behind the desk.

"Good morning, Mr. Price. Welcome to Shadowen Real Estate."

"Good morning." *Or at least it will be if I can get some explanation of what exactly has been going on.*

"Mrs. Shadowen will be with you soon. Would you like a bottle of water or a cup of coffee while you wait?"

"I'm alright, thank you." Derek sat on an armchair and reached for a pile of magazines stacked on the coffee table, passing several real estate publications, the most recent issue of Psychology Today and a half-completed children's coloring book before stumbling onto an unexpected sight.

Thomas Sheridan's face stared at him. The issue of GovTECH was dated over two years ago. The words "WHEN WORLDS COLLIDE" featured prominently on the cover, with "Chimera Technologies Founder Targeting the Private Sector" printed beneath. *Well, that's interesting.*

Derek flipped the magazine to page 32, where he saw a large photo of Thomas and an older woman he recognized as Geraldine Shadowen. *I wonder if this was one of those pay-to-play magazine deals.*

He began reading:

> Chimera Technologies, the brainchild of gov-tech guru Thomas Sheridan, is about to spread its mythological wings.
>
> Sheridan recently announced a partnership with residential development enterprise Shadowen Real Estate to launch Labyrinth Systems, a public-facing business endeavor targeting specifically the real estate and community association management sectors.
>
> "I can't stress enough how grateful and excited I am to partner with a visionary like Geraldine Shadowen on this new initiative," Sheridan said at a launch event earlier this month. "By combining the knowledge, resources and experiences of our companies, we'll show that small businesses can make big differences in both the public and private sectors. "
>
> Labyrinth Systems will leverage Chimera resources and systems for launch, though Sheridan plans to split the new subsidiary into its own entity after the dust has settled.
>
> "We're working with the best development team in the gov-tech market. Not capitalizing on that foundation would

be a mistake — and likely a death knell for our new fledgling enterprise," Sheridan added.

Derek lowered the magazine, his mind awash with questions. *If Labyrinth was this big of a deal, why did Maddie never mention it? Isaiah said Shadowen was Thomas's guinea pig, but this makes them sound like an equal partner?*

"Mr. Price?"

The young woman's voice pulled Derek back to reality. He set the magazine down.

"Follow me, please."

Derek trailed behind as the receptionist led him down a long hallway, which opened up into a spacious setting filled with cubicles. The people working — mostly younger professionals, Derek noticed — hammered away on their keyboards.

He passed a closed office with the blinds drawn on his right. The plaque on the door said "Field Director." *That's an odd title to have at a real estate company.*

Derek noticed an elevator at the end of the hallway, but before reaching it, the young woman directed Derek into a conference room, just beyond the closed office. "Have a seat, Mr. Price. Mrs. Shadowen will be right with you." She paused. "Are you sure I can't get you anything to drink?"

"Actually, I will take a water, if it's not too much of a problem."

Derek walked around the table and chose a seat facing the entryway. *Never take your sight off your exit.* He couldn't remember if he'd learned that lesson from a mafia movie or a squirrelly politician.

He admired the artwork on the walls, aerial photographs highlighting the world's greatest cities. New York. Rome. Paris. Cairo. *Millennia of architectural progress and prowess; that's on brand.*

"Here you go, sir. Can I get you anything else?" The receptionist placed a coaster and bottle of water on the table in front of Derek.

"I should be alright. Thank you."

In a single motion, the young woman walked out the door and an older woman entered, shutting the door behind her. She was shorter than Derek imagined, but her silver hair and welcoming smile were immediately recognizable.

"Good morning, Mr. Price." She extended her hand. Derek stood and shook it. "Geraldine Shadowen. It's a pleasure to meet you."

"Same to you. I appreciate your time today." *Where is everyone else?* "Do we need to wait for the rest of the board?"

The wrinkles on her face scrunched as she laughed. "No, I'm afraid it's just me today. I get to play judge, jury and executioner."

CHAPTER 25
DEREK PRICE
JULY 8, 2018

THE COMBINATION of his stunned expression and non-reply must have been enough.

"My apologies, Mr. Price." He heard remorse in her voice. "I was just trying to add a touch of levity to the situation."

I'm not sure death is such a joking matter for you people. "Well, to be blunt, after my last meeting with one of your employees, I couldn't be too sure."

Geraldine gestured for Derek to sit, as she claimed a seat at the head of the table. "Oh, yes, J.D. told me about your visit. I apologize if he left you with the wrong impression. He means well, but his people skills could use some work." She smiled. "Military men, you know? Even after 40 years of marriage to one of your own, you still can't quite figure out how their minds work."

So, I was right about his background. Derek remained silent, smiling and slightly nodding his head.

Geraldine's demeanor couldn't have been more different than what he'd experienced with J.D. *But I can't let myself get too comfortable; they're both wings of the same bird.*

"Anyway, I appreciate you coming here today. I wish we could have met at the community office, but you know how things are after a long holiday break, right? I didn't want you to wait any longer than necessary."

"I appreciate that." Derek adjusted his position, relaxing his shoulders and uncrossing his feet under the table. "You did catch me a bit off-guard, though. I anticipated meeting with the whole board."

"Well, normally, Jefferson — sorry, J.D. — would join us, as would our other executives, but I wanted to avoid formalities and simply have an honest discussion, see if we can come to a mutual understanding. We've conditioned ourselves as a society to focus on red tape. I prefer to believe we're all better served if we just treat each other as people, Mr. Price."

That's clearly the psychologist in her. Certainly a refreshing take for a business exec. "Works for me."

Geraldine folded her hands on the table and leaned forward. "Well, then, may I start with a simple question?"

"Sure."

"Why do you want to leave Shadow Ridge? Is there anything we could have done to make the community feel more like home for you?"

Derek considered his response before replying. "No, it's not that, not that at all. The community has been great. We've loved our neighbors." His voice broke as he thought about Karen. "My wife loved the activities at the clubhouse." His right hand grabbed hold of his ring beneath the table. "But she died last year. I'm just trying to move on with my life, and part of that is finding a place of my own."

Geraldine's eyebrows flattened; her smile lowered in a show of sympathy. "I'm terribly sorry for your loss. Losing a loved one is never easy, and I certainly empathize with your desire to forge a new path." She paused. "But, as J.D. mentioned, we find ourselves in a precarious position. I hope you understand that we must maintain the integrity of the community."

Here we go again with the "protecting our investment" bullshit. Geraldine's friendly face and amiable behavior had lulled Derek into a false sense of security, but her reutterance of the same propaganda he'd heard from J.D. reinvigorated his frustration.

"With all due respect, Mrs. Shadowen, I've done my research, and I've found this extensive of an application process to be the exception, not the rule. On top of the obvious ethical considerations, I'm not entirely sure this isn't a violation of fair housing laws, as well."

Geraldine rolled her head back on her shoulders. "Mr. Price, I resent the implication of any potential impropriety. I assure you, Shadowen Real Estate operates with the highest degree of integrity and compliance with local, state and federal regulations."

Derek lowered his head. "I'm sorry. I didn't intend any such implications, ma'am." *What would you do if I actually implied you abducted my neighbor from her house in the middle of the night?*

Geraldine nodded. "Back to the matter at hand, I understand your frustration. I really do. I wish I could share more specific details with you, but we must respect the privacy of our applicants, as well as our residents. The information submitted and discovered through the application process is confidential in nature." She paused. "We wouldn't want anyone accusing us of unethical behavior, would we?"

I probably deserved that. "So, basically, you're telling me I drove up here for you to tell me what I already knew? That there's absolutely nothing you'll do to help?"

Geraldine shook her head. "That's not what I'm saying at all. We do want to help. I want to help. But we have to do so in an appropriate manner. There is nothing we can do regarding the past applicants, but I would like to offer a solution. We maintain a list of potential buyers who have expressed interest in our communities across the country. These individuals are all pre-approved, so if any of them are interested in your home, we should be able to expedite the closing process."

Why am I just finding out this is an option? "Would have been great to know that a month ago."

"I apologize for that, Mr. Price."

"So what happens now? Can you share the list or at least have their agents reach out to mine?"

Geraldine smiled. "I promise we'll do everything possible. I must, however, ask for your continued patience. I will ask J.D. to take the lead on this — and to be a little more light-hearted in his approach next time."

"Ask for your continued patience." You mean I should sit down and shut up. "Thank you. I look forward to hearing from J.D. soon."

Derek stood from his chair. Geraldine did the same. The two shook hands.

"It was a pleasure to meet you, Mr. Price. Once again, I apologize for the difficulties you've faced in recent months, especially while still grieving the loss of your wife. I promise I'll do everything in my power to make this right. We'll be in touch soon."

She followed Derek out of the conference room, past the cubicles and into the lobby. Derek stepped into the elevator. He briefly saw Geraldine wave as the doors slid shut.

Well, that was a complete and utter waste of time.

* * *

GERALDINE SHADOWEN

GERALDINE'S PACE QUICKENED as she scurried across the lobby. She headed back toward the conference room but stopped short, standing in front of the closed door labeled "Field Director."

Knocking only out of courtesy, she opened the door, stepped inside and closed it. Jefferson, sitting behind the desk, stopped typing and focused on Geraldine.

"I'm not confident we've solved our Derek Price problem, Jefferson." She hesitated. "In fact, I fear I might have made it worse."

Jefferson leaned back in his chair and clasped his hands behind his head. "What now?"

Geraldine's lips curled downward; her cheeks dropped. "I think you know what we have to do."

"You're positive this is the right course of action?"

She sighed and dropped her gaze to the floor. "It's all we have left, Jefferson. We have no other play." She lifted her head and looked him in the eyes. "Just promise me you'll handle it gently."

CHAPTER 26
Sonia Torres
July 8, 2018

SONIA SIPPED a s'mores Frappuccino through a straw. Sitting at the back corner table of Starbucks, she used her MacBook to research movies inspired by Shakespeare's writings. She checked the computer clock: 9:48 a.m. *I hope he's out of the meeting before my 10:30 class.*

She scrolled the IMDb page for the 2006 movie "She's the Man" starring Amanda Bynes. *Oh, great, another girl-pretends-to-be-a-boy movie. Maybe the backlash to that new ScarJo movie will get the point across.* A message board post confirmed the film's inspiration from "Twelfth Night." She added it to a list that also included 1999's "10 Things I Hate About You" and the Disney classic "The Lion King."

Her phone vibrated on the table. "DEREK'S LAME PHONE" flashed across the caller ID. She answered, "I've been wondering when I'd hear from you. Tell me everything."

"Hey, sorry, hold on. Let me get out of this parking garage so I can hear you better."

"You could have at least waited until you were on the road to call."

She listened to the engine's hum, waiting for a signal.

"What the —?" Derek's voice sounded distant, as if he wasn't speaking into the phone.

"Derek?" No reply. "Derek? Are you okay?" She heard a scratching noise.

"Yeah, sorry. I set the phone on my lap and then some asshole in an Audi almost T-boned me coming into the parking garage. I'm alright, but that was a little close for comfort." *He's been extra cautious since Madeline's accident.*

"Did you give him the finger?" *I would have.*

Derek sighed. "It's like you don't even know me at all, Sonia."

I'm really not sure if that means he did it or not. "Anyway, are you out of the garage yet? Because if you are, I'd like to remind you that your iPhone has Bluetooth, and you wouldn't have to worry about holding the phone while driving." She paused. "I don't want to see you paying to fix any Audis once they actually start enforcing the cell phone ban."

"Ha. You're funny. You should take that show on the road sometime."

Enough of the small talk. "Anyway, tell me what happened."

Derek sighed. "Honestly? More of the same. I mean, Geraldine Shadowen came across as sweet and innocent, but she didn't seem like she wanted to help me any more than J.D. Moore did. She told me her team has a list of pre-approved buyers, but even that came with conditions. I'm starting to have a weird feeling about all of this."

Starting to? I've been telling you that for weeks. "They've had this list of buyers and haven't told you about it? The bullshit continues. So what are we going to do next?"

Derek was silent for a second. "That's what I'm trying to figure out."

"Give me a second." Sonia packed her things and walked outside. "We should reputation-bomb them."

"I have literally no idea what that means, but I'm already sure it's a bad idea."

Someone has to teach these assholes a lesson. "You really need to learn about the world outside of your bubble." She explained the concept of coordinating an orchestrated attack on a company using social media to share negative reviews.

"Wait, why in the world would you want to do that? Do you know the damage you could do to someone's livelihood? Imagine if someone did that to -30-. Do you know what that would do to me?"

Chill, Derek. We're not talking about small businesses. "This isn't targeting people like you, Derek — people who work hard to make an earnest living. This is about sending a message to the one percent who try to control everything in our lives. If they keep getting away with it, it's going to keep happening, and it's going to be people like you and me who suffer." She waited for his response.

"Sonia." He paused. "You know I admire your fire, your passion, but we have to be careful here. Let's imagine there is something out of the ordinary happening. What then? I couldn't live with myself if I let anything happen to you."

Is that why we've hardly talked about this since we found out about Thomas Sheridan? I appreciate everything you've done for me, but I am still my own woman. "Got it."

Another moment of silence.

"I think we should loop Steve in on everything we've found. He knows the ins and outs of this industry and seems to have some knowledge of Shadowen. Maybe he can use his leverage with the paper to get us some answers. What's the worst that can happen?"

Your friend thinks you're insane when you tell him your neighbor was kidnapped and your wife's old boss died in a fire, and you think both might involve your HOA? "Do you think he'll actually do anything to help?"

"You talked to him. You know he's a good guy. I'm sure he'll do whatever he can. I certainly trust him more than J.D. Moore or Geraldine Shadowen."

"Okay."

"Well, I'm still 40 minutes or so out. I'll call Steve when I get home and let you know what he says." Derek paused. "And, Sonia?"

"Yeah?"

"In the meantime, please stay off the internet."

* * *

BRYCE REYNOLDS

"OH, CRAP!" Bryce jerked the steering wheel hard and to the right. *I can't let myself get distracted.*

Let not your hearts be troubled, neither let them be afraid. Pulling the Audi into the parking garage, he nearly collided with another vehicle, a crossover SUV. *Just focus on the work at hand.*

Bryce hated visiting the office. With a skill set suited best for field work, he felt lost in the sea of suits and senior executives. He preferred working alone or with a partner more than with a large team. *But when the boss calls, you answer. And when she wants you at the office, you show up.*

He parked the car and made his way toward a service elevator. His mind replayed the events of recent weeks: the Sheridan fire, the Kim drowning, the Guzman suicide and the two bodies in Andrew Wainwright's home. *She's going to have questions. And explaining why I crashed the company car 100 feet from the office shouldn't be one of them.*

Pressing the button to call the elevator, he closed his eyes and inhaled a deep breath. *It's been a long few weeks, but I have a feeling we're only getting started. Lord, grant me strength to do what needs to be done.*

CHAPTER 27
Madeline Price
Dec. 4, 2016

MADELINE GRIPPED the steering wheel of the silver Honda Civic. She watched the sunset through the rearview mirror. A cool breeze rustled the willow tree in the front yard. She'd arrived home 10 minutes ago but hadn't yet mustered the strength to go inside. Tears streaked her face as she fought back her emotions.

I know he'll understand, but I'm still afraid to tell him. Maybe I should just tell him everything.

The past year had been especially hard for the Prices. Chimera business had kept Madeline away from home more than usual, and Thomas's push to get Labyrinth Systems off the ground only added to her stress. Derek had lost a major -30- client, causing him to also lose sleep worrying about finances.

And, worst of all, the couple had officially found out they'd never be biological parents. In February, a doctor had diagnosed Madeline with Polycystic Ovary Syndrome, more commonly known as PCOS. *He stayed strong through all that. He'll be my rock for this, too.*

Derek had surprised her by suggesting adoption. She'd questioned the expense and intensity of the process, but he'd persisted. Now, returning home from a tenuous two-week work trip, she feared the toll the forthcoming conversation would have on those plans. *Maybe I shouldn't say anything. Maybe I just need to stick it out for the sake of our family.*

Madeline rubbed the tears from her eyes with an open palm, smearing make-up she knew she'd have to clean before seeing Derek. She composed herself, taking deep breaths and forcing her body to stop convulsing. She stepped out of the vehicle and walked to the front door. As she entered the house, she heard Derek on the phone.

"Well, hey, Steve, Maddie just got home, so I need to run. Pre-holiday drinks next week?" He paused, casting a smile and wave Madeline's direction. "Perfect. I'll see you then." Closing the phone, he approached his wife, who still stood in the doorway. He wrapped his arms around her in a giant hug. She lifelessly returned the gesture and choked back tears.

Derek pulled his head back and looked into her watery eyes. "Are you okay?"

I'm really not. She shook her head. Tears flowed from her eyes.

He pulled her body tighter against his and rubbed her back in a gentle up-and-down pattern. He didn't speak. His presence comforted her and reminded her she wasn't facing this alone.

What would I do without you?

She pulled herself from Derek's grasp and forced a smile, mouthing the words "thank you." He followed her through the house toward the owner's suite bedroom, where she sat on the edge of the bed. Derek took a seat next to her. She started to cry again. He put his arm around her.

Leaning her head on his shoulder, she spoke, her words broken as they caught in her throat. "I want to quit my job." She hesitated. "No, I need to quit, Derek. I can't do this anymore." *I can't keep leaving you home while I'm seeing the world. I can't continue playing peacemaker between Thomas and Isiah. I can't keep hiding things from you.*

"It's okay." He let her continue.

"I want to be home. I want to spend more time with my husband. I just want to have a normal life." *I just want us to be happy. I've seen the effects the past few months have taken on Isiah and Katherine. I don't want that to be us.*

"I want all that, too. But, mostly, I want you to be happy."

Madeline pulled her head from his shoulder. "What about money? Will we even be able to pay our bills?" *You work so hard as it is. You can't stress taking on more work to make up for my income.* "And what about the adoption? I don't want to give up the chance to—" Her words trailed off as she cried, crashing her face into Derek's chest.

"We'll do what we always do." He put his hand on the back of her head, stroking her hair. "We'll figure it out one step at a time. Hell, I'll go work at Aldi if I have to."

She laughed through her tears and tilted her head back to see Derek's face. "How did I get so lucky?"

He shrugged his shoulders. "I don't know, but now that you did, I hope you realize there's no escape."

I'm worried you'll be the one who wants to escape if you find out. For the first time since she'd returned home, a smile cracked Madeline's face. "I suppose you're right. That whole 'til death do us part' thing, huh?"

CHAPTER 28
DEREK PRICE
JULY 9, 2018

"HEY, STEVE, how's it going?" Derek stood on his porch staring at Karen Conrad's empty house across the street. *Do I even tell him that part of the story?*

"Deadline's in an hour. You know how that goes. I'm sitting here doing anything but writing."

Steve's always been one of the good ones. I'm glad he's kept his job through all the changes in the past decade. By Derek's calculation, his friend had five years left until retirement. Trying to find a new role with such a short shelf-life wouldn't be the easiest task.

"Oh, I know that feeling. Who down in Springfield managed to get themselves arrested today?" *I wish I'd had more of a chance to cover state politics. Never a shortage of story ideas with Mike Madigan and his cronies running the show.*

"I'm afraid it's nothing that sexy this time. Just an update on expected legislation for the fall session."

"Ah. Well, I don't mean to keep you. I just wanted to let you know I added your name to the guest list at the gatehouse, so you shouldn't have any issues getting here tomorrow."

Steve hesitated. "Shit, Derek. I meant to message you this morning. They need me to help cover the news desk tomorrow night. Is there any way we'd be able to meet up here instead? I'm really sorry about this."

Shit happens, especially in the news business. "Not a problem. My morning is pretty open. Meet for an early lunch? How about The Nook at 10:30?"

"That's perfect. Sorry again for the hassle."

"Seriously not a problem, Steve. You're the one doing me a huge favor here. I'll look for your story in tomorrow's paper."

* * *

Tyler Norris
July 10, 2018

"SHADOW RIDGE: GATE EXIT." The alert popped into the corner of Tyler Norris's monitor. The analyst clicked the button. Derek Price's profile appeared on the screen. *Where's he going now? I thought he had a visitor coming?*

Tyler picked up his desk phone and dialed. Two rings later, a woman answered.

"Thank you for calling the Shadow Ridge community clubhouse. This is Adrienne. How may I help you today?"

"Yes, Adrienne, this is Tyler Norris over at HQ. Is the field director available?"

"I believe so, Tyler. Let me check."

The phone clicked as she placed him on hold. *I hope this doesn't cause a problem.* The phone clicked again. This time, a deep, baritone voice responded.

"Mr. Norris, is there something I can help you with?"

"I just wanted to let you know, sir, that Derek Price has left the community. I know you were expecting him to have a visitor today."

"Thank you, Mr. Norris. We are aware of the situation and have initiated surveillance protocol. Please continue what you're doing and alert me of any other changes."

The call disconnected. *I wish I knew exactly why we cared so much about this guy.*

* * *

Derek Price

RUNNING LATE usually isn't Steve's style.

Derek admired his surroundings while waiting for his friend. During his days at the Daily Herald, the space had been known as The Reading Nook, a locally owned bookstore that prided itself on promoting local authors. The store's reputation as a Chicagoland destination, however, hadn't been enough to keep it afloat during the economic downturn.

"Cup of coffee while you wait?" A middle-aged waitress with scraggly hair and a tired face stood over Derek's table holding a steaming carafe.

"You know what? I will take a cup. Thank you."

After The Reading Nook closed, the building had been vacant for nearly five years before a group of angel investors purchased the space and converted it into a literary-themed restaurant, shortening the name to The Nook. As Derek sipped his coffee, his eyes traced the bookshelf-covered walls.

Maddie always told me I should write a book. Maybe that's a project I can take on when this is all over. A North Star, as Isiah called it. He tapped his hand against the table. His wedding ring made a thumping noise as it hit the wooden surface.

"Refill?" The waitress returned a few minutes later and topped off Derek's cup.

Where is Steve? I'm getting a little worried. He reached for his flip phone, which was sitting on top of the iPhone on the table. He opened it to check the time: 10:42 a.m. *This really isn't like him. I'll give it another few minutes. Maybe he hit traffic.*

Derek picked up the iPhone, unlocked the screen and opened an app called Daily Logic Puzzles that Sonia had installed. Today's "Daily Challenge" came in the form on an anagram puzzle, which required the player to rearrange letters to uncover other words.

He solved the puzzle and checked the clock again: 10:50. *He's 20 minutes late now. I should try calling.* Closing the puzzle app, he dialed Steve's number from the iPhone. *I should use the other phone, but hopefully he'll recognize this number from when we called him last time.* The phone rang four times before voicemail connected.

"Hello, you've reached Steve Erikson, statehouse reporter for The Daily Herald. I'm sorry I missed your call. Please leave your name, number and a brief message, and I'll return your call as soon as possible."

"Steve, it's Derek. I hope everything's alright. I'm here at The Nook, but it seems like something might have come up for you. If another governor has been arrested, I'd appreciate a heads up. Call me when you can and let me know everything's okay. We'll catch up later. Maybe drinks this weekend? Talk to you soon."

The waitress returned to his table. "Are you ready to order or would you still like to wait for your friend?"

"Actually, I think I'll take a check for just the coffee. I don't think he's going to make it."

"You sure I can't get anything else for you? We have our Reuben on special today."

Derek smiled. "No, thank you. I'm alright."

"Well, alright, hun. I'll be right back with your check."

Derek glanced outside, watching cars fly past on the busy street. *I just hope nothing happened to Steve. Work probably got in the way.*

Lost in his own thoughts, Derek didn't give second thought to the black sedan with tinted windows parked across the street.

CHAPTER 29
BRYCE REYNOLDS
JULY 10, 2018

BRYCE LEERED through the window of the Audi, cracked enough to allow line of sight without sacrificing the air conditioning. He'd followed Derek from the gates of Shadow Ridge into the suburbs and watched for almost an hour as his target waited for a friend who would never arrive. *With patience, a ruler may be persuaded, and a soft tongue will break a bone.*

A photo of Derek, a black cloth and a SIG Sauer P226 handgun sat on the passenger seat. Bryce pulled a pair of sunglasses from the overhead visor. He flipped the hood of his jacket over his head and grabbed the firearm. Leaving the window open for circulation, he climbed out of the vehicle and tucked the gun into the waistline of his jeans, draping the jacket to conceal it.

Why did it have to be such a public place? Bryce waited for a break in traffic. *This would have been so much easier at his house.* Finding his opening, he darted across the street and chose a spot on the corner outside the restaurant. He watched through a large plate-glass window as Derek tipped his waitress and headed for the exit.

I *only have one shot. Failure is not an option.* He leaned against the building's brick exterior on the other side of the door. A small group passed, laughing and carrying on conversation.

Ignoring the potential distraction, Bryce watched. He waited. He prayed no one got in his way.

* * *

Derek Price

"ENJOY THE REST of your day, hun."

"You, too." Derek waved to the waitress and checked his phones. *Still nothing.* He slid the iPhone into his rear pocket, opened the flip phone and started to type Sonia a message but stopped. *I'll just call her when I'm on the road.* He took another look at his surroundings, again considering the possibility of writing his own book, and pushed his way through the door.

Stepping onto the sidewalk, he casually glanced each direction before turning right toward where he'd parked his vehicle.

"Hey, Derek."

He stopped as an unfamiliar voice called his name. *That's not Steve. Must be a coincidence.* He kept walking.

"Derek Price?"

Okay, that's no coincidence. He cast a cautious glance in each direction before realizing the voice originated from behind. He turned to see a figure as unfamiliar as the voice. The man wore a hooded jacket, sunglasses, blue jeans and black sneakers. Derek raised a finger to his chest and mouthed an inquisitive "Me?"

The man's face remained stern. He nodded once and cocked his head to the side as if to say, "Come here."

Derek's legs locked. At one point in time, being recognized on the street would have seemed normal. Many in the suburbs knew him from his column in the Daily Herald and sporadic guest spots on the city's TV news. *But that was a decade ago. I doubt anyone up here would recognize me now.*

"Mr. Price, I need to talk to you." The man stepped toward Derek.

Derek stumbled backward. "I'm sorry, but I really have to be going."

Next thing he knew, the other man was at his side with a hand on his arm. "I need you to listen to me. Do everything you're asked, and you'll be fine." The man lifted his jacket to expose the firearm.

What the fuck is happening? Derek's eyes widened; his body shook. He raised his gaze from the weapon to the man's face. *Oh, shit.* "Wait, I recognize you! You're the one who took Karen. You kidnapped Karen! What the hell did you do to her?"

The man used his free hand to remove his sunglasses. His piercing blue eyes stared at Derek. "You need to be quiet. The last thing you want to do right now is create a scene."

I'm not so sure about that. "What are you going to do if I scream right now? If I call for help? Do you see how many people are out here?"

A couple pushing a stroller approached on the sidewalk. The man casually smiled at them. "Have a good day," he said as they passed. He turned his attention back to Derek. "You don't want anyone to get hurt, do you?"

No. I couldn't live with myself if that happened. Derek shook his head. *But what about me? Who knows what they did to Karen.*

"I assure you the last thing I want is for anyone to get hurt. That includes you." The man paused. "Now, my vehicle is parked over there." He tilted his head toward the black sedan. "I need you to come with me quietly. Do so, and we won't have any problems."

Where is he trying to take me? "Why would I go anywhere with you?" His body trembled; sweat ran down his face. *I could scream for help. I could try to break free and run back into the restaurant. I can try to get to my phone and call 9-1-1.* His mind switched gears. *But that puts other people at risk. I just can't do it.*

"All you need to know, Mr. Price, is that I work for some very important people, and they need to speak with you immediately. My orders are to get you to them safely. I can't guarantee that will happen if you don't listen to my instructions."

At this point, what other choice do I have? "Okay. Just promise me no one else will get hurt."

"That's the goal." He removed his hand from Derek's arm. "I'm right behind you."

Derek crossed the street. Arriving at the vehicle, he opened the rear driver's side door and began to climb in. The other man stopped him.

"Phone."

Derek pulled his flip phone from his pocket and handed it to his captor.

"Both of them."

Shit. He'd hoped to be able to use the iPhone in his rear pocket to trigger a call once inside the vehicle. Instead, he removed it and handed it over.

Defeated, he climbed into the backseat. The other man positioned himself behind the steering wheel and locked the doors. He reached for the black cloth on the passenger seat, handing it back to Derek. "Put this on."

Derek hesitated. He looked out the window but couldn't see anything through the tinted glass. *This is how it ends. I'm going to die.* His world went dark, and he hadn't even put on the blindfold yet.

CHAPTER 30
Sonia Torres
July 10, 2018

THAT'S WEIRD.

Sonia pressed the Twitter notification on her iPhone. The app opened to display a tweet from the Daily Herald's official account.

"BREAKING: Bipartisan bill providing tax incentives for development of master-planned communities to be introduced next session. @DHerikson has the story." A link to the newspaper's website followed the tease.

Sonia clicked through to the Daily Herald site and spotted Steve Erikson's byline at the top of the article. *Isn't he supposed to be at lunch with Derek? Maybe he wrote it in advance, and they're just publishing it now?*

A video appeared down midway down the page, featuring Steve standing in the Daily Herald newsroom recapping the article's details. A clock in the background read 10:35 a.m. Sonia checked her phone: 11:07. *He must have gotten called in early. Why hasn't Derek said anything?*

She hit the home button and opened her texts. She typed a message to his iPhone. "Just saw the news. Sucks lunch got canceled. You able to talk to Steve?"

She watched as the message status switched to "READ," but she received no response.

* * *

BRYCE REYNOLDS

THE IPHONE on the passenger seat lit up with a new text alert. Bryce pressed the home button. The screen lit up. *No passcode? That makes it easy.* He read the text from Sonia Torres. *Nothing to worry about.* He tossed the phone back onto the seat.

"Was that my phone?" Derek broke the silence that had filled the car since they'd left The Nook.

Bryce glanced in the rearview mirror. Derek held his body still. *Impressive, actually. If he's nervous, he's hiding it well.*

"Why can't you just tell me where we're going? I'm locked in the car. You know I don't have a weapon. It's not like I can go anywhere."

Bryce continued in silence. He'd spent the past 10 minutes bobbing up and down random streets, in the event his passenger tried mapping his route. *You can never be too careful.*

"Can you at least say something? Tell me your name? Don't I at least have the right to know who's trying to kill me?"

Bryce glanced in the rearview mirror and shook his head. "As I told you, Mr. Price. No one wants to hurt you." He paused. *He's going to learn the truth soon enough, anyway.* "My name's Bryce."

"Bryce." Derek hesitated. "Why are you doing this, Bryce? What's this all about? First, I see you and that woman taking my neighbor from her house in the middle of the night, and now you're kidnapping me in broad daylight and won't tell me where I'm going."

So, Sarah did see something that night. Bryce turned his head, watching the suburban landscape blur past through the driver's side window. *Many are the plans in the mind of a man, but it is the purpose of the Lord that will stand.*

"Do you consider yourself a religious man? Or, at least, a disciple of history?"

Derek hesitated. "A little bit of both, I suppose."

Bryce sensed a nervous tone in his voice. "Then I assume you're familiar with the Knights Templar." *Ten-to-one he brings up "The Da Vinci Code."*

"I'm familiar. I've read Dan Brown's books. But what does any of that have to do with what's happening right now?"

What did I tell you? "I'm talking about the group's actual history, not the conspiracy theory. The Knights originated as protectors of Christian believers, shielding them from attacks as they traveled to Jerusalem. With the Pope's blessing, they even set up their own banks to help these travelers finance their journeys. But the Knights themselves swore an oath of poverty and obedience. They existed to serve others, not themselves."

Bryce looked in the rearview mirror. Even with the blindfold, he knew he had Derek's attention.

"When the Muslims regained control of Jerusalem, the Knights' power and influence began dwindling. Eventually, the king of France turned on them, ordering their outright slaughter. The men who had dedicated their lives to protecting the faithful had become a target. Officially, the Knights' existence ended 700 or so years ago, but that's where we start blurring the lines between fact and Dan Brown fiction."

Derek leaned forward, his head almost touching Bryce's shoulder. "I still don't understand what any of this has to do with me and why I'm sitting back here blindfolded, not knowing where we're going."

Fear has turned to anger, it seems. "What we should take away from the Templars, Mr. Price, is that since the beginning of time, humans have banded together to serve the greater good. And, more often than not, their efforts lead to even more death and destruction. There are forces of evil at play in this world, and I believe we're charged to do whatever we can to protect others from them, no matter the cost."

Derek's face fell away from Bryce's headrest. Bryce looked in the rearview mirror and saw him slouched in the backseat, his blindfolded stare directed out the window.

* * *

Derek Price

FOR THE NEXT 10 minutes or so, Derek sat quietly in the backseat, his eyes closed behind the blindfold, trying to piece everything together. *Shadowen. Chimera. Thomas. And now a psychopath's manifesto on the Knights Templar?*

His body jerked as the vehicle hit something — a speed bump, Derek assumed. *Are we slowing down, or is that my imagination?* Turns became tighter, more methodical. *I don't think we're on the road anymore.* A minute later, the car came to a stop. The sound of the engine dulled.

He heard Bryce's door open and close. The door next to him opened.
"We're here."

Derek stalled. His right hand fumbled to find his left. He slid the wedding band from his finger and gripped it in his palm. As he climbed from the backseat, he slid the ring into his pocket.

A still cool air brushed his skin. He didn't feel the sun's heat beating down on him. *We're clearly still outside but somewhere shaded. It's quiet. Maybe I can make a break for it without putting anyone else at risk.* Bryce grabbed his arm. *So much for that idea.*

"You're doing great, Mr. Price." Bryce led him forward.

Derek could sense solid concrete beneath his feet. *It must be a parking garage.* After about 300 feet, Bryce stopped.

Ding! *An elevator?* He heard the metal doors slide open. *Where the hell are we that no one gets suspicious of a blindfolded man being loaded into an elevator?* Bryce nudged Derek into the elevator. Derek's blood pressure rose along with it.

"C'mon, we're almost there." When the doors slid open, Bryce guided Derek out of the elevator and a short distance down a hallway.
I can feel the AC now. We're definitely inside.

Bryce led Derek into a room and steered him to a chair. He pressed down on his shoulder, instructing him to sit. Derek obeyed, surprised to feel comfortable leather padding beneath him. He heard Bryce move across the room.

The door closed. Derek sensed a third person, who had closed the door quietly behind them. He recognized her voice as soon as she spoke.

"Mr. Price, I'm sorry. You can take that ridiculous blindfold off."

He reached up and pulled the cloth from his face. His eyes adjusted to the light, bringing into focus a familiar scene. A large wooden conference table, aerial photos of world architecture on the walls and the wrinkled, smiling face of Geraldine Shadowen.

Seriously, what the fuck is happening?

"Mrs. Shadowen." The words were barely more than a whisper.

"I apologize for the theatrics." She cast a glare at Bryce. "As I said last time, you can never truly understand the mind of a military man."

"What the hell is going on?" Derek used his palms to push back from the table, standing from his chair. "What am I doing here? I get abducted, fearing for my life, and you bring me to my HOA company's headquarters?"

"Mr. Price, if you'll please take a seat, I promise I'll explain everything." Geraldine lowered herself into a chair at the head of the table.

"I'm not sitting down until you explain what exactly I'm doing here!"

"I know you have questions." Geraldine folded her hands on the table. The inner corners of her eyebrows raised; the outer corner of her lips lowered. "But, first, I believe it's time you learn the truth about your wife."

CHAPTER 31
DEREK PRICE
JULY 10, 2018

THE TRUTH about your wife. The words echoed in Derek's mind.

Sitting in the same conference room he'd visited only days ago, he glanced around the room speechless.

Bryce sat across from him, stoic and reserved. Geraldine reached her hands across the table, as if to offer consolation. "I know this must be difficult for you to hear, but our circumstances have left us no option but to tell you the truth and trust you'll understand the need for secrecy."

The truth? The need for secrecy? He stared, his mouth agape. No words escaped his lips.

"You must pardon my candor. I don't know where it's best to begin." She paused. "Your late wife, Madeline, worked for Chimera Technologies."

Was that a question or a statement? He nodded.

"How much do you know about Chimera, Mr. Price?"

Derek's mind raced to process thoughts and memories, from meeting Madeline to learning about Thomas Sheridan's death. "A fair amount. Besides Maddie, I became friends with several of her coworkers. I know they sold technology platforms to governments. Most of it went over my head, but I knew Maddie was passionate about it."

"And how much do you know about her role with the company?"

Derek snickered. *That was always a running joke.* "She was a business analyst. She had trouble conveying exactly what she did, but I know she was usually the first point of contact for new clients. Our friend Isiah used to say she set them up, and he talked them into the deal."

Derek saw Geraldine's eyes cast a quick glance in Bryce's direction.

"What I don't know, Mrs. Shadowen," Derek continued, "is what any of that has to do with this." He picked up the blindfold and waved it in the air.

Geraldine leaned back in her chair, straightening her pose. She brushed the silver bangs from her face. "I'm afraid you do not know as much about Chimera Technologies as you believe, Mr. Price." Her voice was warm but firm, like a parent having a serious conversation with their child.

She continued, "Like its namesake, Chimera was an amalgamation of multiple parts. One branch did the work you described. They developed, produced and sold software for government solutions. But Madeline worked for the other branch of the company, the less public one."

Less public one? What does she mean? Derek's elbows dug into the arms of the chair; his upper body leaned forward. "I'm still not sure what you mean?"

The top of Geraldine's lips lifted. "Chimera Technologies existed as a shield for a federal intelligence task force operating out of the Pentagon under the shared jurisdiction of the departments of Defense and Homeland Security."

Derek's eyes blinked three times. He shook his head, trying to clear his thoughts. *The Pentagon?* "Excuse me, what? The DoD and Homeland Security? That's insanity! Just tell me what's really going on here."

Waiting for Geraldine to respond, a flood of thoughts washed through his mind. *That would explain Maddie's long trips. But what about Thomas, Isiah, Andrew? Were they all involved with this, too? No, she's fucking lying to you, Derek.*

"I told you this wouldn't be easy to hear, Mr. Price, but I assure you that everything I'm telling you is 100 percent true."

"Even if I were to believe you, what does any of that have to do with real estate development?"

Geraldine took a deep breath. "Much like Chimera, there's more to Shadowen Real Estate than meets the eye."

What, is this a front for the government, too?

"Just as Chimera sold legitimate software, we also sell actual homes. What you won't read in the media, however, is that we limit our clientele to those with backgrounds in government or military service. To those on our side, Shadowen operates under the banner SHADOW — Secure Housing and Domestication of Warriors."

The wheels turned in Derek's head. *J.D. Moore's military background. The story of the Knights Templar. The denied buyers that started this whole mess.*

"Our properties function like any other community association. Granted, our enhanced security resources allow us to better monitor and protect our residents. Thomas Sheridan, who you're no doubt familiar with, helped us establish those systems."

So, that's how Thomas connects to Shadowen. "But, we paid a mortgage. We paid HOA dues."

"Yes, those revenue streams help fund the SHADOW program, as well as community amenities and programs. To keep costs low, we supplement those funds by partnering with entrepreneurs from SHADOW communities to offer low-rent office space. You likely saw the directory in the lobby on your last visit."

The board by the elevator. Now it makes sense why there's a lawyer and an accountant here. "So, does everyone from Chimera live in one of these communities?"

Geraldine gave Bryce another ominous glance. "Not all, but most."

"I'm confused, though. When Maddie and I bought our house, we looked at a dozen homes before we decided on Shadow Ridge. We had no idea we were going to live here."

"Maybe you didn't, Mr. Price." She paused, smiling. "But you should know to never underestimate the influence of a determined woman."

She knew. She was so excited from the time we arrived because she already knew we'd buy the house. The whole time we lived there, she knew she'd manipulated me into the decision.

"So how long did she know?"

"I first spoke with Madeline about two months before you purchased the home. She accepted the offer and signed her agreement to join the SHADOW program about two weeks prior."

"So everyone who buys a house in the community signs this agreement?"

Geraldine nodded.

That means— "Karen." Derek turned his stare to Bryce and leaned across the table. "You want to talk to me about safety and protecting people when I saw him kidnapping my neighbor in the middle of the night?"

Bryce looked at Geraldine. She nodded.

"Agent Reynolds is one of the finest agents SHADOW has. I'll let him share his story."

"The afternoon of the Fourth of July, we received a report that Ms. Conrad had become an apparent danger to herself." Bryce betrayed no emotion. "Agent Evans and I were instructed to assist. We scheduled regular check-ins, and when Ms. Conrad failed to respond, we reported to her residence."

A danger to herself? What did they think Karen would do?

"When we arrived, Ms. Conrad did not respond. We forcibly entered the home through the rear door to minimize disruption to the neighbors. Once inside, we found Ms. Conrad unconscious on her living room sofa. Agent Evans found an empty pill bottle and wine glass on a nearby table. Loose pills were scattered across the floor. I checked her pulse, but it was weak. We didn't have time to wait for an ambulance, so I carried Ms. Conrad to my vehicle and we transferred her to Morris Hospital for immediate evaluation."

Derek thought of the dying flowers and the Amazon boxes piled on the porch. "I don't understand. Why would Karen try to kill herself?"

Geraldine interjected. "Ms. Conrad suffered from post-traumatic stress disorder, an unfortunate remnant of her service in the Middle East. Sometimes, the ghosts of our past continue to haunt our present."

Karen never even told us she'd served. At least, she never told me. "Is Karen okay? Is that why I saw your men there with the truck that morning?"

Geraldine tipped her head. "I'm happy to report that Ms. Conrad is doing well. She has a long road ahead of her, but we have relocated her to a group home where she will receive the personalized care she needs."

Derek sat quietly for a moment. Finally, he mustered the words to speak again. "This is all just so much to take in. I don't understand why all of this had to be a secret."

"I know it's hard for you to understand right now, Mr. Price, but we're finding out now more than ever that some situations require drastic resolutions." She looked at Bryce. Derek followed her gaze. "Agent Reynolds knows that better than anyone."

CHAPTER 32
Bryce Reynolds
June 17, 2018

"C'MON, LANCE, answer the phone."

The pause between each ring lasted an eternity. Bryce's Audi sped down the interstate toward Shadow Farms. The director had requested he meet with her friend, Thomas Sheridan, who claimed to have information of interest to the SHADOW program.

While en route, Bryce's phone had alerted him of a dispatch call for a structural fire on Lone Tree Lane in the community. He had recognized the address as his destination.

"Hello?" A friendly male voice emanated from the phone speaker.

"Lance, it's Bryce Reynolds. I don't have a lot of time. I was headed to meet with a former Chimera agent and dispatch just signaled a fire at his residence. Have your guys been called out to Shadow Farms?"

"Negative. I heard the call, but, so far, we're only on alert. Do you know what happened? Have you made contact?"

No, that's the problem. "Sounds like a gas leak, based on scanner chatter. There's been no suspicious activity at the gatehouse, but I haven't been able to reach my contact, either. I need access to the scene. And if I'm going to get close enough without exposing myself, I need to be in uniform." He paused. "I know that's a lot to ask."

"No need for concern, Agent Reynolds."

Bryce owed his SHADOW career to Lance Anderson. When Bryce had returned home from Iraq, he'd been broken. An errant IED had cost him months of his life recovering, but it had taken much more from three of his squad mates. Lance, who had preceded Jefferson as field director of SHADOW, had since retired and taken a post as a captain with the Coal City Fire Department.

"This may be a matter of life or death, Lance." *Whoever believes in me, though he dies, yet shall he live.* "I'm praying we're not already too late."

Lance's voice never faltered. "Meet me at the empty lot behind U.S. Bank. I'm gathering my gear now."

"I'll be there in 10." Bryce disconnected the call, pressed his foot against the gas pedal and whispered a silent prayer.

* * *

June 26, 2018

"HEY, GUYS, this is Akumi. Leave a message, and I'll call you back."

Bryce sat in his Audi, parked outside Akumi Kim's Nashville home. He ended the call without leaving a message. *She told me she'd be home. Maybe I should check on her.*

Bryce and Akumi's backgrounds couldn't have been more different. He'd finished high school at a private Christian academy and considered the seminary before enlisting in the Marine Corps. She'd grown up in Taiwan and come to the States to study accounting at the University of Notre Dame.

He found the front door of the home slightly ajar. He knocked twice and pushed it further open. "Akumi?" No response.

The two hadn't talked in almost a year, as Bryce had taken a more active role at SHADOW. After Chimera shut down, Akumi had turned freelance, offering her forensic accounting services to any agency with the budget to afford her.

Bryce stepped inside the home. "Akumi, it's Bryce. Are you here?" Again, no response.

He'd reached out when he was assigned to assist with a relocation in Akumi's community, Shadow Run. She'd invited him to her home for drinks and had even offered him a bed for the night, which he had graciously declined.

Something's not right. He pulled the Sig Sauer handgun from its holster and held it at his side. *Be strong and courageous. Do not be frightened, and do not be dismayed, for the Lord your God is with you wherever you go.*

He moved quickly through the downstairs, checking each room — looking behind doors and inside closets. Finding nothing suspicious, he moved upstairs. *Is that music?* "Akumi?" *Maybe she just couldn't hear me over the music.*

He followed the sound to the owner's suite bathroom, stopping short and squaring his back against the wall. "Akumi, it's Bryce." All he heard was the recorded sound of pianos.

He took a deep breath and swung his body around, extending the handgun in front of him in a defensive stance in the bathroom doorway. The room was dark aside from the glow of a lit candle on the counter. But even in the darkness, he recognized the unmistakable form of his friend's body sunk just beneath the surface of the water.

"Akumi," he muttered under his breath.

* * *

June 28, 2018

THAT WAS QUICK.

Bryce glanced at the two police cruisers headed toward the Shadow Grove gatehouse as he made his way to the interstate. *They're going to rule it a suicide. The world's going to think she died a coward, but, man, Nicole was one of the strongest women I knew.*

His phone rang. "Reynolds, talk to me." Jefferson's voice cracked as he spoke.

"I'm sorry, sir." Bryce swallowed. "I was too late."

The evening before, Nicole Guzman had called the SHADOW office to report a strange vehicle she'd believed had been following her. As Bryce had been headed to Charlotte to visit family, he volunteered to detour to Asheville instead and spend a few days with Nicole and her family.

"Nothing from the gatehouse?"

"Nothing out of the ordinary, sir. A few early morning deliveries, a cable installer, but that's it. The only way someone could have gotten in would have been if Nicole had given them her gate code, which would mean we're looking for someone she knew and trusted." *It is better to take refuge in the Lord than to trust in man.*

"Damn it, Reynolds."

I know that's not directed at me. Nicole's death gave credence to a working theory shared only between Bryce, Jefferson and SHADOW director Geraldine Shadowen. In recent weeks, at least three members of Thomas Sheridan's former Chimera team had died under suspicious circumstances.

"I did what I could, sir. He tried to make it look like a suicide, but clearly he is not a professional. I know it's important not to let him know we're onto him, so I finished the scene as best I could, including leaving a few false copies of the note it seems he wrote. The work isn't perfect. You might want to have the director reach out to the local PD. I called in the gunshot as soon as I left the premises."

"Excellent work, Agent Reynolds, but I'm not confident we even know our suspect is male."

He's right. "If we would have known, I would have been more diligent at the Sheridan and Kim scenes." *They all deserve better. They deserve justice.*

"You did everything you could under the conditions presented. You cannot blame yourself, Agent Reynolds."

Yet, I do. "Yes, sir. But I'll do everything in my power to stop this from happening again."

"We all will, Agent Reynolds. There are only three members of the Chimera team left. The director has instructed me to reach out to each of them and offer protective services."

"Where are they located, sir? Tell me where I need to be, and I'll be on my way."

"Unfortunately, only Andrew Wainwright lives in a SHADOW community. The others, Isiah Cross and Monique Duvall, declined to join our program. As for you, Agent Reynolds, we need you to convene with us at headquarters."

"Understood, sir."

Lord, please care for the souls you've already taken and shine a blessing on those who remain.

* * *

July 1, 2018

BRYCE LEANED against a barstool in Andrew Wainwright's kitchen. His gaze shifted back and forth between the phone in his hand and the two bodies on the floor. *I should have been here. That should have been me.*

Bryce had questioned the director's decision to keep him close to headquarters when none of the three presumed targets lived in the area. *It's a three-hour drive. I could have been here with Andrew and still made appearances for briefings.*

He dialed the phone. His call barely rang before being answered.

"Reynolds." Jefferson spoke quietly.

"They're both dead, sir. Wainwright and the agent you sent here with him." *Now's not the time.* His mouth betrayed his mind. "Sir, with all due respect, I should have been here. Andrew Wainwright might be alive if you'd assigned me here."

Jefferson's volume rose. His tone turned tense. "Don't you get it, Bryce? You could just as easily be dead, too?"

Yeah, I've been down this road before. His thoughts turned to the fallen Marines. *I would have taken any of their places, too.* "I knew that risk when I accepted this position, sir."

Jefferson hesitated. "There's nothing else we can do there at the moment. Make your way back to headquarters and we'll assess how to proceed. We have an unrelated issue at Shadow Ridge that may require your expertise."

"I'll be on my way shortly, sir. I want to take one more look at the evidence here."

Bryce disconnected the call. *I don't care what anyone says; this is my fault. Their blood is on my hands.*

CHAPTER 33
Geraldine Shadowen
July 10, 2018

"I'M CERTAIN you have additional questions, Mr. Price," Geraldine said. *I only hope you accept I've been honest with you.*

She watched Derek lean back in his chair. *He seems to be more comfortable.* He placed his elbows on the armrests, clasping his fingers together above his chest.

"I'm just trying to piece everything you're saying together." He hesitated. "Assuming I believe everything you say about Chimera and Shadowen is true, how did the two organizations come together? How did you know Thomas?"

Thomas. I still can't believe he's gone. "Thomas served in the Army with my husband, Randall. When his enlistment ended, Thomas pursued a career in the private-sector until the Pentagon recruited him to lead the Chimera project. They recognized the value in Thomas's background in both military operations and software development as a means of protecting the team's true purpose."

She continued, "After what happened to Randall," she swallowed a lump in her throat, "Thomas presented us with the concept of SHADOW. This had never been the plan. Randall wanted to retire and start a home-building company, but we envisioned nothing of this magnitude. Then the incident changed our perspective. We saw an opportunity to channel our grief and hope into a means of serving others and protecting the brave men and women who sacrifice on behalf of our nation."

We couldn't change the pain Randall endured, but we could help prevent others from suffering.

Derek nodded slowly, listening to her talk. "So, what happened? After Madeline left Chimera, we heard rumblings, and the next thing we knew, Thomas shut everything down. I talked to our friend Isiah, and he said Thomas had ideas that split the team."

At the mention of Isiah's name, Geraldine shot Bryce a look. *Just how much has he told you?* She turned her gaze back to Derek, sighing. "That's one way of characterizing it." She paused. "Mr. Price, I need your word that what's said here today stays between us. I've been transparent because I feel we owe you an explanation after everything you've been through, but you're inquiring about very sensitive matters."

"I understand, ma'am, but my whole world has been shattered in the last 20 minutes. I'm trying to make sense of all of it before I can begin to piece it back together."

I sympathize, but there's some information I simply cannot divulge. "About three years ago, Thomas approached me with a prospect for expanding the SHADOW program's reach and influence. The Chimera team had excelled at developing useful technology for intelligence collection and surveillance. Thomas proposed adapting those resources for the private sector."

Derek's brow furrowed. He scooted his chair closer to the table. "What do you mean the private sector? Like spying on private citizens?"

For one who loved mythology, Icarus had flown too close to the sun. "That was certainly never Thomas's intention, but in the aftermath of Cambridge Analytica, I believe erring on the side of caution proved to be the correct decision. I believe protecting the privacy of others is an essential function of not only the SHADOW program, but the federal government."

"So what exactly did Thomas want to do that caused so much animosity?"

Geraldine smiled. "Thomas was always well-intentioned. He imagined a world where smoke detectors could automatically alert the fire department, or where security systems would trigger alarms based on noise or change in temperature, not just movement. His vision, however, became short-sighted when considering the widespread application of such technology."

"You mean selling the blueprints to the highest bidder?"

Geraldine nodded. "Precisely, Mr. Price. Word leaked through internal channels at the Pentagon, and suddenly Thomas had offers from every federal contractor you can imagine, from Lockheed Martin to General Dynamics. He focused on the potential revenue stream and the rapid expansion it would allow for both Chimera and SHADOW, but he was blind to the harm his product could cause if it fell into the wrong hands."

"Wow." Derek rubbed his thumb against his beard. "So the team split? And that was the end of Chimera?"

"Correct. And, seeing the writing on the wall, I informed Thomas that SHADOW would be terminating our partnership. I'm afraid he didn't handle the news so well."

Derek's eyes squinted; his eyebrows raised. "I noticed monthly payments to Labyrinth Systems in the Shadow Ridge budget. Why did you keep paying him if you had a falling out?"

I couldn't leave him on his own to suffer. That would have gone against everything we believe in. "Honestly?" She leaned forward, placing her hands on the table. "A combination of obligation and pity. When others witnessed the strife his decision caused within his team, as well as the partnership with SHADOW, Thomas was outcast as a pariah. He wanted nothing more than to be a hero, but he found himself the villain."

He had been there for me and Randall when we needed it. I couldn't leave him on his own. "No matter how far apart we drifted, I'd made a promise to always be there for him."

And I was, until I failed him at the very end.

* * *

Derek Price

WAS MADDIE PROTECTING Thomas, too? Derek's mind raced to process everything he'd just heard, though he felt as if he still had more questions than answers. *Isiah will know more. I'll tell him I know everything. Maybe he'll finally be honest with me then.*

"Is there anything else I can answer for you, Mr. Price?"

Derek looked at Geraldine, then at Bryce. "I appreciate you trusting me enough to share this information, but that brings us back to where we started." He paused. "The sale of my house."

Geraldine laid her hand flat on the table. "Your situation has proven rather unique. Admittedly, we were biding our time while we determined the most appropriate course of action."

And there was nothing you could have told me in the meantime to avoid all of this?

"When Madeline entered the SHADOW residency program, our agreement stipulated that, in the event anything happened to her, we would continue providing services to any remaining immediate family. While many of our residents are open about their service, others, like Madeline, kept those details private."

"You mean there are others living a similar lie?"

Geraldine's lips leveled; her eyes held steady. "Most certainly. For many, especially those in the intelligence community, there exists a great deal of concern regarding putting loved ones at risk. Much like Madeline kept secrets to protect you, so do others for the benefit of their families. But we've never encountered a situation such as yours, where a death left behind an unknowing spouse."

Glad I could be of service as your guinea pig. "So what does that mean?"

"While it would be easy to end the agreement we made with Madeline and let you proceed as you wish, we had an obligation, a promise we'd made to her, and we needed to ensure we accommodated everyone's wishes."

"I'm sorry, but shouldn't I be the one to make that choice?"

Geraldine regained her smile. "Absolutely. But Jefferson and I agreed it was important to ensure you were making an informed decision. Jefferson was the one who raised the concern, in fact. He was quite fond of your wife and wanted to preserve her legacy."

Why wasn't he just upfront with me? "So, why the blindfold and the tense ride here? Why not just tell me this at the clubhouse or over the phone?"

"Again, Mr. Price, I apologize for Agent Reynolds's theatrics." She cast another glare in Bryce's direction. "When we learned you had added Steve Erikson to your guest list at the gatehouse, we knew we had to act quickly or we risked the media asking unwanted questions. Agent Reynolds was preparing to visit you at your home when he saw you leaving the community. He followed you this direction, and we had to assume your meeting with Mr. Erikson had been moved."

He followed me from Shadow Ridge to The Nook? Derek's eyes widened as he turned Bryce's direction.

Geraldine continued, "We knew we had to change course. I called in a favor from a contact in the legislature. He'd been planning to introduce additional tax incentives for real estate developers this fall. I encouraged him to leak the story to Mr. Erikson."

That's why Steve never showed up for lunch. "So, let me guess, he waited for me outside the restaurant and, well, you know the rest." Derek waved his hand in Bryce's direction.

Bryce nodded. "Correct. And, being unsure of how well this conversation would go, I did what I felt was necessary to protect the agency."

The conversation lulled. Derek watched Geraldine scribble a note on the back of a business card, which she slid his direction.

"That's my direct line. If I can answer any additional questions or be of assistance, please don't hesitate. Though I need to ask once again for your judicious discretion. Ensuring the integrity of the SHADOW program — a program your wife believed in — may frankly be a matter of life and death."

Death? Like Thomas's fire? "Understood, ma'am."

"Agent Reynolds will return you to your vehicle." She stopped and looked at Bryce. "No need for the blindfold this time."

The three rose from the table. Derek shook Geraldine's hand and thanked her again for her honesty. She left the room, leaving him and Bryce alone.

"If you're ready, Mr. Price."

Derek nodded and led the way. He turned right down the hallway, toward the service elevator.

"This way," Bryce said, heading the opposite direction. "We'll use the front door this time."

CHAPTER 34
Madeline Price
Nov. 25, 2016

"I SAW THE PICTURES of the girls." Madeline's smile beamed from ear to ear. "I can't believe how big they're getting."

Her purse and snacks laid on the seat next to her. Isiah sat across the aisle. Aside from their companion Monique Duvall, who had wandered off in search of a vending machine, and a desk attendant, the flight services building was empty.

With no commercial air travel, the facility exclusively serviced private pilots, a benefit the Chimera team often used to their advantage. The trio would catch their chartered international flight after a layover in Washington.

"They sure are." Isiah avoided Madeline's gaze. "I just hate being away from them this much, especially at the holidays."

"I know the feeling." *I know Derek was upset when I sprung this trip on him. He wouldn't say as much, but I'd promised him I'd be home between the holidays.* "How are things with Kat, by the way? I know you two were in a rough spot last time I saw you."

Isiah looked at her for a second, then he turned his attention to the burnt-orange carpet. "I don't know, Madeline. I really don't know anymore. I feel like I should just confess and tell her everything, lay all the cards on the table and hope for the best. I hate living this double life. I hate hiding who I really am from her."

You're preaching to the choir, my friend. She scooted to the edge of the seat cushion and leaned across the aisle. "But you're so good at it." She smirked.

Isiah lifted his gaze from the floor and smiled when he saw her face. "Lying and manipulating people since 1983. You know me too well."

"Well enough to make you smile." Madeline leaned back in her chair. *The next 10 days are going to be hard enough as it is. We have to keep each other's spirits up.*

Monique Duvall returned from her hunt successful. Her purse slung over her shoulder, she carried a bottle of Dasani water and a bag of peanut M&Ms. "What are you two all smiles about over here?"

Isiah and Madeline exchanged a look. "Well, Madeline was just telling me about this great article she read on the best wardrobes for a 10-hour flight."

Madeline couldn't help but laugh.

Monique let out an exaggerated gasp of disbelief as she looked down at herself, admiring the way her black-and-gray plaid miniskirt and strappy black heels accentuated her dark skin. "I'm changing when we get to D.C." She playfully sneered. "You know I don't make it up here very often. I figured I'd make the most of it and met a friend for lunch."

Isiah raised his eyebrows twice. "Meeting a friend for lunch, huh? Grabbing a little afternoon delight before fleeing the country?"

Monique huffed. "It's not my fault both of you gave up and settled down in yours 30s." She took a seat next to Madeline. "Anyway, what did I miss at this morning's briefing?"

Madeline and Isiah had connected with Thomas Sheridan and Andrew Wainwright earlier, but Monique's flight from Gulf Shores had prevented her participation.

"Seems like the first leg in Germany is pretty straight-forward," Isiah said. "Someone with ties to the NPD has been trying to spread influence among the soldiers at Hohenfels outside of Wolfsburg, about three hours west of Berlin."

"NPD?" Monique asked.

"The National Democratic Party of Germany. Don't let the name fool you; they're considered one of the most extreme neo-Nazi political parties since World War II."

"They sound like swell people." Monique adjusted her position on the hard seat. "So, what's the assignment?"

"I've got this one." Madeline faced Monique. "You and I are leading a course for those stationed at Hohenfels. Routine stuff — handling difficult situations, remaining calm under pressure and basic positioning in public places. NPD seems to target young soldiers at pubs throughout the area, where they stand out from the crowd."

"My job's a little more fun," Isiah chimed in. "I'm preparing a small team to go undercover with NPD." He paused. "And after that? Who knows? Thomas kept a lid on where we're headed next. It makes it hard to tell your wife when you'll be able to check in when you don't even know where the hell you're going."

That's the truth. "Thomas is meeting us in D.C. He had a meeting with the DoD and Homeland. Said he'll have more details when we're on the flight to Berlin."

The conversation ended. Each capitalized on a quiet moment to check their phones. *I should let Derek know we'll be leaving soon.*

Monique broke the silence. "So, I have to ask this here before we meet with Thomas." She glanced both directions to ensure they were alone. "What's your guys' take on this whole Labyrinth project? I've wanted to ask for a while, but it seems like we're never alone."

Madeline and Isiah stared at each other, waiting to see who would respond first. *Wait all you want, Isiah. I'm not losing this one.*

He broke. "You know, I tried to be rational about this and not jump to conclusions. But the more that happens, the more the rumor mill is flying, the more this makes me not only question the project but Thomas's integrity. Sure, it's easy to see a lot of good coming from something like this, but where's it stop? Where do we draw the line? There are days I wonder if Thomas hasn't already driven us straight past it."

Isiah and Madeline both looked at Monique. "Me? Okay." She readjusted her position on the seat as she spoke. "I just try to focus on the positive. You guys know my story. I didn't even think I'd go to college growing up. I never imagined being part of anything like this. But we get to make such a positive difference in people's lives, even if we don't always get to talk about it. As far as I'm concerned, anything that's going to help people is fine by me."

I suppose I'm next. Madeline raised her hand to her mouth and feigned a cough, stalling for time. "Well," she hesitated. "I just—." Her words hung in the air.

Isiah leaned forward and reached across the aisle. "You okay?"

Don't cry. Don't cry. Madeline couldn't stop herself. She burst into tears; her face dropped into her hands.

Monique put a hand on Madeline's back. Isiah moved to her other side and did the same.

"I'm struggling, you guys. I'm struggling with a lot right now, and the mere thought of this makes me so uncomfortable. I don't know what to think anymore. I don't know what to do. I can't help but wonder what Derek would think if he knew. And then I wonder if I should just tell him." *He deserves to know the truth.*

She paused and let the tears flow. "There are just so many variables, so much that could go wrong, and we'd be responsible for it. We could cause so much harm to someone's life."

"I understand the concern, Madeline, and, as I said, I have the same issues." Isiah's words were soft-spoken but powerful. "But look at us. Look at Monique. Look at me. Can you imagine any of us ever being okay with hurting someone? I don't think we could live with ourselves if we let that happen."

I know that's true, but the concern is real. Thomas has lost his focus. "I know. And I love you both because of it."

Madeline wiped her eyes. Monique handed her the bottle of water, which she sipped. Isiah, crouching in the aisle, set his hand on Madeline's knee.

"Listen, Madeline. Let's talk to Thomas on the flight. Be honest. Share your concern with him and see what he says. You don't have to decide your future right this minute. It's certainly not a matter of life and death."

CHAPTER 35
Bryce Reynolds
July 10, 2018

"THE RIDE'S a lot more pleasant in the front." Derek cocked his head toward the driver's seat and smiled.

I did what I had to do. "Sorry again." Bryce had been quiet for most of the drive, despite Derek's attempts at conversation.

"So, you're a military man?"

That question, however, attracted Bryce's attention. "Five years in the Marines. I'd still be enlisted if I could, but I was medically discharged after an incident in Fallujah. Only by the grace of God am I sitting here today." *The others weren't so fortunate.* "You?"

Derek shook his head. "Never served myself, but I admire those who do." He flashed an appreciative smile. "My dad flew fighter jets during Vietnam but didn't talk about it much." He pictured his parents in his mind. "You raised in a military family?"

Bryce chuckled. *Militaristic, maybe.* "No, my old man wasn't keen on serving anyone but himself. I found myself in a bit of trouble as a youth, and my mom sent me away to boarding school. I took an interest in studying history and religion, which led me to considering the seminary."

"Hence the Templar metaphor."

Bryce nodded and continued his story. "I was a just a young kid, though, and I wasn't cut out for the priesthood. I'm sure you know what I mean." Bryce smiled coyly. "I knew I wanted to serve, though, to give back. I figured if I wasn't going to serve my God, I could at least serve my country."

"Well, I appreciate your service, Agent Reynolds. I'm afraid I may have let the circumstances of our meeting leave me with the wrong impression. I hope we can move past that."

Who am I to judge? For we will all stand before the judgment seat of God. "Certainly. But, please, call me Bryce."

The two conversed for 10 more minutes until they arrived at The Nook. Bryce pulled his Audi into the parking lot where Derek's vehicle waited. He shifted to park, turned and offered Derek a handshake.

"Mr. Price, whatever you decide to do, take care of yourself. There's evil in this world that we can't control. You seem like a good man. I know your wife meant a lot to those who knew her." He paused. "Maybe our paths will cross again someday." *Though, for your sake, I pray that I'm wrong.*

Derek smiled and shook Bryce's hand. "I'd enjoy that, Bryce. Thanks for the ride." He opened the car door and exited the vehicle.

Bryce lifted his phone from the center console and typed a message to Geraldine. "Headed back. Tell Jefferson I'll be ready to meet in 30."

* * *

Sonia Torres

"GOOD MORNING, Ms. Torres."

"Good morning, Professor Gregerson." Sonia watched her economics professor enter his classroom. *I swear, he can't be that much older than me.*

She pulled the iPhone from her pocket to text Derek. *It's going to kill me if I don't hear what happened with Steve before class.* Before she finished the message, the phone rang. "Derek?"

"Yeah, Sonia, it's me."

"Where the hell have you been? I've been trying to reach you all morning. I saw a story from Steve on the Herald's Twitter, but you haven't answered any of my messages."

Derek hesitated. "Listen, Sonia, I can't explain it right now, especially over the phone."

You can't talk about it on the phone? What? "Okay."

"I'm still up in the suburbs. Can you meet me at the house in about an hour? This is important."

Sonia pulled the phone from her ear to check the time. She looked in the classroom. Professor Gregerson stood at the podium, preparing to teach. *Fuck.* "Sure. I'll meet you there."

"Thanks, Sonia. I think we finally have the answers we need."

Except the one about whether I'll be retaking econ in the fall.

* * *

Geraldine Shadowen

GERALDINE SAT ALONE in her top-floor office, waiting for Bryce to return. *Hopefully, we can now put Mr. Price's situation behind us and focus on our more pressing issue.*

She reached across her desk and picked up the framed photo of herself and her husband. Randall wore his dress blues and smiled, but sorrow filled his eyes. Standing behind him, her hand on his shoulder, Geraldine's smile appeared forced.

Our system failed you. It failed young Tony Wallace, too, and Randall still hasn't let that go. I promised we'd do better, that I'd ensure no one else suffered as you did. Now I'm the one who failed.

"Mrs. Shadowen." The young woman's voice pierced through the speaker of Geraldine's desk phone. "Agent Reynolds has returned."

"Thank you. Please send him up."

She placed the photo back in its place on the desk and tidied up her workspace. She moved to a small, round table on the other side of the office. Earlier, she'd prepared the space with necessary files and a notepad. A knock on the open door drew her attention.

"Come in, Bryce. Have a seat."

"Yes, ma'am." They both sat down. "How do you think our meeting went?"

Geraldine forced her lips into a half-smile. "I'm worried, Bryce. I really am."

"Worried who he'll talk to? I'm sure that reporter will wonder what he'd wanted to meet about."

Our secrets leaking is the least of my concerns at the moment. "I don't know. Based on my limited interactions, I hesitate to believe Derek Price would rush to that type of behavior. I'm certain he'll consider what his wife would want if she was here." She paused. "But, my greater concern is our situation with Isiah Cross and Monique Duvall."

Bryce nodded. "It's been over a week since we assigned agents to their homes, and so far, everything's been quiet, right?"

Geraldine clasped her hands, resting her wrists on the edge of the table. "Ms. Duvall believes she heard someone trying to break into her house last evening. Agent Colton found no evidence to support it. But Ms. Duvall is understandably on edge. Jefferson has arranged for both her and Mr. Cross to be transported here. We will house them at Shadow Ridge until we resolve this matter."

"And they're both okay with this?"

Geraldine's lips turned downward. "While Ms. Duvall agreed immediately, Mr. Cross resisted. He had reservations about uprooting himself for an uncertain length of time. Who could blame him?"

Bryce nodded silently.

"Thomas's team has suffered so much. Ten of the 12 members of the Chimera project are dead. Jefferson and I believe there's credence to the theory they're all connected. A majority of the deaths have been in the past six months, as you're aware, but we question whether they may date back further. Perhaps even beginning with Madeline Price." *And, if so, do I dare reveal that news to her husband?* "Ms. Duvall and Mr. Cross are the only ones left."

"We'll do everything we can to keep them safe, ma'am. You have my word."

Geraldine smiled. "As the Psalms say, 'Your word is a lamp to my feet and a light to my path.' I know with all my heart that you will do everything you can. But I can't help but feel responsible. SHADOW exists to prevent atrocities such as this."

Bryce leaned across the table. "You know you can't blame yourself for any of this. Every man and woman who signs up to serve our country knows the level of risk involved. We commit ourselves to our cause, knowing it may require sacrifice. I've lived with visions of laying on that roadside in Fallujah, helplessly watching my friends die around me, knowing my faith was the only thing keeping me alive. Yet, I have absolutely no regrets about the decisions I've made."

You remind me so much of Randall when he was young.

The receptionist's voice rung through the speaker of the phone between them on the table. "Mrs. Shadowen, I have Field Director Moore on the line."

Geraldine looked at Bryce and nodded. "Put him through." She heard a click. "Jefferson?"

"Yes, Madam Director."

"Agent Reynolds is here with me. I've informed him of the relocation plan. Can you update us on our status?"

"Certainly. Ms. Duvall and Mr. Cross will arrive tomorrow evening. Keith Farley will transport Ms. Duvall from her home in Gulf Shores. Mr. Cross requested to drive his own vehicle, but I convinced him otherwise. Shea Edwards will fly him here from Kansas City."

Geraldine held her chin in her hand as she listened. "And you will transport them directly from the airport to Shadow Ridge, correct?"

"Correct. Agent Reynolds, I would like for you to be their primary point of contact. The site team is preparing two vacant homes for our use. Ms. Duvall will have her own unit, while you will stay with Mr. Cross. I wish I could speculate how long this quarantine will last, but we still have no reliable leads as yet."

Bryce leaned closer to the phone. "I'm not worried about it, sir. This is my top priority until we catch the bastard responsible."

His language took Geraldine by surprise. *That may be the first time I've heard him swear.*

"Very well," Jefferson replied. "Plan to meet at The Barracks at 7. That will allow our guests time to settle in before dinner. Thank you, Agent Reynolds."

"It's what I was born to do, sir."

Such passion and commitment for a young man. "Thank you, Jefferson." Geraldine disconnected the call and looked at Bryce. Her lips formed a partial smile, but her eyes exposed her worry. "Promise me you'll take care of yourself, Bryce."

"I promise, ma'am." A half-smile of his own crossed his face. "Just as soon as I'm sure they're safe."

CHAPTER 36
DEREK PRICE
JULY 10, 2018

"THAT'S SOME SERIOUS Blackwater-level bullshit, Derek!"

You need to calm down. Derek had arrived home to find Sonia waiting in his driveway. Her standing placement on Derek's guest list allowed her to bypass either the need for a gate-access decal or a call to Derek.

He'd taken the long route, allowing himself time to process everything before unloading it on Sonia. He'd anticipated she would have opinions, but after explaining everything to her in detail, she had unleashed a vitriol response that barely let Derek get a word in.

"Sonia, please settle down. We have to be rational about this." *Maybe I should have kept this one closer to the chest. I knew she'd have concerns, but I didn't expect this.* "Being angry is only going to make this harder."

Her arms flailed as she paced across the great room floor. "Make this harder? Was it ever easy to begin with? You call me out of class to come down here, and then you just casually drop a bomb and tell me your wife — who I considered my second mom — was some kind of black-ops spy for the government! And you expect me to just sit here and say, 'Okay?' You have no business telling me how I should react."

I thought maybe we'd talk about it like adults. "Can you stop for a minute and imagine how I feel?" *I've watched you grow so much, but you're still just a teenager.*

Derek stood from his seat on the couch. "Sonia, I'm sorry." He reached out a hand. She turned and walked toward the kitchen, turning her back on him.

"What am I supposed to do now? Do you expect me to leave here and go work on school projects and pretend none of this ever happened? We've spent three weeks trying to find answers, and now we have them, and it's just over? These people have been screwing with your life, Derek! That's not right. How do you not see that?"

"You're right. I can't expect you to do anything." His hand fell to his side in resignation. "All I can do is ask you to trust me, to give me time to figure things out on my side. You think this has affected you? I just found out the past 10 years of my life have been a damned lie."

Maybe I need to bring someone with more perspective into the mix. Someone like Steve. Or Isiah. But he was part of this, too. Is he even really my friend?

Sonia spun around, facing Derek again. Her anger turned her tan skin a reddish brown. Her hair was tussled where she'd run her fingers through it. "Are you really okay with all of this? These people have been manipulating you, playing you, stopping you from moving on. The fucking government just told you that you can't sell your house! I thought your party was the one yelling 'Freedom!' from the street corner for anyone who would listen."

They're not the government. You're too emotional to deal with any of this right now. "I'm not saying I agree with anything, Sonia. I'm saying it's been an hour, and I don't have all the answers yet. Is it that hard to understand?"

He waited for her response, which never came. He slid his wedding band, which he'd put back on after the SHADOW meeting, up and down his finger. "This hits close to home, okay? We need to take our time and be smart about any response before we do anything irrational."

"Yeah, because invading people's privacy and trying to control their lives is the completely rational thing to do."

Derek sighed. "Listen, I love razzing you about your political beliefs, but that's not what this is about. This isn't the Patriot Act or Edward Snowden or Russia interfering in the election, Sonia. This is about me. This is about Madeline and the people she worked with, people I considered my friends."

Sonia's arm shook as she opened and closed her fist repeatedly. "They're your friends? What the hell does that make me, Derek? Everything you knew about them was a lie."

Derek winced but stayed quiet.

"You don't even know what they were really doing on those trips. Did they give you specifics or just the bullshit you told me about being 'part of the intelligence community?' You know the crazy shit our government has done in secret. We injected pregnant women with plutonium in the '40s. We intentionally exposed soldiers to Agent Orange in Vietnam — and then lied about it. We trained foreign dictators and warlords in Georgia, for fuck's sake. Would you turn a blind eye to all of that? Would they still be your friends if they were involved in that?"

"Maybe you need to lay off the conspiracy theories for a while." Derek raised a hand to his forehead and pushed back his hair. *That probably went too far.* "Listen, Sonia, I think we need to put this conversation on hold. Neither of us is in the right frame of mind to talk about this rationally right now. There's enough going on. The last thing I want to do is start a fight."

"Bit late for that, don't you think?"

I don't think you know how much that hurts.

Sonia moved toward the front door. "I'm going home to focus on the term paper I've been neglecting in order to help you with this stupid investigation. I'll get back to the Sparrows' ad campaign tomorrow and email you the art concepts. After that, maybe I need to take a break from -30- for a while."

Neglecting your schoolwork? I've always made it clear your mom and your education were your top priorities. Have I been pulling you away too much?

"Sonia, please, just take a few days and think about things. Don't rush into any decisions." *She just needs time to cool down.* "Please tell your mom I said hi."

She walked out the door without saying another word.

* * *

SONIA TORRES

SONIA SLAMMED the apartment door shut as she entered, startling Luciana.

"Mija? Is everything okay?" Luciana, sitting on the living room loveseat, swung her torso to face her daughter.

"I'm fine, mamá." Sonia's pace quickened as she crossed the room. "I'm just not feeling well. I'll be in my room."

"Is there anything I can get for—?" The slam of Sonia's bedroom door cut Luciana off mid-sentence.

I still can't believe the way he acted. He's trying to make everyone happy like he always does, but he's not seeing the bigger picture here.

A knock at the door pulled her from her thoughts. "Sonia, honey, are you sure you're okay?"

"I'm sure. I just need some space."

"Did something happen at school?"

I only skipped class — again — and probably sealed the deal on a failing grade, just to get in a fight with Derek and probably cost myself a job, too. "No, mamá. It's just—." She hesitated, searching for a response. "It's nothing. I'll be fine."

"Well, I'm here if you need anything."

Not even you could help me out of this one, mamá. "Thanks."

Sonia pulled her MacBook from her backpack and powered it on. She opened a web browser and navigated to Reddit. She checked the news, celebrity gossip and the day's political commentary before following a link to one of her favorite message boards: r/conspiracy.

'*Maybe you need to lay off the conspiracy theories for a while.*' *Maybe you just need to open your damn eyes to what's happening in the world, Derek.*

She clicked various discussion threads, reading but not commenting. *See, these people understand. Sometimes the conspiracy is easier to believe than the truth.* She moved the cursor to the homepage menu and created a new post.

Her fingers flew furiously across the keyboard, typing "Security vs. Privacy: Where Do You Draw the Line?" *If Derek won't be the voice of reason in this, I'll find someone who will.*

CHAPTER 37
Sonia Torres
July 11, 2018

BEEP! BEEP! BEEP! Sonia's phone vibrated as her 6:45 alarm woke her. She tossed and turned for nine minutes until the snooze alarm triggered. *I told Derek I'd have those concepts to him today. I need to take care of that before class, so I can see Em tonight.*

She rolled onto her back and scooted to an upright position, stretching her arms out and yawning. *I could really use a few more hours of sleep, though.* She rubbed her eyes and reached for a bottle of water on her nightstand. Emptying it, she tossed the bottle into a small blue recycling bin next to her dresser and picked up her phone.

Holy shit. The screen lit up to unveil notifications of over 200 responses on her Reddit post. Clicking the latest alert, her post about privacy and security filled the screen of her phone. *Oh, fuck.*

She read the post again:

> Turning to this community because, honestly, I don't know where else to go. This is going to sound completely unreal, but I swear to you every single word of it is true. Today, my best friend was abducted by a paramilitary organization that claims they're

promoting safety and security while they've been monitoring his family for years without his knowledge.

He learned his wife had lied to him about their relationship. That she secretly worked as a spy for the government. And that the people she worked with were venturing into "private-sector" surveillance. I thought he'd be as furious as I am, but he's trying to push this off as nothing. I can't understand how he can be so wrong. How could anyone be so wrong about something so obvious?

I'm supposed to be silent, to lay low while he figures out how to handle it. But I just can't do it. This is tearing me up inside, sitting here right now writing about it. I have to do something. But I'm scared. I'm scared to lose my friend. I'm scared they'll come after me if I'm found out. I don't know what to do. I need help.

If you had information to share, what would you do? Where do you draw the line between security and privacy? How much do the American people have a right to know? If anyone can understand where I'm at, they're here in this group. I know you won't let me down.

Oh my god. I was so angry, I wasn't even thinking. Derek is going to kill me. She scrolled to the comment section. The pit in her stomach grew wider.

"Not only should you tell the truth, you're obligated to do so. Start naming names! You know we have ways of finding out who you really are."

"Do you have any idea we thwart hundreds of potential terrorist attacks each year because of surveillance? You'd probably be singing a different tune. Besides, I bet you have an iPhone. 'Hey, Siri, can you explain that we sacrificed privacy for convenience years ago?'"

"Can we move this thread to r/thatneverhappened, please?"

They just keep going. She scrolled through the comments, stopping about halfway. *What the hell did I do? What do I do now? Should I delete it? Ignore it and hope it goes away?* She inhaled and closed her eyes. *Do I tell Derek? Do I run away and never show my face around here again?*

She tossed the phone on the bed, buried her face in her hands and cried.

* * *

Isiah Cross

"WHAT'S UP, Derek?"

Could your timing have been any worse? Isiah covered one ear with his hand as he pressed the phone to the other. The engine of the Cessna 172 rumbled behind him. He watched as the pilot, Shea Edwards, inspected the exterior of the plane, preparing for their departure.

"Isiah, can you hear me?" Derek's voice crackled through the speaker.

"Yeah, buddy, I hear you." Isiah walked down the tarmac. "I'm just getting ready to catch a flight."

"Oh, sorry to bother you. If it's easier to talk when you land, that's fine."

Isiah spun his head on his shoulders. Shea continued his preparations. "It's all good, Derek. I've got a pretty busy agenda when I land. Something I can help you with?"

"I met with Geraldine Shadowen." Derek's voice was devoid of emotion. "She told me everything."

Isiah stopped pacing. *How much of everything?*

"I know about Chimera. About Thomas. About SHADOW. I know about all of it."

Do you know that being a member of Chimera has become a common cause of death in the past few months? "Derek, buddy, I'm sorry. I wish I could have told you."

"I wish you had. I wish Maddie had told me. I wish I understood why this is all a big secret."

Maybe you should be glad you didn't know. Isiah looked over his shoulder. Shea had disappeared from his line of sight. *He's probably checking in with the hangar before we head out.*

"Listen, Derek, I owe you answers, buddy. Probably a few rounds of drinks, too, if we're being real. But my pilot's waving me down. I'm going to have to let you go. I'm actually headed up your way for a few days. Let me see how things go when I get there, and maybe we'll get together and talk through everything."

"That sounds great, Isiah. Have a safe flight. Hopefully, I'll see you soon, then."

Isiah tilted his head backward and mouthed, "Thank God," as he disconnected the call. He dropped his arm to his side and shook his head. *Derek, buddy, there's so much you still don't know.*

* * *

Sonia Torres

SONIA BARELY HEARD the phone ring over the running water of the faucet. She stood in the kitchen, hand-washing dishes to distract herself. *I can't let it keep bothering me. It's over. I deleted the post.*

The responses to her Reddit entry, however, hadn't stopped. With the original post removed, she'd started receiving direct messages from other users.

"Why did you take the post down? We have a right to know."

"Stop being a little bitch. You know we can find out who you are, right?"

"Are you okay? Did they find you?"

It's probably just more stupid messages. I need to just delete the app or shut off my phone completely. Glancing at the screen, she saw a text message alert. She grabbed a kitchen towel and dried her hands before picking up the phone.

It's from Derek.

"How's it going today?"

My life's a total shit show right now, and I'm pretty sure you'll never trust me again. Thanks for asking. She tossed the phone aside and went back to the dishes.

Luciana entered the room in time to see the phone bounce across the counter, landing in front of the microwave. "Oh, mija, what's wrong?"

Sonia shook her head. Luciana crossed the room to stand behind her, placing her hands on her daughter's shoulders and leaning over them to look at her face. "Something has upset you since you got home yesterday. You know you can tell me anything, right?"

Sonia's body quivered in her mother's embrace. Tears formed in her eyes as she tossed the dish towel down. "I messed up, mamá. I messed up real bad this time."

Luciana turned Sonia away from the sink and wrapped her in her arms. "I don't know what you did, mija, but it doesn't matter. Everything will be okay. You will find a way to make it right."

I hope so, but I seriously doubt it this time.

CHAPTER 38
Jefferson Moore
July 11, 2018

"WELCOME BACK, Mr. Cross. I hope you had a pleasant flight."

Jefferson led Isiah from the small flight services building to his black Chevy Suburban, parked right outside the brick office. *And I'm relieved you arrived safely. I hope Ms. Duvall has the same experience.*

"Little bumpy, and I missed the free peanuts, but I got where I needed to be. Even after years of flying in and out of here, I'm still not sure I'll ever get used to small planes, but, hey, at least I didn't have to take my shoes off at security."

Jefferson pressed a button on the remote in his hand to unlock the doors. He walked to the back and opened the hatch. "If you'd like to store your luggage, we have about 20 minutes until Ms. Duvall arrives."

"Sounds good." Isiah lifted his rolling suitcase and backpack. "I can't wait to see Monique. I haven't seen her since I left Chimera. We've got some fond memories involving this crappy little airport."

We couldn't take the risk of a commercial flight. "I only wish you could reconnect under more ideal circumstances."

Isiah nodded. "I just need to grab a few things out of here, and I'll be good to go." He unzipped the backpack and removed a Butterfinger and a Copenhagen chewing tobacco can. "Vices, right?" He grinned sarcastically.

Jefferson closed the hatch. "We can either wait inside or here in the vehicle."

"Seemed kind of stuffy in there when I passed through. Maybe staying out here with the AC would be best."

The two men climbed into the Suburban. *He appears to be in high spirits despite his reservations.* "I'm sorry about your colleagues. I know it's never easy to lose those closest to us." Jefferson glanced across the center console.

Isiah stared out the windshield. "Thanks."

"We're doing everything in our power to assist with the investigation. Director Shadowen has been in constant contact with our colleagues in Washington. We'll find the son of a bitch responsible and ensure that justice is served."

Isiah nodded.

"Do you have any theory as to why this killer is targeting members of your team specifically?"

Isiah directed his stare into Jefferson's eyes. "To be honest, Chimera hurt a lot of people. We were never meant to be on the frontline. We weren't combat-ready. But we still helped take down cartels. We played a part in bringing charges against the Proud Boys in Texas. That's not even mentioning any foreign diplomat we might have wronged. I'm sure there's a lot of bad blood out there. But it seems pretty clear this has gotten personal."

Jefferson's phone chimed. As he checked it, Isiah opened and bit into the Butterfinger, which had melted in his luggage.

The message from Monique read, "On the ground. Need a bathroom break. Meet you inside." Jefferson locked the phone without replying. "Ms. Duvall just landed and needs to use the restroom before we leave. She said to meet her inside."

Jefferson reached to stop the engine, but Isiah stopped him, holding up a chocolate-covered hand. "Why don't you stay here and keep the air running? If I know Monique, the first thing she's going to do is complain about the weather. Besides, I could use a bathroom myself."

"Very well. I'll be here when you're both ready."

I hope they're quick. Agent Reynolds is expecting us.

* * *

Isiah Cross

ISIAH ENTERED the building and paused, watching Monique and her pilot unload two full-sized suitcases and a carry-on bag from the single-passenger aircraft. She wore a free-flowing sundress and heeled sandals definitely not suited for air travel. *That's Monique for you.*

He headed for the bathroom, where he washed the chocolate from his hands and dried them with paper towels. Finished, he waited just inside the doorway, listening.

"Do you need help with your bags, ma'am?"

"No, thank you. I've got a friend meeting me here. I'll make him take them to the car for me."

That's about right, too.

"Very well, ma'am. I'll leave them right here outside the restroom for you. I hope your visit goes well."

"Thank you."

Isiah listened as the door to the women's restroom opened and swung shut. He pulled the tobacco can from his pocket and strolled down the hallway. Checking to see if anyone had seen him, he entered the women's restroom.

Monique leaned over one of the sinks, checking her makeup in the mirror. A pile of paper towels Isiah assumed she'd used to clean the sink before touching it were piled on the shelf beneath the mirror. *Oh, Monique.*

She looked up, grinning in the mirror, presumably to check for food in her teeth. Her eyes squinted; her brows pulled together. "Isiah?"

She'd clearly seen his reflection in the mirror. "You know this is the women's room, right?"

Isiah's hands tightened around a thin metal cord he'd removed from the tobacco case. "Hi, Monique. Long time, no see."

As she began to turn, he charged her, pushing her into the counter. Her ribs collided with the hard edge of the laminate. She winced in pain. Isiah kicked the back of her knee. She dropped to the floor, clipping her forehead on the sink.

She reached a hand to her head. "What the hell, Isi—." Her words turned to strained breath, as Isiah slipped the metallic cord around her throat and pulled back, pressing his knee into her spine for leverage.

The bottom edge of the mirror caught the reflection of her face. He watched as she tried hopelessly to grip the cord and free it from her throat. The life in her eyes faded.

She stopped struggling. Her body went limp in Isiah's arms. He released his grip and let her fall to the floor.

I'm sorry it came to this, Monique, but we all have a penance to pay.

Isiah checked his hands. The tension of the cord had sliced his palms. Blood oozed from the straight-line cuts in his skin. He clenched his fists. *The pain is temporary. The satisfaction will last forever. The shrink said the hardest steps would be the first and the last, the alpha and the omega. What do you know? She was right.*

He dragged Monique's body into the handicap stall and returned to the sink to rinse the blood from his hands. *That was easy enough. But I suppose I have another problem to deal with now.*

Isiah collected the metallic cord, bunched it up and jammed it in his pocket. Spotting Monique's purse, he tore it open and poured its contents on the tile floor. He rummaged through her belongings, tossing aside a container of Tic-Tacs, a tampon and her eyeliner.

He opened her nail kit and inspected the items inside. Pulling out a set of clippers, he slid out the sharp-tipped file inside. *This will do.*

Standing and admiring himself in the mirror, Isiah rolled up the sleeves on his shirt to hide the unavoidable remnants of blood.

Satisfied, he nodded to his own reflection, left the bathroom and walked out the front doors.

The last time I was here, I was flying to Germany with Madeline and Monique. How things have changed.

Now, both women were dead, and their blood was on his hands.

CHAPTER 39
Isiah Cross
April 6, 2017

THE LONG-SLEEVED DRESS SHIRT FLEW across the room, landing on the edge of a plastic hamper, rocking it with imbalance. Isiah pulled a white undershirt over his head, scuffling his curly red hair. He tossed the shirt toward the same hamper. This time, he nailed his target. *Boom goes the dynamite.*

Bare-chested, he stood in front of an oscillating floor fan. He tilted his head back and closed his eyes. *I've never been so glad to be home.* He grabbed the commemorative Kansas City Royals World Series T-shirt from the bed and pulled it on.

"I'm just about ready, Kat." No response. He looked out the open bedroom door but didn't see anyone. *Maybe she didn't hear me.*

The past few months of work had made Isiah cherish his moments at home with Katherine and their daughters, Kelsey and Deandra. His relationship with his boss, Thomas, grew more unstable by the day. And he had to navigate troubled waters without his best friend and partner in crime, Madeline Price, by his side. *None of that matters right now. This weekend is all about my baby girl's 10th birthday.*

He tugged the bottom of the T-shirt, admiring himself in the headboard mirror. *Not too shabby.* Moving toward the bedroom door, he called out, "Who's ready for Paradise Park?" *No response from the girls? Kat must be loading them in the car.*

Isiah left the bedroom, walked down the hallway and stopped at the dining room entryway. Katherine leaned against the back of a chair, her head bowed, crying. "Kat, what's wro—." Isiah stopped as he looked at the table.

The flowers he'd brought home were surrounded by several items he recognized: two passports, a driver's license, credit cards, a black notebook and an envelope he knew contained recent receipts from hotels, restaurants and bars. The name Alexander Kensington appeared on all the documents, as did Isiah's photo.

Oh, fuck. "Katherine." He slouched against a chair on the other side of the table. His head drooped; she couldn't see the remorse in his eyes.

"Isiah, don't." The tension in her tone spoke volumes.

"But, how did—."

"How did I find this? Does that even matter, Isiah?" Tears burst from her eyes. "Deandra was in your office. I told her to stay out of there, but she wanted to leave a note for you to find. They've missed you so much, Isiah. They've asked every day when you're coming home."

He lifted his head. Tears formed in his eyes.

"She knocked a stack of papers off your desk. I worried they were important, and I didn't want you to blame her. So I cleaned them up. When I was down there, I saw a loose floorboard. I thought maybe we had mice or a leak or something was wrong with the house. I wanted to check it out, make sure we didn't have a bigger problem. When I touched it, the board moved. I lifted it up, and this is what I found inside."

Isiah moved around the table. Katherine threw up a hand, signaling him to stop. "Kat, I can explain." *I just need to tell her everything. I don't care what happens. This isn't worth ruining my marriage anymore.*

"Just admit it. You're doing it to me again, aren't you? I don't want any more of your lies and your bullshit excuses. For once, just tell me the damn truth, Isaiah." She glared at him. "You're fucking around with another woman again, right? Let me guess." Her voice grew louder. "It's Madeline Price, am I right? I knew you two had something going on."

"What the hell, Katherine? Even if you think I could pull something like that, you know Madeline better than that! You really think she could do that to Derek? She's like a sister to me!"

Silence hung between them. Isaiah looked around for the girls. *I hope they're not hearing this.*

"They're waiting in the car, Isaiah. We're leaving, and when we get back, I want you gone. And I don't want to see you here again. I'll text you a time you can come pick up your shit."

"Damn it, Kat. I'm not going anywhere! Will you just stop for a minute and listen to me?"

He darted around the table, grabbing for Katherine's arm. She jerked backward and stepped toward the front door.

"Kat, please give me a chance to explain."

"You've had your chances, Isaiah. I'm done with the secrets. I'm done with the lies. I'm fucking done with you."

Damn it, Kat. You don't really want to do this.

She burst into full-blown tears as she barged through the door and powered her way to the white Kia Rio in the driveway. Isaiah chased her onto the front steps and saw Kelsey and Deandra buckled in the backseat. *My girls.*

"Kat, will you please stop?"

She ignored him and slammed the car door shut.

He rushed into the house to retrieve his truck keys from the kitchen counter, making it back outside in time to see Katherine pull out of the driveway. He fumbled with his keys, trying to unlock the driver's door of his decade-old Dodge Ram. Once successful, he climbed inside, fired up the engine and began his pursuit.

She'll probably go to her parents' house. He sped down 79th Street, rehearsing in his mind what he'd say when he caught up to Katherine. *I'm sorry, Kat. There are things I should have told you a long time ago. I'm done lying. I don't want to hide the truth from you anymore.*

Spotting Katherine's car in the distance, approaching the intersection at Mission Road, Isiah pressed his foot against the gas pedal. *Thank God the road's empty, at least.* Katherine's car was only a few hundred feet ahead. The light turned red.

I'll jump out of the truck, run to her window and beg her to listen.

Katherine's vehicle didn't slow down.

What is she doing?

Isiah looked northward and spotted a semi-truck barreling down Mission Road. *No. No. No.* He watched as the Rio blew past the light and into the intersection. *Oh my God. Stop. No. Stop!*

He slammed on his own brakes, screeching to a halt as the collision played out through his windshield like a movie on a theater screen. The noise — the crunch of metal on metal — reverberated down the street and echoed in his mind.

No. No. No. This can't be happening. This isn't happening. Katherine.

The truck driver leaped from his rig and rushed forward. Even from the distance, Isiah saw the blood streaking his face. *Wait, he's not going to the car.* Isiah followed the man's movement. That's when he saw Katherine lying on the asphalt about 10 feet away. *No. No. Dear God, no.*

Isiah dropped to his knees. His body shook. Adrenaline surged through his veins. Tears flowed freely. *No. This can't be happening. Katherine. Kelsey. Deandra.*

He pulled his phone from his pocket, intending to call 9-1-1. His fingers hovered over the screen. He dropped the phone to the ground and buried his face in his hands.

In that moment, his world faded to black, and he found himself engulfed in a darkness he wondered if he'd ever escape.

* * *

May 9, 2017

"HAVE YOU GIVEN any thought to our discussion from last time?"

Isiah relaxed in the oversized blue armchair. *I still feel like I should lay down for this.*

Dr. Darlene Ferraro sat across from him in a purple armchair of her own. Filled bookshelves lined one wall, while the other featured an expansive window offering a bird's-eye view of downtown Kansas City.

Isiah swung his left leg over his right and rustled his fingers through his curly red locks. "As a matter of fact, I have." He smiled. "I think I've found a project that will both keep me busy for a while and bring about a personal sense of satisfaction, as you'd recommended." *Just don't ask for specifics. I don't want to lie to you.*

Dr. Ferraro smiled and clapped her hands together. "That's wonderful, Isiah. You're a smart young man, and I'm proud of the progress you've made so quickly. Now, with a North Star to guide you, I believe your potential is endless."

"Thank you. I really owe my success to a friend of yours, Geraldine Shadowen. After what happened to Kat and the girls, she reached out to me. We'd met a few times through work. She recommended I contact you. I'm glad she did. I feel like I'm ready to live again."

"Geraldine is a good friend. I'm sure she will love to hear about your successes."

I'm sure she'll hear about a lot more than that.

"Just a word of caution as you embark on this new journey, Isiah. The road will not always be easy. There will be challenges ahead. There's an old saying that the hardest step of any journey is the first. I like to add that the last can be just as difficult."

The first and the last. The alpha and omega, straight out of Greek mythology. Oh, wouldn't Thomas be so proud? "I'll be sure to remember that." Isiah slid forward on the chair. "Dr. Ferraro, I really can't say thank you enough. Before I met you, I wasn't sure life was worth living any longer, but now, I have a clear path and hope to help make the world a better, safer place."

"You deserve all the credit yourself, Isiah. It's difficult to pick oneself up after a tragedy like you endured, but you've come so far. I look forward to our next visit and hearing how your project is progressing."

"Sounds great. Thank you again for everything."

The first and the last will be the hardest. The alpha and omega. The first and the last. Madeline and Monique. It has to be.

CHAPTER 40
Isiah Cross
July 11, 2018

ISIAH WALKED confidently to the waiting Chevy Suburban. He couldn't see Jefferson through the tinted windshield, but he knew the older man was watching. Isiah smiled and shook his head as he approached.

Whatever happens next, I know I've done my part. Thirteen months after embarking on his personal vendetta, Isiah had taken his last step. Only, he was realizing his journey wasn't complete yet. *Those were about justice; this one's a matter of inconvenience.*

Making his way toward the driver's side of the vehicle, Isiah paused, reflecting on the night his quest had begun. *I hardly feel like the same man. I lacked confidence. I lacked discipline. I lacked courage. But look at me now. I've finally accepted who I was always meant to be.*

* * *

June 19, 2017

AM I REALLY *going to do this?*

Isiah's pickup truck pulled out of the grocery store parking lot and onto the two-lane road.

Can I really do this? No, it's not a choice. It's not about what I want to do. It's not about what I can do. It's about what I need to do.

He followed Madeline's silver Honda Civic from a safe distance through town. *Was it really her fault? She had the courage to walk away from it. She had the courage I never did. No, I'm not the weak one. I'm the only one with the strength to do this, to ensure no one else suffers the way I did.*

He trailed the Civic south down Route 53 from Braidwood. While not Isiah's home turf, he'd visited the area enough to know his way around. *It's not too late to stop. No. Just a little further. There's nothing between here and that next shitty little town. The first step is the hardest. It will get easier from here.*

A few minutes later, away from town and on an open stretch of tree-lined roads, Isiah pressed his foot against the gas pedal, tapping the rear bumper of the Civic. The vehicle swerved, but Madeline corrected herself. Isiah saw her head lift toward the rearview mirror. *She recognizes the truck. She recognizes me. Fuck, I can't do this. No. I have to do this. She saw me. She'll ruin everything.*

He slammed the gas again and pulled into the other lane. He angled the truck alongside her vehicle and watched her expression through the window. *She looks so confused. So scared. That's how I feel, too. No. Put the emotion away. Focus. They'll never hurt anyone again.*

Isiah jerked the steering wheel to the right. The echoing crash of metal on metal rung through the air. The Civic veered off the road, but Madeline corrected its course and tried speeding away. *It's too late to turn back.* He sped up, aligning the truck's front bumper with the rear panel of her car. He pulled the wheel to the right again.

This time, the Civic spun out, veering off the road and into a ditch, where it rolled and landed upside down. Isiah slammed the brakes. *Was that enough? Do I stop and check? What if she's alive?* He spotted a vehicle approaching in the distance. *Shit. I can't stop.* Eyeing a small gravel service road leading into the backside of a trailer park, Isiah took the opportunity to disappear.

Either she's dead or I am. The first and the last. The alpha and omega.

* * *

JEFFERSON MOORE
JULY 11, 2018

JEFFERSON OBSERVED Isiah approaching the vehicle. *He's alone. Where's Ms. Duvall?* He assessed his subject. *He's rolled up his sleeves. Possibly the weather, though he should be accustomed to Midwest summers.*

He shook the thought from his head. *This whole situation has gotten the best of me. He's here for our protection.*

Isiah knocked on the window and opened the rear door. "Monique's taking her sweet time. She'll be out in a minute, I'm sure."

Jefferson nodded. He kept his sights trained on the front door of the flight services building. "What about her luggage? Does she need assistance bringing it out?" He looked in the rearview mirror. Isiah glared back at him, his body shifting in the backseat.

"She said she had it under control. Probably wants to feel independent. You know how women are." He paused. "While we're stuck here waiting, can I ask you a question?"

"Of course." Jefferson watched Isiah's reflection in the mirror with interest, though he could only see his passenger's chest and above.

"You were raised in a Southern family, had a promising football career. And you threw that away to join the military. After that, you could have retired and been set and revered as a hero. But you chose this life instead."

"Yes, I saw this opportunity to continue serving my country. I've never considered this position a job. I've always looked at it as a privilege. Why do you ask?"

"It's nothing, really. I just wondered how a man of your age and stature ends up here playing chauffer. Seems like life could have taken you down a better path."

Jefferson remained silent as he reached to adjust the rearview mirror.

* * *

Isiah Cross

ISIAH MOVED QUICKLY. With Jefferson's hand reaching for the mirror, he saw his opportunity. He swung the nail clippers upward from between his knees with the metal file extended outward, driving the sharp edge into Jefferson's exposed neck.

Jefferson screamed in pain, instinctively grabbing for the wound. Isiah slid the metal cord around the left side of his victim's neck. He shoved his right hand around the headrest, trying to secure the other end of the cord. Jefferson's arm blocked his reach. *Damn it.*

Isiah swatted at Jefferson's arm to no avail. *Motherfucker's strong for his age.* Isiah changed his approach, instead applying pressure to Jefferson's head, pushing it toward the driver's side window. Jefferson groaned, struggling to keep his wound protected. Eventually, he released his palm from his neck. Blood dripped from his hand as he reached for the firearm at his side.

Now or never. Isiah grabbed the other end of the metallic cord and jerked backward. The pain seared in his hands as the wire dug deeper into the slices left from attacking Monique. Blood oozed, dripping onto his pants and the vehicle's charcoal interior.

Jefferson grasped for the wire at his neck, unable to slip his fingers between metal and skin. Isiah positioned his bottom on the edge of the rear seat, leaning back for leverage. He closed his eyes, gritted his teeth and focused. After seconds that felt like an eternity, the resistance stopped. Jefferson's hand fell from his throat to his side.

"Holy shit," Isiah muttered aloud. He released his grip on the cord, which fell to Jefferson's lap. Isiah threw his head back against the seat and inhaled a deep breath. He clenched his fists, aggravating his pain.

What now?

CHAPTER 41
Bryce Reynolds
July 11, 2018

THE LACK OF PERSONAL EFFECTS in Jefferson's office at The Barracks amused Bryce. *The man really knows how to add a personal touch.* While the field director spent most of his time at SHADOW headquarters, maintaining an appearance of normalcy for Shadow Ridge residents remained critical. *He could at least have a picture of his wife.*

A calming quiet filled the community clubhouse office suite. Most of the team, aside from lifestyle director Heather Ryan and Adrienne Palmetto at the front desk, had left for the day. *We're in the middle of hunting a serial killer, but life goes on.* He tapped a pen against the wooden desk. *Yet you do not know what tomorrow will bring. What is your life? For you are a mist that appears for a little time and then vanishes.*

Bryce's phone vibrated. He pulled the device from his pocket and checked the caller ID. *Geraldine? I expected it to be Jefferson.*

"Geraldine. I'm glad you called. I haven't been able to reach Jefferson. I thought they would be here by now."

Silence hung in the air. "Bryce." Her voice cracked. "Jefferson is dead."

Bryce dropped his fists onto the desk in front of him. He switched the phone to speaker and set it down. "What the hell happened? What about Monique Duvall and Isiah Cross? Were they hurt?"

"Ms. Duvall is dead, too. And I'm afraid Mr. Cross is the one we've been looking for."

What? I thought he was a target, too. The realization sank in. *We brought the predator right to his prey.*

"Cross fled the scene, Bryce. The attendant at flight services heard Jefferson's vehicle speed out of the parking lot. When he stepped outside, he found Jefferson's body on the ground. His firearm is missing."

Bryce ran his fingers through his hair, tightening their grip in frustration. "And Ms. Duvall?"

"The attendant found her body in the women's restroom. After finding Jefferson, he remembered seeing her enter but never exit. She'd been strangled to death."

If you do wrong, be afraid, for he does not bear the sword in vain. For he is the servant of God, an avenger who carries out God's wrath on the wrongdoer.

"That should have been me. I should have been the one handling their transport. I could have taken care of myself. I could have stopped this." His voice grew louder. "Jefferson would be alive if I'd be the one to go to the damn airport."

Geraldine hesitated. "You can't blame yourself, Bryce."

Just say it — I could have been the one dead instead.

"I shouldn't have let him go. I loved the man like the father I wish I'd had, but he wasn't fit for fieldwork at his age, especially with stakes this high."

"He knew the risks, Bryce. He always knew the risks. I tried moving him to Shadow Ridge full time, but you know how bullheaded he could be."

Bryce cracked a smile. *That's the truth.*

"All we can do now is find Mr. Cross and ensure he's brought to justice. For Jefferson, as well as the others."

"Do we have any leads? If he took Jefferson's Suburban, can we track the GPS?"

"We located the vehicle abandoned in a trailer park south of Braidwood." She paused. "The site isn't far from where Madeline Price died."

Bryce leaned his head backward, staring at the ceiling. "Were there any witnesses?"

"We have a team headed that way, but so far, nothing. This is a law enforcement matter now, Bryce. It's out of our hands. We've done all we can do, and I'm afraid that doesn't appear to have been enough."

Bryce's voice softened. "You can't blame yourself for this, either, Geraldine. There's only one man responsible, and I'll do everything in my power to find him. There's no reason for me to sit around here waiting anymore."

Geraldine waited to reply. "Actually, Bryce," she stalled. "I fear that isn't entirely true."

Cross wouldn't come here — to Shadow Ridge — would he?

Geraldine answered his question. "When we met with Derek Price, he mentioned he'd been in contact with Mr. Cross, that they were friends. Now, we have every reason to assume Mr. Cross was implicit in Madeline Price's death. I can't explain why, Bryce, but I worry Derek Price may be in jeopardy."

Even my close friend in whom I trusted, who ate my bread, has lifted his heel against me. "I suppose it's not unreasonable that he confided in Cross after our meeting. If he needed someone to talk to, he might have called someone who already knew. Would you like me to contact Mr. Price?"

"Not yet. We've put the poor man through enough already. I'd rather not worry him until we have more concrete cause for concern. Stay nearby, watch the community. I'll have the team monitor his activity from our office. If we don't locate Mr. Cross soon, I'll reach out to Mr. Price myself."

"Understood. I'll maintain my position and alert the gatehouse."

Both sat in silence for a moment. "Bryce, thank you. I hope you know Jefferson was proud of the man you've become. Take care of yourself. We'll talk soon."

Bryce ended the call and reached across the desk for the wooden nameplate that greeted visitors. His fingers ran across the engraved letters spelling "J.D. MOORE." Closing his eyes, he felt the first tear form. He blinked to fight the others back.

Reclining in Jefferson's chair, he whispered a silent prayer. *Father, he's in your hands now. I trust you will shepherd him to your flock and ask that you bless me with the strength and courage to honor his legacy in everything I do.*

* * *

Derek Price

DEREK STARED at the half-filled box. *Do I even want to keep any of this?* The notebooks, Post-its and random loose-leaf pages represented the end of an investigation. Instead of pride, though, Derek found himself overwhelmed with regret. *I don't know what to believe anymore. And with Sonia angry and Isiah not answering, I don't have anyone I can talk to about it.*

He pulled the cobalt band from his finger and tossed it in the air, catching it as it fell. He repeated the process several times, stopping only when he nearly missed. *What would Madeline have wanted me to do? Do I even really know? I don't know what to think.*

Closing the cardboard flap, Derek picked up the box and carried it to the office, setting it on top of a pile on the closet floor. He spotted the iPhone on his desk and tapped the screen, hoping a notification for a message from Sonia would appear. *Still nothing. She must really be mad.*

He started to toss the phone back on the desk but stopped. *I'll give it one more try.* He typed slowly, double-checking each character. "I'm sorry if what I said upset you. I'm going to put this phone up for now. Please call me on the other line when you're ready to talk. Hope you're doing okay."

Gripping the phone, he stared at the screen, hoping for an immediate reply. When none came, he set the device on the top shelf of the desk, hit the light switch and plunged the office into darkness. He made his way to the great room and assumed his position on the couch.

Let's see what Gibbs is up to today.

* * *

Roxie Mills

"EVENING, SIR. What can I do for ya tonight?"

The middle-aged woman stood behind the front desk in the nondescript motel lobby. Roxie Mills wore an oversized tie-dye shirt and jeans two sizes too small. Her hair was pulled up in a bun, and her smile accentuated her missing canine.

He's kinda cute, especially those ginger curls. She leaned on the counter, watching the weary visitor with both curiosity and concern. *But sure looks like he's seen better days.* The man carried a backpack, rolled a carry-on suitcase and donned a Kansas City Royals World Series T-shirt doused with sweat. *At least he ain't no dirty Cubs fan.*

"I need a room, please." He avoided direct eye contact. "Just one night."

"Single king, non-smoking work for ya, hun?"

The man nodded without response.

The quiet type, I see.

"I just need an ID and a credit card."

The man patted each of his jeans pockets, turning his head to look behind him. He sighed and finally made eye contact. "My car broke down, and they towed me to a repair shop. I must have left my wallet inside. I've got cash in my bag, but my license is in the wallet. Sorry, it's been a hell of a day."

The broke-down car story. An oldie but a goodie, I suppose. "For a handsome young fellow like you, I think we can make that work." *This ain't exactly the Hilton.* The clientele of the rundown motel usually included truck drivers, transients and the occasional prostitute. *Maybe a little "I help you, you help me" action later tonight?* "What's the name for the room?"

"Kensington. Alexander Kensington."

"Alright, Mr. Kensington, it'll be $40 for the night."

The man swung his backpack from his shoulder and set it on the counter. He unzipped the bag and dug around inside, pulling out a wad of cash. The woman squinted, peeking intently at the other contents, including what appeared to be a balled-up dress shirt stained with blood and the handle of a firearm. *Ain't none of my business.*

"Here you go." The man handed her two $20 bills. She passed him a small metal key on a tattered maroon chain in exchange.

"Thank you kindly, hun. You'll be in room seven, right out the door and to your right." She smiled, exposing her missing tooth. "Can I get ya anything to make your night a little more comfortable?" *Perhaps some company?*

He zipped the backpack shut and slung it over his shoulder. "Just a little privacy, please."

She couldn't help but notice the cuts on his hands as he handled the backpack. She wished him well and smiled as he walked out of the lobby and toward his room.

I wonder what his story is.

CHAPTER 42
Isiah Cross
July 11, 2018

ISIAH ASSUMED the fiberglass shower had been white at one time, though it appeared more of a faded mauve as he stood beneath a stationary showerhead, rubbing no-brand motel shampoo across his scalp. His signature curly locks were now spread across the bathroom vanity and trash can. Remnants of red hair fell to the shower base, where he'd placed a towel on the shower floor to protect his feet.

This place is completely disgusting, but after today, I couldn't care less. After ditching Jefferson's Suburban in the Hidden Acres trailer park, he'd spent the afternoon on foot, crossing corn fields and following back roads to avoid being spotted on a major thoroughfare. He'd secured a room at this dilapidated motel, rested for a bit and gone to work changing his appearance.

The shower took care of any loose hairs the trimmers had left behind. *My hair hasn't been this short since—.* He stopped, leaned his hand against the shower wall and closed his eyes. *Since the honeymoon, when Kat made me shave it before we went to the Bahamas.*

He slammed his palm into the fiberglass. *Damn it; I miss her. We should be at home, tucking the girls into bed. We should be getting ready to cuddle up and watch some dumbass reality show she loves.*

Turning the shower knob off, he shook his head, stirring loose any remaining trimmings. He opened the sliding glass door and reached for a towel from the rack. *They ruined that. They took that away from me, and I'll never get it back. They deserved everything that happened to them, everything I did to them. They'll never hurt anyone again.*

Isiah tossed the frayed off-white bath towel onto the counter by the sink. He stopped in front of the mirror, admiring his reflection. *The best I've felt in a long time. Physically and mentally. Dr. Ferraro was right. With this behind me, I feel like a new man.* He walked out of the bathroom and grabbed a pair of plaid boxers from the rolling suitcase laid open on the tattered flower-patterned comforter.

Sitting on the edge of the bed, he pulled each leg through the holes of the underwear. He collapsed backward. The mattress had no give. *It's probably a good thing. I shouldn't stay here long. They probably have the entire world looking for me by now.*

He laughed. *They'll paint me as the villain, tell the world I'm a fucking psychopath. But I know the truth. I know they're the ones who have ruined countless lives. Taken people away from those they love the most — all in the name of protecting others. What a crock of shit.*

His eyes grew heavy, his breathing labored. Darkness shrouded his mind like a shadow. *SHADOW.* His body jerked upright in the bed. His eyelids flung open.

Don't fall asleep yet. You still have work to do. There are others with a penance to pay. It's time for the world to see what they've done.

* * *

Roxie Mills
July 12, 2018

ROXIE MILLS'S LEGS WOBBLED across the motel lobby. She stopped, raised an open palm to her mouth and yawned. *I'm ready for the sack. Where the hell is Tessa?*

The box of gas station donuts in her arms — continental breakfast, as the motel billed it — had been dropped off minutes ago. Few guests came back to the office in the morning, but those who did generally enjoyed the sugary sweets. She set the box on a table near the front door and reached for a nearby TV remote.

Roxie didn't care much for the morning news, but the occasional guest took an interest in the day's events. *Oh, honey, that shirt makes you look fat.* She kept her eyes on the young twenty-something anchor as she grabbed an apple fritter and shoved it in her mouth.

Returning to her station behind the front desk, Roxie prepared to hand operations over to her replacement. *If she'd ever bother showing up. I'm not staying past 7. I know that much.* She opened the cash register, removing a stack of bills from a plastic tray inside. *$20, $40, $60, $80, $100, $120.* She stopped, took the last bill and slid it into the pocket of her ripped jeans.

The news broadcast's background music changed, catching Roxie's attention. She lifted her gaze to the screen to see the older, male co-anchor addressing the audience. *What I would give to get me a piece of that.* A small photo appeared on the screen. She immediately recognized the man's red curls. The word "WANTED" stretched across the photo in blocked red letters.

"Authorities are searching for Isiah Cross of Overland Park, Kansas. Cross is wanted in connection with the murder of this man." The photo changed to one of a stern-faced, older black man. "Jefferson Moore was found dead yesterday evening at a private Cook County airfield. We'll have more on this story as it develops throughout the day."

Roxie's jaw hung open. "Well, twist my tits," she whispered under her breath.

Wasting no time, she beelined for the front desk phone and dialed.

"9-1-1. What's your emergency?"

"Yeah, I was hoping ya could tell me what the reward is for that sly young fella on the news this morning." Excitement filled her voice.

"You know, the one who offed that geezer at the airport. He's been right here with me all night."

* * *

Derek Price

THE SHRILL RINGTONE WOKE Derek from his sleep. He rolled over, tossing the pillow tucked under his arm to the floor. *What time is it?* The clock on the nightstand read 8:12 a.m. *Damn.* The phone rang again.

Who's calling this early? Maybe Sonia finally came around. He didn't recognize the number on the caller ID but answered anyway, his voice groggy. "Hello?"

"Mr. Price, it's Geraldine Shadowen. I'm sorry if I woke you."

At least she waited until 8. "No, I was just getting up anyway."

"There's something very important I need to talk to you about."

Derek pushed the comforter aside and swung his legs over the edge of the bed. Reaching a seated position, he switched his phone to his left hand and used his right to scratch an incessant itch on his back. "Well, to be honest, Mrs. Shadowen, I've given this as much thought as I can. I think it's best to stick with my plans to sell the house."

Her silence caught Derek off-guard. "I'm afraid this isn't about your home, Mr. Price. Forgive me; I'm struggling with how to say this, but I wanted you to hear it from me before you see it on the morning news."

He noticed an unsettledness in her voice he'd not heard before. *The news?* He straightened his posture, still seated on the bed. "I just woke up. What did I miss?"

"Authorities are currently searching for a friend of yours, Isiah Cross."

Derek hunched forward. "What? What do you mean? Is Isiah okay?" *What the hell happened?*

"No, I'm afraid not." She cleared her throat. "Isiah Cross is wanted for murder."

"Murder!" He forced himself to his feet and paced the room, running a hand through his hair. "What do you mean murder?"

"There was an incident last night at a private airport outside the city. Mr. Cross viciously assaulted both Jefferson Moore and a woman I believe you know, Monique Duvall."

Monique? Why was she even here? This can't be right. There has to be more to this.

"I'm certain you have questions. We all do."

"But why would Isiah hurt Monique? They worked together. They were friends." *Maddie and I hung out with them a lot. They were like family.*

"To be completely candid, we suspect these were not Mr. Cross's first victims."

Not the first victims? What does that mean? This can't really be happening? Am I dreaming again?

"We have reason to believe Mr. Cross has been targeting former members of the Chimera team for months."

"Targeting? What do you mean by targeting?"

"For death, Mr. Price. Everyone who worked for Chimera is now dead."

Thomas. The fire. Wait. No.

"How long did you say this has been happening?"

Geraldine hesitated.

She knows but doesn't want to say.

"We believe it's been happening for about a year."

Just say it. Just fucking say it.

"I know what you're thinking. I wish I could answer with certainty, but we simply don't have all the facts yet. I know this isn't easy for you to hear."

Derek looked down at his nightstand. His cobalt wedding band sat next to the alarm clock. He picked it up, gripped it tight in his hand and sat on the edge of the bed. He lost control. Tears flowed.

"I just don't understand. They were friends. We were friends. I admired Katherine. And those girls, I watched them grow up. I just, fuck — none of this makes any sense. None of it makes any damned sense."

"I wish I had the words to take away your pain, Mr. Price, but all I can offer is an open door if you ever need to talk. For now, I implore you to stay close to home and take care of yourself. Mr. Cross's last known location was in Braidwood last night, so we assume he's still in the area."

Oh, shit. Derek's chest suddenly felt heavy. "Mrs. Shadowen, I need you to be honest with me. Should I be worried? I talked to Isiah the other day. He told me he was coming here and that we should get drinks."

Geraldine paused. "I've asked Agent Reynolds to remain at Shadow Ridge. I will send you his number when we're off this call. If you need anything, even if it's just someone to talk to, please reach out. He's one of the finest agents — and men — I know. I'd trust him with my own life."

And mine, too, apparently.

CHAPTER 43
Sonia Torres
July 12, 2018

"SO, BRAD'S BRINGING his friend Joey. He's super funny and good looking. I told Brad to talk you up, Sonia."

"Great." Sitting on the tan leather seat in the back of Emily's Camaro, Sonia's mind wandered. *I can't believe I forgot my damn phone. Hopefully mom doesn't need me.*

From the front passenger seat, Torrie spun the volume knob to the right. "It's our jam. Crank it up." She and Emily leaned their heads toward the center of the car, bellowing the first line of the chorus of Toto's "Africa" in unison with Weezer's Rivers Cuomo.

Sonia chimed in with the next line from the backseat, leading all three girls to burst out laughing.

"We should have put the top down before we left," Torrie interjected during one of the song's slower verses.

"We'll take it down for the ride home," Emily replied. She looked at Sonia in the rearview mirror. "So, now that you're back with us, what do you think about Joey?"

Sonia blushed. "I don't know, Em. I told you I just have too much going on right now to stress about a relationship."

Torrie turned her head, smiling. "Are you sure he's just not too young for you? We know you're into older men, after all." She and Emily looked at each other and cackled.

That's really not funny. Sonia wanted to enjoy a day with her friends. She'd consciously tried putting Derek out of her thoughts. *I need to talk to him, though. If nothing else, we need to figure out what's happening with -30-. Maybe I'll text him tomorrow.* She ignored Torrie's remark and changed the subject. "So, what's the plan, anyway?"

"We're meeting the guys for breakfast at Silver Spoon, then we figure we'll hit the mall for a bit, grab lunch and do a movie at 1:15. That way Torrie can get home for her shift at The Garage tonight. That work for you?"

"Sure." Sonia put her head back against the seat. *Just tell me where we're going when. I feel completely lost without my phone.*

* * *

Isiah Cross

"YOU CAN'T catch me!"

The young girl, maybe 3 or 4 years old, waited at the base of the slide for another child — a boy, probably 2 — to reach the bottom. Based on their curly golden hair, Isiah guessed they were siblings. The girl ran across the mulch chip-covered playground, as the boy chased her.

I remember Kelsey and Deandra playing like that. Isiah watched from a metal bench across the park, periodically shifting his gaze between the children and the two adult women standing nearby. *I can still hear Kelsey's squeal when Deandra would catch her. The memories are all I have left. They took the rest from me.*

He yawned. His body needed rest, but his mind wouldn't allow it. He'd spent the night in darkened silence in the motel room, contemplating his next move. *Programs like SHADOW enable people like Thomas to commit atrocities against others and then go back to a normal life, pretending their actions have no consequences,* he'd told himself. *They hide the guilty behind metal gates and entertain them like kings. They forget about the wrongs they've committed. There's no accountability, no justice. That has to change.*

"I'm a princess, and you will treat me with respect!" The girl's shrieking call broke his spell. She stood over the boy, sprawled on his butt before her.

Respect. That's what people like Geraldine Shadowen lacked. They talk about service. They talk about honor. But they're just a bunch of damn cowards.

Isiah noticed the woman stealthily point in his direction. He knew his attire — a black jacket, jeans, baseball cap and sunglasses — wouldn't keep him hidden forever, but he'd needed respite. He'd left the motel around 5 a.m. and had yet to find a safe place to secure food or water.

Time to go. I'll find somewhere else to lay low, see if I can find something to eat. I need to clear my head, to think. Getting this far was easier than I thought, but now they know. They'll have a fucking army protecting her. I'll never get through.

Grabbing his backpack from the bench, he stood up, stretched and diverted his gaze. Walking away from the crowd, toward the parking lot, he stopped, turned and took one last look at the children. *Stop thinking about them. They're gone. They're never coming back. Thomas made sure of that, and Geraldine protected him.*

Isiah weaved through rows of parked cars, occasionally looking back at the two women, ensuring they'd lost interest in him. The further he moved away, the less they seemed to care. Distracted, he banged the bumper of a blue Ford with his knee. Looking at the vehicle's windshield, a small vinyl sticker with the letters BCR and a picture of a fisherman caught his eye.

He smacked his hand on the hood of the car with his palm. A full-length smile crossed his face. *How did I not think of that sooner?* He didn't so much as look back at the women. He crossed the parking lot with a skip in his step. *Derek, buddy, I think it's time for a visit.*

* * *

Derek Price

DEREK FELT RELIEVED to hear a familiar voice. "Hey Steve, what's going on?"

"Well, first, I wanted to apologize again for missing lunch the other day. As much as I enjoy covering Springfield, these politicians have a tendency to make announcements at the most inopportune times."

Derek laughed out of courtesy. "Nothing to worry about. I know how crazy the news business can be, especially now that you're doing it with basically half the staff we had." *Now, tell me why you're really calling.*

"That's the truth." Steve paused. "But, Derek, there's another reason I'm calling."

Bingo.

"I'm sure this isn't a surprise, but we're working every lead we can on this murder at the airport. We're now finding out there were two victims, including a woman who'd just flown in on a private plane from Alabama."

Poor Monique. I still can't believe Isiah did this.

"One of the victims, Jefferson Moore, was the community manager at Shadow Ridge. I know that's your neighborhood, so I just wondered if you might have anything to share we could use in our coverage?"

Boy, do I ever. "You know, Steve, I'd never met the guy until the whole deal with the house started. My interactions with him have been professional. He seemed to care about the people who lived here." *Or at least the people who knew why they lived here.* "But I've never been overly involved. I've always kind of laid low. I was sad to hear what happened, though." *And terrified knowing why.*

"That's fair. What's the vibe like in the community right now? Do people seem scared? Concerned?"

"I haven't really talked to anyone. I've been hunkered down at home all day dealing with some personal stuff." He rubbed his thumb against his wedding band. "But if I get out and about and hear anything, I'll definitely give you a call." *I feel awful lying, but I have to think about this before I tell him.*

"That would be great, Derek. Let's try to grab lunch next week. If you still want to talk about your house issues, I'm happy to help."

That all seems so insignificant right now. "I think that's behind us now, but I appreciate it, Steve. I'll talk to you soon."

Derek hung up the phone. *That was a nice distraction. I wish it had been Sonia, though. She's on her phone nonstop. She has to have seen the news. I just need to know she's safe. I just want to tell her everything's going to be okay. What's one more lie at this point?*

* * *

Bryce Reynolds

"TWO PEOPLE ON for all shifts. When you're ready for rounds, one of you can go, but call me before you do. I'll head up this way. I don't care what hour of night it is, I want to know before either of you leave this building."

Bryce stood inside the small brick gatehouse at the entry to Shadow Ridge, lecturing two of the community's gatehouse attendants. He looked around the cramped quarters, noting the open cans of Monster and half-empty bag of Cheetos. *I wish we could have called in professionals.*

The role of a gatehouse attendant was predictably mundane. These employees monitored incoming and outgoing traffic, signed in visitors and delivery personnel, and conducted routine patrols throughout the community.

Tonight, however, protocols had changed. Given the circumstances, the automated gate entry system had been disabled. The two on-duty attendants were expected to greet every vehicle entering the community and manually open the gates for residents and approved guests.

Tonight of all nights, we need more than part-time employees. Bryce saw nervousness in their eyes. They'd obviously pieced together the need for concern. *The fear of man lays a snare, but whoever trusts in the Lord is safe.*

"You gentlemen understand the importance of tonight's assignment, correct?"

The two men — a thin older gentleman in his 60s and a stocky middle-aged man — glanced at each other and nodded.

"Any questions?"

"No, sir," the men responded in unison.

Bryce walked out of the guardhouse and into the evening air. Raindrops fell from the sky. He climbed behind the wheel of his black Audi and drove toward The Barracks.

But the Lord is faithful. He will establish you and guard you against the evil one. He shook his head. *I sure as hell hope so.*

CHAPTER 44
Sonia Torres
July 12, 2018

"WHAT DID I tell you? Joey's pretty cute, huh?"

Sonia and Emily sat on stools around a high-top table. Torrie had ventured off to talk to a co-worker at the bar. "Yeah." *Too bad he also seems like a self-absorbed tool.*

The Garage bustled with activity as the evening rush reached its peak. Emily had talked Sonia into extending their plans for the day to include dinner. Torrie's shift had just started, but she stopped by their table every few minutes to bring refills and gossip about the day's events.

Sonia looked at a clock on the wall, hanging just below a neon Guinness sign. *Shit. It's already after 6:30. Mom has to be wondering where I am.*

"Hey, Em, I should probably head home soon. I wasn't planning to be gone this late."

Emily's nose scrunched; her forehead wrinkled. "Really? I'm heading back to campus next week. Can't I at least enjoy one night with my bestie before I go? C'mon, let's play a game of darts."

You know, she's right. I needed a day like today. "Fine. Loser pays for dinner."

* * *

Isiah Cross

ISIAH SQUATTED with his knees bent, his back leaning against the red metal case of the video rental box. He nursed a bottle of Aquafina he'd purchased from the vending machine on his other side.

Hurry up.

He waited for a woman who had entered the store about 10 minutes ago. He'd spotted his signal as she'd pulled into the parking lot. Exercising patience as she'd exited the vehicle and walked to the store, he'd confirmed his expectation.

The lower passenger side of the PT Cruiser's windshield sported a vinyl barcode decal with the Shadowen Real Estate logo and a special design for Shadow Ridge. *I'd recognize that logo anywhere.*

Isiah reached behind his back. He could feel the cold metal of the Glock 22 he'd taken from Jefferson against his skin, but touching the weapon with his own hands sent tingles through his spine. *I'm fucked if she doesn't come out soon.*

Two minutes later, his wish was granted. The woman — early 40s with cropped black hair — pushed her cart with one hand, holding her cell phone with the other. She moved quickly, passing through the sprinkling rain falling from the sky. Isiah crept behind her, keeping his distance, holding his head down.

She opened the vehicle's hatch and loaded bags of groceries, two cases of soda and a giant pack of toilet paper. As she reached to pull the door down, Isiah made his move. *This is it.* He waited for her to open the driver's side door and approached her from behind, trapping her between himself and the door.

"Excuse me, ma'am?" He reached a hand outward. She turned around, a surprised expression on her face.

"Can I help you?" Her eyes moved from the baseball cap to his jeans, wet from a mix of oppressive summer humidity and the ongoing rainfall.

She probably thinks I'm homeless. Might as well use it. "Would you be able to help a poor soul out?" He stepped closer to her. She raised her guard.

"I'm sorry. I don't have any money." She started to climb inside the vehicle.

Isiah pulled the Glock from the waistband of his jeans and pointed it at her, holding it low enough that the vehicle shielded it from view. "I don't want any problems. Just listen to what I say." He stepped even closer and pressed the gun against the woman's stomach. "Hold out your purse." She hesitated. He pushed harder. "I said hold out your purse."

The woman complied. Isiah used his left hand to find a keyring inside, then snatched the purse from her grasp and tossed it on the ground. "Now ditch the phone." She listened immediately this time and threw her phone near the purse. "Get inside and put your hands on the steering wheel."

Isiah stepped back, opened the rear door and assumed a position behind the driver's seat, keeping the firearm trained on the driver. "Now, listen to me. Don't try anything stupid, and we won't have any problems. Just pretend everything is normal and drive home."

She looked up in the rearview mirror, her eyes wide and watery, her lips trembling. "What is this all about? Why are you doing this? Why me?"

Wrong place, wrong time. For you, anyway. "You're a means to an end, lady. You get to decide how you want to play this. I don't want to hurt you. Believe me, I really don't, but I need your help. If you can do that for me, everything will be just fine and you'll be putting these groceries away soon enough. Get me inside the gates, and I'll be out of your life forever."

The woman's eyes widened; her jaw tightened. "You're him," she muttered, barely loud enough for Isiah to hear. "The man from the news. The one who killed J.D."

Isiah remained resolute, silent.

"Paul didn't want me coming out tonight. He told me it was dangerous. I didn't listen. I told him it didn't make sense for a criminal to stay around here. It's too easy to stand out in a small town. I was sure they'd flee to the city, that you'd—."

Just shut the fuck up already.

"I'm telling you lady," he cut her off. "I don't really need you. I just need your damn car and that." He nodded toward the gate access decal. "If you'd prefer, I could just leave you here." He pushed the handgun into the back of the seat. "Or you can shut the hell up and start driving."

* * *

Bryce Reynolds

BRYCE PULLED his vehicle to the curb and shifted it to park. He looked out the passenger window at the empty house once occupied by Karen Conrad. *I need to ask Geraldine how she's doing.*

He turned his gaze to the left, looking out the driver's side window at Derek Price's home. The front of the house was dark, but he noticed a light near the back. *Either the owner's suite or the office, if I remember that floor plan.*

Rain beat down on the car, picking up momentum as storm clouds darkened the evening sky.

Let each of you look not only to his own interests, but also to the interests of others. I should check in on him, make sure he's doing okay.

Bryce's phone rang. Grabbing the device from the center console, he checked the caller ID: Shadow Ridge Gatehouse.

"This is Reynolds."

"Uh, yeah, Agent Reynolds, this is Frank Faraday up at the gatehouse."

He recognized the voice as the middle-aged attendant.

"Donnie's wife called with some kind of emergency at home. I told him to go ahead and take care of it, that I'd call and have you swing by when you have a chance."

Damn it. I told you not to leave until I was there. "You mean he's already gone? Why am I just hearing about this?"

"He's only been gone two minutes or so. She sounded panicked. I told him I had it covered."

I gave you explicit instructions. "Has there been much traffic into the community?"

"Nope, been pretty slow going, actually."

Thank God for that, at least. "I'm on my way." The frustration in his voice was obvious.

"Sounds good, Agent Reynolds. There's a car coming in now, so let me go check them in. I'll see you when you get here."

Bryce glanced at Derek's house as he shifted the Audi back to drive. *I'll come back later tonight and check on him. I've got to fix this mess first.* He pressed the gas pedal and raced toward the entry gate.

* * *

Isiah Cross

"YOU'RE GOING to need to calm down."

Crouched in the backseat, covered with a dog hair-laden blanket, Isiah could no longer see the woman's face. "You're doing great, just be calm. It's almost over. Just a few more minutes and you'll be on your way home."

He heard the woman's labored breathing. *Bitch better not still be crying.* The car slowed as it approached the gate, which Isiah expected. He hadn't, however, anticipated coming to a complete halt.

Something's wrong. This is taking too long. The gate should be open. Wait, what is she doing?

Isiah heard an electric hum as the driver's side window rolled down.

"Is there a problem, sir?"

Shit. The guard.

"No, ma'am. We're just being extra cautious tonight with everything on the news. Where's home?"

Just stay calm and give him your address.

"1245 W. Adams St. Doherty residence. Paul and Beverly."

"I'll just need to look that up in our system, ma'am, and we'll have you on your way."

Isiah peeked from beneath the blanket, seeing the stocky guard pushing buttons on his iPad. He pulled the blanket back over his eyes.

"Are you traveling alone tonight, ma'am?"

"I am. Just on my way home from the grocery store."

Isiah noticed a tremble in her voice. *Did he hear that, too?*

"Do you mind if I look in the back?"

Damn it. The woman stammered. Isiah flinched beneath the blanket.

"Ma'am, I'm going to need to take a quick look before I let you in."

The rear driver's side door opened. Isiah thrust himself upward, sending the blanket to the floorboard. He pointed Jefferson's Glock at the gatehouse attendant and pulled the trigger. The sound echoed in the car's cabin. The driver screamed in terror. The guard stumbled backward. Isiah fired again.

Isiah moved quickly, reaching out the door to grab the iPad the attendant dropped. The gate access system remained open on the screen with the Labyrinth Systems logo in the corner. He pressed a circular green button, and the mechanical arms of the gate went to work. Seeing the gates open, Isiah dropped the iPad.

The driver gripped the steering wheel, bawling. "I'm sorry it had to come to this." Isiah pressed the firearm against the cushion of the driver's seat and pulled the trigger. The woman screamed. Isiah didn't care. He hurriedly climbed from the vehicle and ran on foot through the narrow opening of the gate.

He paused, watching the gate close and ensuring no one could follow. As the mechanical lock clicked shut, he increased his pace and ran further into the community.

Time to say hello to an old friend.

CHAPTER 45
BRYCE REYNOLDS
JULY 12, 2018

BRYCE SPED down Shadow Ridge Drive toward the gatehouse. *Damn it. No.* Even from a distance, he could see the carnage ahead. A car stopped outside the gate with its doors open. A portly man's body sprawled on the asphalt. No sign of movement.

Muttering under his breath, Bryce accelerated the vehicle until he reached the back of the gatehouse. He threw his car into park and leaped from the driver's side door in a single fluid motion. He grabbed the knob of the rear door on the community side of the gate. *Locked.*

He took two steps backward and charged the door, lifting his foot and using its force to knock the door loose. The gatehouse was as messy as he'd left it hours earlier, but this time he was the only one inside. Wasting no time, he crossed the small space, headed for the other door which opened on the street side of the gate.

Rain splattered against his body as he squatted next to the gate attendant. He rolled the man onto his back. His shirt was soaked with blood. *Two entry wounds.* He placed two fingers on the man's neck. *No pulse.*

A faint moan drew Bryce's attention to the PT Cruiser. He left the attendant's body and dashed to the driver's side door of the vehicle.

The driver, a woman in her 40s, slouched over the steering wheel. Bryce immediately spotted the entry wound on her back. *He shot her through the seat cushion.*

He leaned down, trying to see her chest and stomach without moving her body. *No exit wound.* The woman groaned.

"Ma'am." Bryce looked at her face. Her eyes were closed, her breathing strained. "Ma'am, can you hear me?" No response. "Ma'am, just stay with me. I'm here, ma'am. You're going to be okay." *Lord, don't make a liar out of me.*

He stood up, pulled his phone from his pocket and dialed.

"9-1-1. What's your emergency?"

"I need you to listen carefully. I'm a federal agent with clearance at the DoD and Homeland Security. There's no time for protocol. I'm at the entry gate to the Shadow Ridge community in Grundy County. I have a gunshot victim, a woman in her 40s, shot in the back with no exit wound. I need an ambulance ASAP."

The young woman on the other end of the call faltered. "Are there any other victims, sir?"

"One other gunshot victim, fatally wounded. Suspect is believed to be Isiah Cross, subject of an ongoing manhunt. He's likely still in the community and should be considered armed and dangerous. Send anyone you can. We're going to need all the help we can get."

"Units are on their way, sir. Can I do anything else to assist?"

"Pray no one else gets hurt."

* * *

Geraldine Shadowen

"YOU'VE BEEN quiet tonight."

Randall Shadowen rolled his wheelchair next to Geraldine. Sitting on the back patio of her home, Geraldine let the cool breeze wash over her. The moon's beams shined through the clouds, reflecting on each falling raindrop.

She looked at her husband and smiled. "Do you remember that silly expression my dad always quoted? There's always light in the darkness." She laid her forearm on the armrest of the chair. Randall put his hand in hers. "I'm sitting here hoping it's true."

"We've survived every challenge life has thrown our way, and we're still here. We'll get through this one, as well, my dear."

"Even if we do, how many didn't? How many lives have been lost because I failed to uphold my promises to them?" *SHADOW exists to protect people like them. We couldn't do that. I couldn't do it.*

Randall patted his wife's hand. "I couldn't protect Tony, either, and I've carried that weight on my heart and soul for more than 10 years. Every day, I hope the guilt will fade, but it never does."

Geraldine turned and looked at him. "What happened to Tony wasn't your fault."

Randall had met the young soldier, Tony Wallace, in 2006. While Randall hadn't been his supervising officer, he'd developed a relationship built on mutual respect with the boy. When he'd learned others in Tony's squadron had been harassing him under the guise of "initiation," Randall had reported the incident to Tony's commanding officer. They had taken no official action.

As Christmas had drawn near, tensions had been heightened, and Tony had found himself involved in a physical altercation that resulted in a fractured skull for the instigator and a dishonorable discharge for Tony. Raised in a low-income family, the military had been Tony's hope to escape the life he'd known and forge his own path.

Randall had spoken on Tony's behalf at the hearing, but his life sentence to a wheelchair served as a reminder he'd not done enough. Days after the shooting at the Shadowen home, police had caught Tony Wallace robbing a convenience store. The former soldier was killed in a shootout.

"If I'd fought harder, they might have given him a second chance. He didn't start the fight; he was defending himself. Instead, I signed the young man's death sentence. And I'll pay that price for the rest of my life." He squeezed his wife's hand. "He was just a boy. He didn't know any better. Your people were adults. They made their own choices. They knew the risks. You did everything you could to help them, and I'm sure they'd tell you the same."

Before Geraldine could reply, her phone rang, vibrating the glass-top patio table. She looked at the screen. "It's Bryce. I need to take this."

Randall nodded and rolled his chair back into the house, giving Geraldine privacy.

"Bryce."

"Geraldine, he's here." His voice sounded tense, his speech hurried.

Her heart sank in her chest. "My God, Bryce, are you alright?"

"I am. But I'm at the gatehouse waiting for backup. One of the gate attendants is dead. A woman — I believe she's a resident — has been shot. She's alive, but if the ambulance doesn't get here soon—." His words trailed off.

Geraldine put her elbow on the table, holding her head in her hand. Her stomach turned. She felt an acidic taste in her mouth, as if she could vomit.

"This is your call, Geraldine. Do I wait here or do I go after him? He couldn't have beaten me here by much."

He's right. I have to make the choice. I can't put that on him. "There's a woman fighting for her life, Bryce. I can't just tell you to leave her and let her die alone. I can't carry that weight on top of the others. I'll have the office issue an emergency text alert telling everyone to stay inside. If there's anyone at the clubhouse, we'll gather them in the auditorium."

"Understood."

"Isiah Cross is smart, Bryce, but he's not invincible. We have him trapped. As soon as paramedics arrive, I want you on the streets."

"Do you think he's here for Derek Price?"

I hope not, but it's the only plausible explanation. But why? What does he want with Mr. Price? He didn't even know the truth about Chimera until days ago.

"I don't know, Bryce, but wherever he's heading, let's pray he doesn't leave a trail of bodies in his wake."

* * *

Derek Price

"HELLO?"

"Luciana, how are you?" Derek stood in his home office, leaning on his desk. He held the flip phone to his ear.

"Oh, Derek. I'm so happy to hear you are safe."

"You've seen the news then?"

Luciana's voice deepened. "Oh, yes, I've been thinking about you all day. I'm sure if Sonia knew, she'd be worried sick, too."

If Sonia knew? "Is she not at home? I've been trying to reach her."

"She went out shopping and to the movies this morning with friends. She was supposed to be home for dinner, but I've not heard from her, either. I'm hoping she's home soon. I'm beginning to worry."

Thank God. If they went to the movies, they're either in Morris, Joliet or Kankakee. As long as they're away from here, they should be safe. "I'll try to text her again. But if you see her, please ask her to call me. Take care of yourself. I hope you're feeling well. We'll have dinner one of these nights."

"That would be wonderful, Derek. Take care of yourself, as well. I will have Sonia call."

Derek closed the phone to end the call and reopened it to send a text. "Just me again. Little nervous with everything going on. Please call when you can." He set the flip phone on the desk shelf next to the iPhone that Sonia had given him last month.

I should have left town myself. I could have gone up to stay with Steve, if I needed to. But there would have been too many questions. And Geraldine told me to stay here. Even after all of this, I can't help but trust her. Of course, I trusted Isiah, too. Maybe that's the real problem. Sonia always says I have to stop trying to see the best in everyone.

Derek looked at the box on the desk chair. He'd pulled it out of the closet earlier in the day and now found himself drawn to it again. When he'd first opened the box a few weeks ago, he'd simply been looking for answers about Labyrinth Systems and the connection between Thomas Sheridan and Shadowen Real Estate.

Now, he hoped it might contain insight into a new set of questions. *How much did I really not know about Maddie's life? About the people she worked with? About our own relationship and home? Why did she hide it all from me? Would she have ever told me the truth?*

On top of the pile inside the box was a familiar photo taken at a Chimera Christmas party. He looked across their faces. Madeline. Thomas. Monique. *So much personality, so much spirit. Gone.* Isiah. *Such heart and vigor, the life of the party. A serial killer. I still don't know how this happened. What triggered him to lose it like this?*

A phone dinged. Hopeful Sonia was reaching out, Derek grabbed the iPhone. *I should have known to text her from this one.* The screen lit up, showing no new notifications. *Damn.* He opened the text message thread between them and read the last message, sent yesterday: "I'm sorry if what I said upset you. I'm going to put this phone up for now. Please call me on the other line when you're ready to talk. Hope you're doing okay."

I really need to talk to her.

He started to set the phone down but stopped, hearing a noise behind him. *What the fuck was that?* Before he could turn around, a familiar voice stopped him dead in his tracks, preventing him from seeing the emergency alert from Shadowen Real Estate on his flip phone.

"Derek, buddy, how about those drinks?"

CHAPTER 46
Madeline Price
April 16, 2017

HAUNTING ECHOES of pre-recorded organ music reverberated throughout the church sanctuary as mournful visitors came and went. Three caskets — one larger than the others — waited at the front of the room. Between them, a table displayed framed photos of a loving family, two stuffed bears and a vase of flowers.

Madeline and Derek tucked themselves away in the back corner, watching their friend Isiah greet each guest passing by the receiving line with a handshake and what she could only assume was a forced smile.

I've never known anyone who could control their emotions like him. I suppose that's what makes him so good at what he does. "I still can't imagine what he must be feeling."

Derek looked into Madeline's eyes. "I know. I don't know what I'd do if I ever lost you. But to lose Katherine and the girls—." He didn't finish the thought. "And yet, he looks at peace standing up there."

You didn't see him before the services started, when it was just the two of us. "That's Isiah. He's the type who thinks he has to be strong for everyone else's sake. That's why I appreciate you staying. I want to talk to him again after it's over, make sure he's okay."

A few minutes later, a familiar face entered the church. Monique waved and weaved her way through the crowd to join the Prices.

"Madeline, it's so nice to see you." The women hugged. "Work hasn't been the same without you."

"It's great to see you, too, Monique." She pulled back from the hug but left her hand on Monique's arm. "I just wish it was different circumstances. How have things been going?"

"Oh, honey, not good. I know this probably isn't the right place for work gossip, but since you've left, Nicole and Akumi have already bailed for new opportunities. I probably won't be far behind them, and who knows what will happen with Isiah after all this." She turned her head and looked toward the front of the church.

I'm not surprised. Thomas has been driving everyone apart for months. "I'm sorry to hear that. I hope everyone lands on their feet somewhere."

"No need to worry at all. We all have to do what's best for us, right?"

Madeline and Derek both nodded.

"Have things been any better with Thomas?" *I mean, other than what I heard about Isiah showing up drunk at the office last week yelling that he's responsible for what happened to Katherine and the girls.*

"I haven't heard much since Isiah told him he was leaving." She shot Madeline a knowing glance. "We're not sure if he meant that, though, or if he'll be back. We all just kind of chalked it up to a heated moment of grief."

Derek put his hand on Madeline's shoulder. "Well, we might be about to find out." He pointed past Monique to the entryway of the sanctuary, where Thomas Sheridan and his wife, Colleen, picked up a memorial program from a small table.

Oh, no.

The three watched trepidatiously as the Sheridans lined up with other guests and moved toward the front of the room. Madeline knew the moment Isiah saw them. He kept his smile, but his lips pursed, his eyelids tightened. *This isn't going to be good.*

She looked at Derek. "I think we're going to have a problem."

Before either Derek or Monique replied, Isiah's voice rang out through the chambers of the church. "What the hell are you doing here?" He moved from his position in the receiving line, placing himself between Thomas and the caskets.

"I'm going to go see if I can diffuse this situation before it gets worse." Madeline scurried across the room, excusing herself as she weaved through huddles of alarmed guests. *Just keep your calm, Isiah. You don't want to do this. Not here, not now.*

Thomas waved his hands in the air as he spoke, but she couldn't hear his words. No one in the room, however, missed Isiah's retort.

"After everything that's happened, you really think I want you here? You think anyone wants you here? No, I want you gone, you fat piece of shit! I want you out of here now! I want you and your fucked-up ideas out of my life forever!"

Madeline approached Isiah, putting a hand on his shoulder. "Isiah, please. Let's take a walk. Let's get some fresh air." She noticed Derek and Monique had followed her. Monique led Colleen Sheridan away from the scene. "We can figure all of this out later, Isiah. This isn't what Katherine would want."

At the mention of his late wife's name, Isiah pulled himself away from Madeline and charged at Thomas, shoving him backward. "We wouldn't be worried about what Kat wanted if she was still alive."

Thomas held up his hands defensively. "I don't want any problems, Isiah."

Isiah charged him again. "Then you never should have shown your fat fucking face here today!"

The two men scuffled. Thomas's size provided a distinct advantage, but Isiah fought with adrenaline and passion. Madeline held her hands to the sides of her head, watching the two grapple for control. *Both of you need to stop. Damn it. Just stop.*

Derek moved to pull the two apart, but as he did, Thomas shoved Isiah with enough force to send him backward, where he stumbled into Derek and lost his balance. Isiah's body tumbled downward, hitting the memorial display table on his way to the ground.

Oh, no.

The table wobbled. The stuffed bears toppled over. Picture frames fell forward over the edge of the table. The vase of flowers rocked and tumbled to the ground, sending an echoing shatter throughout the sanctuary.

Oh my God. Madeline and Monique rushed to Isiah's side, helping him up from the ground. Derek ushered Thomas toward the rear of the church.

"Isiah, are you okay?" Madeline kept hold of his hand. They both looked at the shattered glass and flower petals strewn across the floor.

"No, Madeline, I'm not. And I won't be until that fat bastard pays for everything he's done. My life is ruined because of his damn ego trip." Anger gave way to sadness. Isiah cried. "I just want them back, Madeline. I want my family back. I want to hold my baby girls and tell them how much I love them."

Things must have really gotten worse with Thomas. But it seems like Isiah blames him for what happened. I don't understand; the crash was an accident. "I'm sorry, Isiah." Madeline held her friend, letting him cry on her shoulder. "You know I'm here for you. We're all here for you."

Monique put her hand on his shoulder. "Tell us what we can do to help, and we'll be the first ones at your side and the last ones to leave."

Isiah pulled his head from Madeline's shoulder, wiping tears from his eyes. "I think I just need a minute." He looked around the room. Some people blatantly stared, while others poorly hid their efforts to not do so. "I just made this entire day worse. I'm going to go outside for a minute. I'll be back."

"Do you want us to come with you?" Madeline glanced at Monique.

"No, I need to be alone."

He walked down the center aisle of the church and out the door, silently passing Derek on his way. Derek pointed over his shoulder and mouthed, "Is he okay?"

Madeline shook her head. *No, he's really not.*

"Any idea what that was about?" Derek asked when he rejoined the women.

"There's been more tension between them lately, but I never expected it to get physical," Monique said.

I've never seen either of them like that before. "Emotions are high right now. We should probably help clean this up," she gestured to the floor, "and finish the service so we can all put this behind us."

Derek nodded. "You're right. But I have to ask, do we need to worry about Isiah? Do we think he could hurt anyone else, even himself?"

Madeline and Monique exchanged a glance. Madeline replied, "Well, I've never seen anything like that before, but this is Isiah we're talking about. In the grand scheme of things, he's practically harmless. I don't think he'd intentionally hurt a fly."

CHAPTER 47
Sonia Torres
July 12, 2018

SONIA SWUNG the front door of the apartment open, stepping inside and seeing Luciana in the kitchen. Her mother finished drying the plate in her hand, set the dish and towel on the counter and hustled to the living room.

"Oh, mija, dear. I'm so glad you're okay." She wrapped her arms around her daughter's waist.

"Is everything alright, mamá?"

Luciana released her grip and looked at Sonia. "So you haven't heard? Derek has been trying to reach you all day."

Haven't heard what? Did something happen to Derek? "Mamá, tell me what's wrong."

"A man from Derek's neighborhood was murdered last night. Police are still looking. It's been all over the news."

I didn't have my phone. What man was murdered? Who died? Is Derek okay? She raced toward her bedroom and flung the door open to see the glow of her phone illuminating the otherwise dark room. "DEREK'S IPHONE" appeared on the screen. She hastily answered the call.

"Derek, I just heard. What in the world is going on?"

She didn't hear an immediate response. Her heart raced. "Derek?"

Then she heard his voice. "How could you do this? How could you do any of this?"

Do what? It sounds like he's talking to someone else. Did he mean to call me? Pocket dial? Is he on the other phone? Then, she heard another man's voice she didn't recognize, fainter than Derek's. She switched the phone to speaker and turned the volume to its max.

"They ruined my life, Derek. They took everything from me. They had to know the pain they caused me. Their families had to understand what it feels like to lose everything that matters in their world. They had to pay for the suffering they caused so many others. Someone had to show them exactly what they'd done."

Sonia's body trembled listening to the man speak. His voice was loud and high-pitched. *What the hell is happening? Who is that? What does he want with Derek?*

"You fucking murdered them, Isiah. You killed them in cold blood. They were your friends. I was your friend! And—." His voice went silent for a moment. "Madeline."

Holy fucking shit.

* * *

Derek Price

DID THE CALL go through? Does it even matter? She wasn't home to answer.

Derek tried to focus on Isiah's face, but every few seconds, his gaze shifted toward the weapon in his assailant's hand. The two stood on opposite sides of the office. *What the hell can I do? I'm trapped in here.* He closed his left fist and rubbed his thumb against his wedding band.

"Madeline." Tears ran from his eyes, but he dared not move his hands to wipe them away. "How could you do this to Madeline?"

"I'm sorry, Derek." Isiah's voice was cold, firm. "I loved Madeline. She was like a sister to me. But even she couldn't see it. She just didn't understand. She palled around with Thomas and the others, doing their bidding with no regard for anyone but themselves."

"You know that's not even true!" Derek took a step forward. Isiah raised the Glock. Derek stopped. "She came home in tears after her last trip. She broke down in my arms, telling me she couldn't do it anymore. She quit her damned job, left Chimera behind. You can't stand there and tell me you honestly believe she was responsible for any of this."

Isiah waved his hand with the Glock in it. "They were all responsible, Derek. We were all responsible. They went on with their lives and pretended nothing had changed. Madeline left Chimera but still didn't tell you the truth. She still couldn't come clean about who she really was. Why do you think that was, Derek? Why did she continue peddling secrets when it no longer mattered? Because they were all part of the problem!"

She was doing a job. She was protecting me. "And what does that make you?"

Isiah laughed. "Haven't you figured that out by now, buddy? I thought journalists were supposed to figure this shit out on their own. The answer's right in front of you, but like you've always been, you're blinded by seeing the best in people." He paused. "Me? I'm the solution, Derek. I'm the one atoning for my sins and exposing the truth to the world. By the time we're done here tonight, there will be no more hiding in the shadows."

Shadows. SHADOW. The word hit like a brick. *The way Geraldine talked about SHADOW. This is what she meant.* "Is that what this is all about? Some kind of vendetta against Geraldine Shadowen and SHADOW?"

"That wasn't always the plan, no. Originally, this was about revenge against that motherfucker Thomas and his merry band of misfits. But last night, I had a revelation. You're right, I realized this is bigger than Thomas, bigger than just Chimera. People like Geraldine Shadowen spend their lives enabling people like Thomas, giving them a perfect life after they've ruined those of so many others."

She protected them from psychopaths like you! "And how am I supposed to help you with that? I didn't know a thing about SHADOW until two days ago!"

"Buddy, you told me you met Geraldine Shadowen, right?"

Derek didn't respond. Isiah pointed the gun at his chest. Derek nodded.

"Such a sweet, harmless old lady. On the surface, at least. She's not taking the losses she's suffered too well, Derek. She laid her cards on the table when she arranged a protective detail for me here in Shadow Ridge. I tried resisting, but the old bitch can be relentless. So, I figured I'd let her help, let her bring me and Monique together. Save me some trouble and a trip to the wastelands of Alabama."

I still don't understand what this has to do with me?

"You're right, though, you didn't know about any of this. If Madeline was alive, you probably still wouldn't know. She would have kept you in the dark and drug you along like she did for a decade. You're the definition of innocent in all of this, Derek. People like me and Madeline took a risk when we signed our lives away in the name of so-called 'public service.' The worst you did was fall in love with the wrong woman." He paused, letting the words ruminate. "Now, imagine, do you think Geraldine Shadowen could let anything happen to someone like you? No, I hope it doesn't come to that. Poor old Geraldine would never be able to live with herself. Am I right?"

You're out of your damned mind. Do you really think they'll let you anywhere near her? "So what's the plan? You use me as leverage to get to her and then kill me, too?"

Isiah laughed. "Derek, buddy, this isn't Hollywood. I'm not going to stand here and tell you my whole damn plan." He pointed the handgun at Derek's head. "No, fuck that. I'll tell you what you need to know when you need to know it. Now listen carefully."

Tyler Norris

THE RINGING PHONE PULLED Tyler's attention from the game of Candy Crush on his phone. He'd volunteered to cover the night shift at the Shadowen Real Estate office, which generally entailed answering calls about broken water lines and burned-out streetlights.

I hoped tonight would be more exciting. He answered his desk phone. "Shadowen Real Estate after-hours emergency line. How can I help you?" His voice was sluggish, unenthused.

The woman spoke loudly and with urgency, catching Tyler by surprise. "I'm calling with the location of Isiah Cross."

What the hell do I say? "Ma'am, have you tried calling the police? I believe you've reached this number by mistake. This is an after-hours number for Shadowen Rea—."

She cut him off. "Listen, I don't have time to explain. My name is Sonia Torres. I'm friends with Derek Price. Isiah Cross is in Shadow Ridge. He's at my friend's house."

Sonia Torres? Why do I know that name? Oh crap — from his guest list. "Thank you for the call, Miss Torres. I'll handle it." He hung up.

His fingers flew across the keyboard as he accessed Derek Price's profile in the SHADOW database. He picked up the phone and dialed.

"This had better be important."

"Agent Reynolds, this is Tyler Norris at HQ. I believe I have a location for Isiah Cross."

"We know he's in Shadow Ridge. I'm on patrol now."

"I'm sorry, sir. I should have been more specific. I have an exact location. The Derek Price residence at—." The call disconnected. "Agent Reynolds? Sir?"

CHAPTER 48
DEREK PRICE
JULY 12, 2018

"ARE YOU READY to listen, Derek?"

Derek stared down the barrel of the Glock. His tears had stopped; his shaking body stilled. *I'm not just going to let him kill me, too. There's a way out of this. There has to be. But what is it?*

He considered his adversary. *He's younger, probably faster. But he has to be exhausted. He's been on the run all day. If I can get past him, maybe I can outrun him. If I can get outside, I can yell for help.*

"I asked if you're ready, Derek." Isiah stepped his right foot forward, closing the gap between himself — and his weapon — and his captive prey.

Derek didn't flinch. "Ready when you are."

"Okay. We're leaving through the front door, getting in that nice car of yours out there, and you're taking me out of here. I'll give you more instructions when we're in the car. Don't even think about trying anything stupid."

Derek patted his hand against the keys in his pocket. *How does he expect me to get him out of the community?* "Are you out of your mind? They have to know you're here by now. Don't you think they'll have this place swarming with cops?"

"That's my problem, not yours."

Sure, because I'm nothing but collateral damage to you. "And, assuming we make it that far, how are we getting through the gate? Do you expect to just smash right through it?"

"You drive. Let me worry about the rest of it. If you've got a fucking problem with that, I'll just shoot you now and take your damn keys." Isiah waved the gun wildly.

Do they even know he's here? Did I call the wrong bluff? Did the call even going through? If it did, I'm sure it went to voicemail. There may not be anyone out there. The realization dawned on him. *Agent Reynolds. Geraldine said Bryce is here. If I can break away, I can find him.*

"C'mon, buddy, we don't have all night."

Derek's feet skittered across the floor toward Isiah. He looked into his captor's eyes as he passed. The warmth and welcome he'd once seen there had been replaced with a dark emptiness. *How did it come to this?* He stepped into the hallway, lit only by the radiance of the office light. The house ahead remained shrouded in black.

"You don't have to do this, Isiah. You could just let me go. We can call the authorities, and this would all be over. No one else has to get hurt; no one else has to suffer. No one can blame you for the grief you're feeling. They can get you the help you need."

Isiah scoffed. "Damn it, Derek. I don't need anyone's help! I've made it this far on my own just fine. Besides, how do you still not realize this isn't about me? That I'm not the one with the problem. I'm the one with the solution. I'm the one who's going to light the fuse and blow this powder keg apart. Now shut the hell up and keep walking."

Thunder rumbled in the distance. *It's so dark. Maybe I can use that to my advantage.* Derek remembered the stacks of boxes strewn across the living room, where they'd been for weeks given the delay in selling his house. *That's it; that's my only chance.*

"I'm serious, Isiah. We can end this now. Just say the word."

"For fuck's sake, Derek. I told you to shut up!"

Reaching the end of the hallway, Derek stopped and closed his eyes. *Now or never.* He opened his eyes and bolted ahead, navigating the maze of packed boxes with precision. Without stopping to consider their contents, he tipped a stack of boxes.

"What the hell are you thinking, Derek?"

He shoved a second stack to the ground and heard Isiah stumble. *Just keep moving. Don't stop.*

"Motherfucker, Derek!"

He could have shot me. No, he needs me as bait. They won't hesitate to kill him if they catch him alone.

Derek focused on escape, shoving a third stack of boxes onto the floor. He didn't hear Isiah move. Suddenly, a bright light shone in front of him. *Shit. His phone. Don't stop. Just go. Just get outside and find help.*

He reached the front door, twisted the handle and bolted outside. *He can't be far behind me. I can't stop and look. Just keep running.* He leaped from the porch, his feet missing both stairs, and ran into the night.

* * *

BRYCE REYNOLDS

BRYCE LEFT the engine running as he climbed from the Audi onto the curb outside Derek's home. The front door of the house stood open. The room beyond appeared dark and lifeless. *Shit.* He pulled his weapon, holding it in front of himself with his elbows locked and his arms extended.

He slowly ascended the steps and landed on the porch, stepping toward the front door with reservation. Reaching the entryway, he glanced inside and saw no signs of movement. Looking down, however, he saw boxes and their contents — framed photos, trophies, decorations and more — scattered across the floor.

"Derek?" He stepped forward. "Derek, it's Bryce Reynolds. If you can hear me, don't panic." No response. He took another step and felt something crunch beneath his foot. *What was that?* Stopping, he squatted down and saw the shattered ceramic figure. He picked up an intact piece shaped like the head of a lion. *Hopefully that wasn't important.*

Bryce dropped what remained of the ceramic figure, resumed his stance and moved again, sweeping his eyes across the kitchen before heading toward the light emanating from the office. "Derek, it's Bryce. I'm coming down the hallway now."

Either he's not here or—. No, don't think like that. If you faint in the day of adversity, your strength is small. He stopped and scanned the office. *No signs of struggle.* Entering the owner's suite bedroom, he found the same. He crossed the room and checked the bathroom. *They're not here.*

Isiah Cross had clearly been inside Derek Price's home, but now, both men were missing.

* * *

Sonia Torres

WHAT IN THE ACTUAL FUCK? Flashing red and blue lights lined Shadow Ridge Drive. Two squad cars were positioned horizontally across the road, blocking Sonia from entering.

She parked her Cavalier on the side of the street and turned on the hazard lights. A deputy approached as she lunged out of the vehicle.

"Miss, this is an active crime scene. I'm going to have to ask you to leave."

She pressed forward. The deputy extended his arms outward to block her path.

"No, you have to let me in. My friend's in trouble. I have to make sure he's okay."

"I understand your concern for your friend, miss, but this area is under lockdown at the moment. I'm going to need you to move on and leave the area."

I'm not leaving. I'm not going anywhere until I know Derek's okay. She pushed forward again. The deputy physically restrained her. "No, you can't do this. You have to let me inside." Tears burst from her eyes.

The deputy waved to alert a nearby female officer, who rushed over. "Is everything okay, miss?" She put a hand on Sonia's shoulder. Sonia shook her head. "What's your name?"

"Sonia Torres." She pushed through the tears. "My friend Derek Price lives here. He's in danger. I need to know he's okay."

The male deputy ran toward the gatehouse while the female officer led Sonia to a patrol vehicle and invited her to take a seat out of the rain. She sat quietly, listening as Sonia talked.

"I haven't talked to Derek in a few days. I feel like such as asshole. I've been avoiding him since we got into a fight. It all seems so stupid now." She caught her breath. "I got home tonight and my mom said something was going on. Derek was calling me but when I answered I could hardly hear him. Then I heard someone else there, too, someone Derek said killed Mad—." She broke down, unable to finish the thought.

The deputy returned and whispered in the officer's ear. She nodded. He turned and left again.

"Miss Torres, we've contacted Shadowen Real Estate. They confirmed your connection to Derek Price. I'm afraid I can't let you beyond this point, as we're still looking for the suspect, but you're welcome to stay here, out of the rain. Can I get you a bottle of water?"

Sonia nodded and mouthed, "Please. Thank you."

The officer walked away from the vehicle, leaving Sonia alone. She buried her face in her hands and cried.

I'm so sorry, Derek. For fighting with you. For posting that bullshit online. For ignoring you when you needed me. Fuck. I'm sorry for everything.

* * *

Derek Price

WHERE IS EVERYBODY? Running down Harrison Street, Derek's legs propelled him forward, his mind reminding him Isaiah couldn't be far behind. His eyelashes batted away raindrops. His feet focused on maintaining traction on the wet asphalt.

There's no one on their porches, no doors even open. The adrenaline he'd used as he burst through the front door faded. His legs ached; his breathing became labored. *Don't stop. I can't stop.* He turned on Sycamore Lane. *Where the hell am I going? It doesn't matter, just run.*

"Damn it, Derek, won't you just fucking stop?"

Shit. He sounds close. He didn't turn to look. He couldn't chance losing his balance and slipping on the wet road. He bit his lower lip and pushed himself to pick up speed. In the distance, he spotted the glowing lights around the tennis courts and event lawn illuminating The Barracks. Closer, though, he noticed a porch light shining at a two-story home.

Derek rushed toward the lit home, knocking over a large plastic trash bin on the curb. The bin clattered as it bounced from the sidewalk to the street.

"You asshole, Derek!"

That might have bought me some time.

The door of the two-story house swung open. *Thank God! But what then? He'll go after them, too.*

"Hurry, get inside!" A broad-shouldered man in jeans and a white undershirt stepped onto the porch, waving for Derek.

Bang! A gunshot reverberated through the rainy air. The man ducked back inside the house.

No, I can't put them in danger. "Get back inside! Protect your family!" Derek's words were laden with distress and exhaustion, but the message came across. The man closed the door of his home. Derek kept running.

His eyes focused on the monstrous building in the distance. On an ordinary day, The Barracks stood as a symbol of community. Tonight, the massive concrete walls represented Derek's last hope for salvation.

CHAPTER 49
BRYCE REYNOLDS
JULY 12, 2018

BRYCE'S PHONE RANG as he reached the front porch of Derek's house. "Talk to me."

"Agent Reynolds." The same young man who'd called earlier with Isiah Cross's location spoke. "We have reports of a single gunshot near the intersection of Harrison and Sycamore. Witnesses reported two men on foot headed toward the amenity center."

The Barracks.

Bryce ended the call without responding. He jumped from the porch and raced to his car. Once in motion, he ignored the stop sign at the end of the street. His eyes squinted, searching for signs of life through the pouring rain.

Oh, crap! He swerved to avoid a trash bin that had fallen onto the road but kept his eyes on the concrete building ahead.

He's smart. That's where I'd be headed, too. A secure facility with Access ID-controlled entry, staffed by SHADOW personnel, seemed the safest place imaginable at the moment.

I just pray I'm not too late.

* * *

Derek Price

DEREK'S HAND FUMBLED for the keyring in his pocket. The east entry to The Barracks' fitness center loomed less than 300 feet away, but the keyring snagged the fabric of his jeans. *Are you kidding me?*

He saw the red light on the black pad next to the door, glowing like a beacon on the horizon. His hand gripped the keys, and he pulled. Finally, the snarled thread snapped, sending his keys flying out of his jeans and into the night air.

Derek reached out and closed his fist around the keys. *Thank God.* Ahead, the lights of The Barracks shone like those at the end of a tunnel. *One way or the other, this is it.* He reached his hand for the electronic plate. If he made it inside, he'd have a chance. If not, he'd be trapped between the glass-plated door and his assailant.

Come on. He extended his arm, waving the keyring in front of the black panel.

Click. The light turned from red to green. The locking mechanism disengaged. Derek flailed his hand toward the door handle, pulled it open and stepped inside. The fitness center was empty.

Seriously, where the hell is everyone?

Hearing Isiah behind him, Derek grabbed the inside handle and tried to pull the door shut. Just before the lock latched, Isiah snagged the outside handle, igniting a battle of upper-body strength. Derek propped his foot against the doorframe for leverage and pulled as hard as he could. His muscles burned; his legs ached. *Just a little more.*

Outside the door, Isiah raised the Glock to his side and fired. The trajectory of his shot placed the bullet into the nearby grass, but the sound and threat were enough to break Derek's concentration. He stumbled backward and fell to the floor, his ankle writhing with pain.

Isiah threw the door open, clutched the weapon under his arm and clapped slowly three times. "Derek, buddy, did you really think that was going to work?"

* * *

Isiah Cross

WELL, SHIT, they definitely know where I am now. No problem. This will be over soon enough.

Isiah hovered over Derek, who scuttled backward across the floor on his hands and feet like a crab. Derek muttered something under his breath.

Isiah stepped forward. "What was that, Derek? What do you have to say for yourself?"

Derek whispered again.

Loud enough so I can hear it. "I asked you what you have to say for yourself!" He leaned down in Derek's face, snarling.

"I said, 'Just another foot or so.'" Derek's arm swung upward, clocking Isiah in the face with something heavy and solid.

Motherfucker. Isiah raised a hand to his pained jaw. He looked to the ground and saw a five-pound free weight. *That fucking hurt —and he barely clipped me.* Derek was on the move, skittering across the fitness room floor.

I should just shoot you right now and get it over with. He watched Derek knock over a stack of cones and a basket of balance balls. *But there's no fun in that, is there? Besides, I need you alive if you're going to be of any use to me. I need leverage or else I'm a dead man.*

He watched as Derek reached a crossroads, forced to decide whether to turn left through the double doors toward the lobby or continue straight to the locker rooms. *You're either a sitting duck in an open space or trapped with nowhere to run. It's over, Derek. Just give up.*

Derek hobbled toward the men's locker room. Isiah sauntered behind, still rubbing his jaw.

Injured prey. Like a gazelle running from a lion. This is almost too easy. Isiah entered the locker room, finding Derek about halfway across the empty space, leaning on a porcelain sink for support. Isiah laughed and raised the firearm toward a bank of lockers, pulling the trigger.

Derek cowered. Isiah's ears rang. "That's your last warning, Derek. You have nowhere left to go."

Undeterred, Derek hobbled his way across the locker room floor. He balanced himself with the wall as he rounded a corner, leaving Isiah's sight.

Isiah followed Derek methodically. A smile beamed across his face. Emerging from the locker room corridor, he stood about 10 feet from the edge of the community's Olympic-sized swimming pool. *This is it, Derek. You and me, buddy. I didn't want to hurt you. I wanted you to help me, to understand they've hurt you, too. But you're just fucking like them. Oh well, I suppose that makes this easier.*

* * *

Derek Price

DEREK STUMBLED backward. The space between him and the edge of the pool lessened by the step. "Please, Isiah, you don't have to do this."

Isiah smiled and lurched forward, gripping the Glock in his hand. "That's where you're wrong, Derek. This is my purpose, my North Star; without this, I have nothing to live for. I thought you of all people would understand, would sympathize with the nights I spent with a knife to my wrist or a bottle of pills in my hand, wondering how I could live a life without Katherine, without Kelsey and Deandra. I wanted to fucking die, Derek. I wanted to be with them again. But then I saw the light. I realized this wasn't about my suffering. No, it was about so much more than that."

I miss Madeline every day. I've wondered what I'd do if they ever caught the bastard who did it. I never imaged it would be like this. "You're a fucking psychopath, you know that, right? This is absolute insanity! Katherine and the girls died in an accident. Thomas didn't do that. Madeline sure as hell didn't do that. How can you blame them for what happened?" Derek rubbed his hands together, coyly sliding the wedding band from his finger, gripping it tightly in his hand. *I'd give anything to hold her hand one last time.*

Isiah stopped. "You don't know what you're talking about, Derek. Once again, all you know are the lies they wanted you to believe. If you'd open your damn mind instead of your mouth, maybe you'd understand."

He reached his hands for his head, trying to pull what Derek remembered as curly locks. "I killed them, Derek. I fucking killed them. Katherine was trying to leave me. I chased her down the street, trying to make amends. She didn't stop, Derek. She didn't fucking stop."

My God. Derek tightened his grip around the cobalt ring. "But, why? You two seemed so happy together."

"Don't you get it, Derek? It's because she found out the truth. She learned that I'd spent our lives lying to her about who I was and what I did. And she wouldn't listen when I tried to explain. That wasn't what I signed up for. I never agreed to throw my whole life out the window for that fat piece of shit and his ego trip."

He blames Thomas, but it was the life he chose. The life Maddie chose. What would I have done if she'd told me?

"I never meant it to come to this, Derek. I just needed you to get me to that old bitch at SHADOW and make a trade. But you wouldn't listen. You forced my hand. You've become a liability. I'll find someone else. I'll find another way." He lifted the firearm, pointing it at Derek. "I'm sorry, buddy. I really am. Tell Maddie I said hi."

Derek bent down and sprinted from his position. His twisted ankle seared with pain, but he forced himself forward, wrapping his arms around Isiah's torso. The momentum sent both men tumbling to the ground. In the midst of the scuffle, Isiah pulled the trigger.

Oh, fuck. The bullet grazed Derek's arm. He winced with pain. *It burns. Focus. No, I can't do this.* His fist unclenched, sending the wedding band crashing to the floor. He watched it bounce and roll away for a second until Isiah's fist pummeled his face. Isiah forced his weight on top of Derek, pinning his victim to the pool deck.

Derek forced himself to roll over, putting pressure on the gunshot wound but freeing himself of Isiah's grasp. Isiah reached for Derek, grabbing him by the injured arm and tugging. Derek felt the world fall from beneath him. *What the—?* Isiah pulled him downward. Before Derek knew what happened, both men were submerged in the pool.

Water washed over Derek's face as his body sank beneath the surface. He struggled to breathe as Isiah held his head under water. The chlorine burned in his open wound. *This is it. I'm going to die.* His head bobbed above the surface long enough to take a single gasp of air and to see a fleeting vision of what appeared to be boots on the edge of the pool.

Isiah squeezed Derek's wounded arm. Derek opened his mouth to scream; his mouth filled with water. *Just let go.* He released the little hold he had on Isiah. The surrounding water turned red with blood. He could no longer see the surface.

Was that a gunshot? The thought faded as Derek began to lose consciousness. His eyes closed, but he could see. There, surrounded by a field of white light, stood Madeline, just as beautiful as the day they'd met. The white background shifted into a familiar scene, the great room of their home at Shadow Ridge, empty of the life they'd built together. She smiled and reached out her hand.

Madeline.

For the first time in more than a year, Derek Price felt at home.

CHAPTER 50
DEREK PRICE
JULY 12, 2018

RAINDROPS GLISTENED shades of red and blue as they fell from the sky outside The Barracks, illuminated by the flashing lights of emergency response vehicles. Shadow Ridge residents gathered at a distance. Those who had been inside the auditorium during the incident now huddled outside. Police and EMTs worked the scene.

The rear doors of an ambulance in the parking lot hung open. Paramedics circled the vehicle. Derek laid still on a stretcher outside the vehicle, wearing a sleeveless shirt with the word "LIFEGUARD" printed across the chest and covered with blankets. Medical tape was wrapped around his arm, protecting his flesh wound. The rain didn't bother him; he'd been soaking wet when they'd found him.

His eyes were closed, his thoughts elsewhere, when he heard a familiar voice.

"You doing okay?"

He opened his eyes, pushed himself to a seated position and smiled at Bryce. "Only because of you." *At least that's what they tell me.*

"We all got lucky tonight." Bryce smiled. "You know what they say, 'Death doesn't discriminate between the sinners and the saints.'"

"I don't recognize the verse. Which book is that from?"

Bryce chuckled. "'Hamilton,' actually."

Derek nodded.

"But, you know, I think someone else had your six tonight." Bryce tilted his head upward.

"If I wasn't a man of faith before tonight, I think I will be now, Agent Reynolds."

"Please, call me Bryce."

"Fine, then. Bryce," he paused, "is there any update on the woman shot at the gate? I think they said her name was Doherty?"

"She's alive, Derek. I'm not going to lie, though. She probably has a rough road ahead, but they expect her to make a full recovery."

Thank God for that. "Thank you." He bent his neck to look past Bryce. "Have you heard any more about my friend Sonia? The other agent said they'd check."

"I haven't heard, but I'm happy to ask around. From what I understand, she's the one who called in your location. She sounds like a good friend."

I hope we're still friends. "The best."

Bryce pulled his phone from his pocket. "While I go check on that, there's someone else who wants to talk to you." He dialed the number queued on the device and handed it to Derek. He walked away, leaving Derek to enjoy a private conversation.

* * *

"MR. PRICE, I know there's much on your mind at the moment, and I'm sure you want to rest. But, please, if there's anything at all I can do, don't hesitate to reach out. I hope we're able to connect in the coming days once the dust has settled."

"I appreciate that, Mrs. Shadowen. I'm sure we'll be in touch. And, please, call me Derek."

"Very well, Derek. I also want to express my condolences. I know Isaiah Cross was your friend."

Was. "The Isaiah I knew died in that crash with Katherine and the girls. I didn't recognize the man I met tonight at all. Grief hits each of us differently, I suppose. I just regret that his came at such a cost. I guess we never truly know what someone's capable of."

"We reveal our true selves in the face of adversity, Derek. You're a good man. I didn't know your wife that well — though I wish I had — but I knew her well enough to know she'd be proud of what you did tonight. You put yourself in harm's way to protect others. That makes you a hero, Derek."

I might be a fool, but I'm certainly no hero.

* * *

Bryce Reynolds

BRYCE WALKED the perimeter of police tape, scanning the crowd. Working off a rough description — Hispanic female, late teens with dark hair and brown eyes — he didn't plan to leave the scene until he found his target.

That must be her. The girl's eyes were wet not only from the rainfall; her mouth clinched tight with her top teeth biting her lower lip. "Sonia Torres?"

Her head popped up; her eyes widened. "That's me."

"There's someone here waiting to see you." He lifted the police tape. She ducked under. "I hear I should be thanking you for your call."

She looked at him and smiled. She brushed wet bangs from her face and turned her gaze away. "Is Derek alright?"

"Given everything he's been through tonight, I'd say he's doing okay. I'm sure he'll be doing even better when he sees you, though."

The corner of Sonia's lip curled, making Bryce smile. "Were you here when it happened?"

"I've been in the community all night. After we got your call, I headed to Derek's house and followed them to the clubhouse. He'd put up a hell of a fight on his own. But I'm thankful I arrived when I did."

He traced her gaze toward the life-size black bag lying on a gurney near a second ambulance. They both stopped. He turned and looked at her.

"I'm sorry, I feel like such an idiot. I never even asked your name." Her face glowed under the overhead streetlight.

"Reynolds. Bryce Reynolds. But you can call me Bryce."

"It's a pleasure to meet you, Bryce." She smiled and extended a hand.

He returned the gesture. "Pleasure's all mine, Miss Torres. Or should I call you LatinaDragon?" He smiled coyly, referencing her Reddit username.

Sonia's open palm flew to cover her mouth. "Oh my God, you know about that?" She started to turn and walk away.

Bryce gently grabbed her arm, chuckling. "Listen, don't worry about it. After everything we've all been through, it's the least of our worries. If we concerned ourselves with every half-baked conspiracy theory that gets posted to the internet, we'd never have time to do our actual jobs."

Sonia's mouth opened and closed twice, but no words escaped.

I hope I didn't scare the poor girl. "By the way, one of the agents found this by the side of the pool. I thought you might want to give it to him." Bryce reached into his pocket and pulled out a cobalt wedding band. "I'm sure he'll appreciate having it back."

* * *

Derek Price

DEREK SMILED as Bryce led Sonia in his direction. The closer she approached, the more her pace quickened until her arms were wrapped around his body, squeezing.

Watch the arm. Pain shot through his body when she touched the injured limb, but he didn't complain.

Sonia pulled her head back, keeping her hands on his arms, and stared him in the face. Tears burst from her eyes. Her smile radiated a sense of joy Derek hadn't seen in weeks. "I'm just glad you're okay," she blubbered.

"I'm just glad you answered the phone."

Neither could help but laugh.

The two enjoyed a moment of quiet, embracing each other's presence.

Sonia broke the silence. "I'm sorry I blew up on you. I'm such an idiot. There's just been so much going on lately between Mom and school and -30- and everything with the house. I felt like I could break at any moment, and I just pushed myself too far."

"Sonia," he grabbed her hand. "I've felt awful since it happened. I shouldn't have acted the way I did. But why didn't you tell me you were under so much pressure? You should have let me help. I could have at least taken some work off your plate."

Sonia's head dropped. She pulled her hand loose and wiped her eye. "I didn't want to let you down."

"You never have to worry about that, you hear me?" Derek fought back his own tears. "But maybe you need to spend more time with friends your own age. Enjoy being a teenager while you still can." *I hope you still make time for me, though. I don't know what I'd do without you.*

"Oh, shit." Sonia reached into her pocket and pulled out the wedding band. "That agent, Bryce — he asked me to give this to you." She handed him the ring.

Is she blushing? "Thank you. I worried they wouldn't find it."

He held the ring between his thumb and index finger and stared. Lifting his gaze to Sonia's face, he spoke. "I saw her, Sonia. When I was trapped under the water, certain I was going to die, I saw Maddie."

Sonia nodded but didn't speak.

"We were in the house, but it was empty, like it was before we moved in. She took my hand. I held hers and looked into her eyes. She looked back at me and smiled. She told me she was home, but it wasn't time to join her yet." He paused. "That's the last thing I remember before everything went black. I woke up on the pool deck with Agent Reynolds standing over me."

Derek and Sonia both cried renewed tears. She leaned in for another hug, patting Derek on the back. "She's always been home, Derek. She's home inside all of us who loved her, who cared for her."

But did we really know her? "I just can't help but think about the secrets she kept from me, from us." Derek looked for answers in Sonia's eyes.

"She was real, Derek. The way she loved you was real. She might have lied about her job, but you can't fake love like that. And that's the part of her we'll never let go."

Epilogue
Derek Price
Aug. 15, 2018

"SHE ALWAYS LOVED her birthday."

Clouds blocked the morning sun. A breeze blew through the cemetery, rustling the leaves of the giant oak trees lining the metal perimeter fencing. Derek and Sonia huddled together, admiring the ornate black granite headstone engraved with "PRICE."

The left side of the stone bore Derek's name and his birthday. The right side featured Madeline's name and the dates "Aug. 15, 1977 – June 19, 2017."

Derek looked at Sonia. "Have you ever been told about the dash?"

She smiled and shook her head from side to side.

"It's a way of saying that it doesn't matter how long someone lived, but rather how they lived."

"Well, Madeline definitely knew how to live." She put her hand on Derek's arm.

He smiled. "She sure did, didn't she?" He pulled the iPhone from his pocket and checked the time. "We should probably get going. Your mother won't let me forget it if you're late for her appointment."

"Take your time."

Derek turned his attention back to the headstone. He squatted to eye level, reached his left hand to his lips and touched it to the stone. "I'll always love you, Maddie."

He lifted his gaze and saw the realization on Sonia's face. She pointed toward his naked hand. "I thought it was finally time to put it in the safe with hers."

Sonia's wide smile exposed her teeth. "I'm proud of you." She took Derek by the arm, leading him away from the gravesite.

"I hope you know I'm proud of you, too. I'm bummed you won't be helping with -30- as much, but I'm glad you're taking care of yourself. Classes start again soon, don't they?"

"Yeah."

"What's on the schedule for the fall?"

"Financial accounting, advanced advertising strategy, international politics and—." She stammered and looked away. "Macroeconomics — again."

Derek chuckled. "Well, I'll try not to rope you into any crazy conspiracies this time around. But, speaking of accounting, I've got something for you. It's in the car."

He quickened his step until he reached the CR-V, throwing open the driver's side door and grabbing a sheet of paper from the passenger seat. He closed the door and scurried back to Sonia's side.

"What is it?"

"Just look."

Sonia held the paper, printed on Shadowen Real Estate letterhead, up to her eyes. "Holy shit. Is this legit?"

"The payment cleared yesterday. All $10,000 of it."

"Derek, I don't know what to say. How can I ever thank you enough for this?"

"You can hug your mom, hold her tight and tell her we'll do everything we can to help her through this. Geraldine promised me that wouldn't be a one-time donation."

Sonia threw her arms around Derek's shoulders. Tears welled in her eyes.

"Don't cry. You don't want to ruin your makeup, do you? Especially if you're seeing him again tonight."

Sonia pulled back. Her cheeks blushed a dark shade of brown. "I won't see him again until this weekend. I don't know, though, Derek."

"Don't know about what? Bryce is a great guy, Sonia. I owe him my life — literally. And he's become a good friend."

Her face flushed; her lips curled. "He's so sweet." She wiped the bangs from her eyes. "I really like him, Derek. I think I'm just afraid it's getting too serious."

Derek nodded slowly and snickered. "Is it that whole working for the enemy thing you two have got going on?"

She playfully smacked his arm. "Funny. No, I'm just worried it will cause problems for you, especially if it doesn't work out between us. And, God knows, I've caused enough problems for you already this summer."

Derek put his hands on her shoulders and looked her in the eyes. "Listen, we're all adults. If something happens and it doesn't work out, it wasn't meant to be. But, please, don't let worrying about me get in the way of your happiness." He paused. "Besides, it's okay. I know the boss."

* * *

DEREK'S CR-V SAT in its designated parking space with the engine running. A voice played through the car's speakers.

"What's up, Derek?"

"I just wanted to follow up and see if you needed anything else from me before our meeting this afternoon."

Steve Erikson laughed. "A little heads up as to what the hell we're meeting about would be nice."

I still hate keeping secrets from Steve, but he'll know soon enough. "I wish I could tell you, but even I'm embargoed until this afternoon. Just be assured when I tell you it's worth the front page and that you've got the exclusive."

"If you've taught me anything, Derek, it's that I can trust you."

After the last month or so, I wouldn't be so sure. "Sounds great. We'll see you this afternoon, Steve."

Derek turned off the engine and ended the call. *I can get used to this Bluetooth thing.* He crossed the parking garage, headed for the main entrance. While he had access to the private service elevator, he preferred building relationships with the security guards working in the lobby.

He looked both ways as he entered the open circular space. An older gentleman behind the desk rose from his seat. "Good morning, Mr. Price. How are you today?"

"Doing well, Ben." He smiled and shook the man's hand. "Today's the big day, you know."

Ben smiled in return. "Oh, yes, sir. We'll be ready for the press conference tomorrow. We'll have you set up in the Sheridan Room."

"Perfect. Thanks for stepping up lately, Ben; it hasn't gone unnoticed." Derek waved and turned to his right, approaching a bank of elevators. He hit the up button. As he waited, he looked at the blackboard directory with removable white letters. *I'm still not used to it.* Wedged between listings for an attorney and a financial advisor, plastic characters spelled "-30- PUBLIC RELATIONS | DEREK PRICE."

Ding! The elevator opened. Derek stepped inside. He kneeled down as the door closed and reached inside his leather messenger bag, pulling out a folder labeled "ANNOUNCEMENT" and checking the papers inside. Satisfied, he put the folder back, zipped the bag and slung it over his shoulder as he stood.

Reaching the ninth floor, the elevator doors opened. Derek stepped out into the upper lobby of the Shadowen Real Estate office. "Good morning, Mallory. How are you today?"

"Oh, just living the dream," the young woman behind the front desk answered. "Mrs. Shadowen is waiting for you in the conference room."

"Thank you." Derek crossed the lobby and moved down the hallway. He stopped outside the closed door labeled Field Director, pausing for a moment to remember J.D. Moore. *I wish I'd had a chance to know him better.*

Entering the conference room, Derek glanced at the aerial photos on the wall. The two others in the room both stood from their seats at the table. "Director Shadowen." He shook Geraldine's hand. "And Field Director Reynolds." He reached across the table and clasped hands with Bryce.

"You're officially one of us now, Mr. Price. Please drop the damned formalities." Geraldine's face wrinkled as she smiled.

"I'll get right on that, Director. Just as soon as you start calling me Derek."

All three took their seats. "Is everything prepared for this afternoon?" Geraldine asked.

Derek set his bag on the empty chair next to him and removed the folder. Flipping it open, he collected two copies of a document and slid one to each of the others, keeping a third copy for himself.

The top of the page featured the Shadowen logo with large, bold font beneath it reading: "Shadowen Real Estate Announces Historic Partnership with U.S. Government." A smaller subheading added, "SHADOW Program to Provide Affordable Housing to Military, Government Employees."

Derek looked at Geraldine. "I confirmed with Steve Erikson that he'll be here this afternoon. Steve's a good guy. We can trust he'll do the story justice. And we're set for the news conference tomorrow. I've heard from a few people who will be coming, but I think once the Herald hits the streets in the morning, we'll have a lot more interest."

Geraldine and Bryce exchanged a pensive glare.

"This is the right move." Derek leaned on the table. "There will be a lot of questions early on, but we're ready for it. Senator Durbin is planning to release his statement of support tomorrow, and the agencies are set to follow suit. Residents have all been informed, as well."

"Any update in that regard?" Geraldine looked to Bryce for an answer.

"A few families have opted to relocate. We've been working to finalize arrangements for them until they can find permanent homes. But, for the most part, everyone has been supportive."

Derek raised his hand to interject. "We've even had several people offer to share their stories with the media. After nearly a decade, this has been good motivation to actually meet more of my neighbors."

Geraldine smiled and nodded. "Very well. I don't know if I've truly done enough to earn your trust, Derek, but you've been gracious enough to share it. The least I can do is trust you on this matter."

Derek's gaze shifted from Geraldine to Bryce and back. *We've come a long way from the first time we all sat in this room together.* "Well, I should go check everything one more time before Steve comes in." He stood from his seat.

"And I'm going to head back down to Shadow Ridge." Bryce rose, too. "Heather's working on the rededication. I'm not sure what I can really add, but I want to do my part. Next week, we'll officially be working out of the Jefferson D. Moore Community Center. I'll be in touch about the ceremony, Derek."

"Sounds good, Bryce. Thank you for everything, as well." He winked. "I know how happy she is."

Bryce's cheeks flashed the slightest shade of red. He left the room without replying.

Derek and Geraldine were alone in the conference room. "Derek, before you go, I wanted to say thank you again for everything you've done these past few weeks. You experienced a great trauma and have handled it with courage, compassion and care. And now, to help us — to help me — take this next step, I can never repay you."

Derek's body tingled. "It's my pleasure, Geraldine — my honor, really. Madeline kept this part of her life secret, but I know she did it with the best intentions. She found our home and never once talked of leaving. She obviously believed in what you're doing, and I know she'd be here with us if she could."

"You're a good man, Derek Price. Our world could use more people like you." Geraldine reached out and patted Derek on the shoulder as she left the room.

Standing in the empty conference room, surrounded by photographs of the world's greatest cities, Derek inhaled a deep breath and closed his eyes.

The whole world's changed so quickly. My world has changed. Madeline. Despite the lies, despite the secrets, I've come to realize you're always at my side. Sonia. I never could have done this without you. Isiah. The friend I thought I knew. You showed me what my life could have become.

Derek opened his eyes and stepped toward the door. For the first time he could remember, he put the past behind him and focused entirely on the future.

We walk a dangerous path, carrying the truth from the shadows into the light. All we can do is take it one step at a time.

Acknowledgements

While "To Live and Die at Shadow Ridge" is my debut novel, it's far from the first one I've tried to write. When I finished the second draft, I stopped and asked myself, "What was different this time?" At first, I credited the extra hours at home and free weekends that resulted from the COVID-19 pandemic. But that's not it.

The truth is that, for the first time, I realized that while mine is the name of the cover, I didn't write this book alone. This project would not have been possible without the input, guidance and support of so many others. I don't know if I can ever adequately express my appreciation to everyone who helped make this happen. But I'm going to try. My eternal gratitude to:

- My beautiful wife, Anna, for picking me up every time I felt like this story wasn't worth sharing and for sacrificing her free time to allow me to write. She helped inspire this story in ways I can't publicly disclose; you never know who's listening.
- My parents, Jim and Raelene, for encouraging me to write, from childhood through adulthood. Without them, there wouldn't have been a dream to be fulfilled. Sharing this experience with them has made it even more meaningful.
- My alpha readers, Sandy, Karen, Kathy and my critique partner and aspiring author K.A. Pardon. They read my first draft and somehow stuck around for the second. Their feedback and perspective helped improve the story and made me a stronger writer.
- My beta readers and sounding boards, including Kerensa, Dawn, Quinne and future best-seller C.A. Kennedy. Your feedback helped me polish the final product for publication.
- My work family, especially my teammates Nicole and Jennifer, for continued support, both personally and professionally. You

continue to make the experience of working in community management fun and memorable, even on the mundane days.
- My late friend Becky for always inspiring me to chase my dreams and for reminding me that everyone has a story to tell. I only wish you were here to see this one come true.
- The creators of The Hero's Journal, which I used to develop a writing routine early in the process. And the members of the Hero's Quarters, the affiliated Facebook group that has reminded me to always look at the positive side of adventure. This experience also led me to create The Bards of Hero's Quarters, a digital writing group for any heroes looking to help each other on their quest.
- The members of the Mystery Writers and NaNoWriMo groups on Facebook, who answered questions, provided perspective and developed this story.
- Everyone who gave this book a chance, whether you quit after the first Donald Trump reference or you're still reading. I never imagined there would be an audience for my writing, but you've all proven me wrong.
- Codex Art and Apparel for an amazing cover design and my best friend Adam for his proofreading services. These vital elements of a successful book often go underappreciated.

I'm sure there are many others I'm forgetting, and I apologize. Just know that if you've so much as said "good luck" or "congratulations" to me, I consider myself fortunate to have you in my life.

The success of this endeavor belongs to all of us. Don't let anyone or anything stop you from living your own dreams.

ABOUT THE AUTHOR

Adam Testa spent his childhood in and around rural Grundy County, Illinois, as depicted in "To Live and Die at Shadow Ridge," where he dreamed of writing and publishing a novel. R.L. Stine's "Goosebumps" captivated him as a child, while Dan Brown's Robert Langdon series influenced his adult writing style.

Testa has six years of experience in the community association management industry, most recently serving in corporate communications for a national service provider. Prior to working with HOAs, he served as a multimedia reporter for a mid-sized regional news outlet covering local government, higher education and arts and entertainment.

He resides in Phoenix with his wife, Anna, and son, Zachary. When he's not writing, Testa enjoys following pop culture, watching comic book movies and tolerating "Baby Shark" for the umpteenth time.

Follow Testa's adventures as he embarks on his next writing project, "The Brennan County Journal Trilogy," at facebook.com/AdamTestaAuthor.

Made in the USA
Monee, IL
21 November 2020